1

Girl on the Run

Sarah Tucker Redux

Jim Knoedel

Published by Jim Knoedel, 2023

ALSO BY JIM KNOEDEL

A Golden Era – A Tale of Two Runners

A Long Road Ahead – A Tale of Two Runners Redux

*Run Like a Girl – A Tale of a Distance Runner
During Title IX*

Front Cover Photography: Lauren Stanley

Back Cover Photography: Northwestern University Archives

Cover Design: Mary Sullivan

GIRL ON THE RUN – SARAH TUCKER REDUX

First Edition: August 23, 2023

Copyright © 2023 Jim Knoedel

ISBN: 979-8-35091-772-7

www.taleoftworunners.com

This book is dedicated to athletes I coached whose lives ended much too soon. They are gone but not forgotten.

Brian Casey
Jennifer Darrow
Crista Fabrycki
Jennifer Goebel
Jim Janak
Monieka Thompson
Diana Wight

Title IX

"No person shall, on the basis of sex, be excluded from participation in, be denied the benefits of, or be subjected to discrimination under any education program or activity receiving Federal financial assistance."
June 23, 1972

Chapter 1
August 22, 1982

I sat on the giant boulders along the Lake Michigan shoreline, the blocks of limestone stacked in random piles at the water's edge, staring eastward across the water at clouds hovering low over the lake, trying to digest my first weekend on the Northwestern campus. My roommate was taking a nap, but I was restless, walking across campus, drawn towards the water without thought.

Cross country camp officially began Monday the 23rd, our first meet at UW-Parkside in three weeks, classes for the first quarter not getting underway until Thursday September 23rd. I was grateful to focus on running before the schoolwork began, my concern about the demands of classes more unnerving than any worry about running.

In early August I got the news Coach Capriotti was leaving and Mike O'Shea would be taking his place, the change was quite a shock so close to the cross country camp. We didn't know a thing about him other than he was twenty-nine and ran at Michigan. I worried he wouldn't want me, possibly cutting my athletic scholarship – even though mom and dad claimed it wouldn't happen. But you never know.

Jennifer Hernandez was my roommate at Hobart House, the dignified 3-story dormitory like a fifty-year-old dowager – elegant but old. And I mean old. We bought matching bedspreads, managing to fit a small loveseat along the window for any sleepovers, pinning posters of Chariots of Fire and Richard Gere in "American Gigolo" on blank walls, a purple African violet on my desk and a macrame plant hanger I knotted from twine dangling from the curtain rod, the spider plant desperately in need of water.

Later that afternoon, I walked to Giordano's with Jennifer to meet the rest of the team, Coach O'Shea waving us over as we circled through the revolving door, nervously smiling as we approached our new teammates. I was excited but scared, clinging to Jennifer as though we were attached at the hip, both of us worried about being accepted by the girls. And by our new coach. He hadn't recruited us.

My concerns were all for nothing, our teammates treating us like old friends, already making plans for activities on campus and trips into Chicago before school began. Coach O'Shea was personable and dynamic, his enthusiasm inspiring everyone, expressing to Jennifer and me that he was excited to have us on the team.

After we finished eating, he went over the schedule, new 1982 NCAA rules, times for physicals, and then jumped into the day-to-day routine.

"Until school begins on September 23rd, we'll meet each morning...except Sunday, at 9am at Anderson Hall. Some days we'll go off campus, others we'll do workouts around here. Bill Jarvis, the equipment manager will hand out practice gear and give you a locker after Monday morning's practice...so tomorrow come dressed to run."

He looked around the table after finishing his talk.

"Any questions?"

Anita Keller smiled and waved her hand like a second grader.

"Hey Mike. Coach. Is it true you're going to take us shopping at Old Orchard after we get lockers?"

Everyone broke out laughing, the grin on Anita's face telling us she was joking...sorta.

Monday morning Jennifer and I jogged the half mile to Anderson Hall from our dormitory, Becky Beach and Joanne Sloan already sitting in the grass when we arrived. Becky shaded her eyes with a hand and smiled.

"Good morning. Did you two think of bringing a dry tee shirt? You're going to need it. The woods are always steamy, and you'll sweat like a stuck pig."

10

Jennifer and I twisted sideways, the profile of our backpacks answering her question.

If you gotta pee, do it now." Joanne pointed at the hallway. "There's one in Anderson Hall. They have portable toilets on the trails, but you don't want to use them – no toilet paper and they're all gross."

We both shook heads. From behind us Anita approached at a jog, wearing a black t-shirt with a headshot of Debbie Harry, her sleeves haphazardly removed with scissors, smiling when she slowed to a stop after hearing Joanne's statement.

"So, which of you two." Anita pointed back and forth between Jennifer and me. "Has taken a nature pee?"

We all laughed, my hand creeping into the air, a blush filling my cheeks.

"So do you use the squat technique or…"

Her head turned, tossing a quick wave to Coach O'Shea as he burst through the Anderson Hall door like he was late for a meeting – Janelle, Alice, and Terry trailing behind. He was carrying an orange Gatorade cooler and a sleeve of cups, the tilt of his shoulders indicating the container was certainly full. Anita grinned and covered laughter with a hand, winking at me as she took a sip from her water bottle.

"Okay, okay, enough chatter ladies." He jiggled the van keys. "Let's load up." Coach turned to Anita. "I see you already picked up your practice gear." He rolled his eyes at her shirt, unlocking the van so we could jump in.

The dirt trail in Glenview meandered alongside the Des Plaines River, the path wide enough we could run in groups of two and three, chatter continuous at first, petering out as the heat began to overwhelm us – in spite of the shade provided by huge oak and cottonwood trees. I enjoyed the setting, through a break in the trees spotting a blue heron standing still in a shallow part of the river, waiting for a guileless fish to swim by.

On the ride to the trail I was a bit nervous, afraid I would get buried by the workout tempo, but after Coach O'Shea told us no faster than 7:30 pace my worries disappeared. This was

11

my first opportunity to show them I was made of the right stuff.

As we ran through the forest the steady rhythm of foot strikes was hypnotic, my mind drifting to the conversation with mom at Dane's Dairy last June. I knew she wanted to spend more time with me before I left for school in August, though a bit surprised when she spoke the unspoken words about Thorsten which I had been thinking of for weeks.

"I think Thorsten is a great boy. He's polite, very motivated, and has a good head on his shoulders." Mom smiled. "And if I was your age, I wouldn't mind having him on my elbow." She burst into laughter.

I rolled my eyes.

"But we need to talk about you two getting intimate."

I blushed, turning side to side to make sure no one overheard, more embarrassed by her words than I was by the awkwardness of the subject she was broaching. It was as if she could read my mind. Recently, I had been thinking about it much more, wondering if I was ready. Wondering if this was the time. That Thorsten was the one.

"First, I want to remind you to always keep me in the loop. I'm on your side…no matter what." The way she looked at me I could read the words that she didn't say. That she didn't want me getting pregnant.

"Second, I don't want you having intercourse but also realize everything in your body is saying how badly you want to. So, if you need birth control pills tell me. We'll get them when you want. It's your decision…just don't wait until it's too late." She put her hand over mine and squeezed it. "But if you can wait…please do. The intimacy changes some boys…has an effect on relationships that even I failed to realize."

I looked up into her eyes, the openness of her words shocking. She pursed her lips and nodded.

"You're young. I'm not saying Thorsten isn't the one…but you need to think about where your paths are going. He has three more years in Missouri, and you have four in Chicago. The two campuses are four hundred miles apart and your weekends will be busy with cross country and track. A long-distance relationship is much harder than you think…I know." Her head dropped. "So." She smiled. "Let me know what you decide."

We stood and embraced for an extra beat, mom finishing with a kiss on the top of my head.

Now the summer is gone. Memories of camping with Thorsten last weekend were still fresh in my mind. It made my heart ache. *How was I ever going to survive our separation?* That evening we sat around the campfire and stared into the flames, his arms around me as I leaned back into his body, feeling so contented – like I had died and gone to heaven.

Thorsten left for his internship at the *Daily Tribune* in Columbia in early July, running miles the only thing filling my aching heart, a final trip to Knoxville in August for the 1982 AAU meet merely something to divert the sadness. My boyfriend was gone.

At Saturday's practice we drove to Swallow Cliff Forest preserve to get miles on the dirt trails in the southwest suburbs, pulling into the parking lot and everyone climbing out, the team looking at a hill three times the size of Evanston's Mt. Trashmore – the hill we ran repeats on last Tuesday.

"Holy shit." It was Anita. "This hill is like Trashmore on steroids." Her eyebrows rose.

"See those chutes." Becky pointed at the u-shaped tubes. "They're for toboggans. The chutes are longer than a football field…supposedly you can get up to fifty miles an hour."

"Hey Mike…coach." Anita grinned. "Do you think we could bring out roller skates next time?"

Coach O'Shea rolled his eyes.

"Okay ladies. We're doing the eight mile loop. Keep in mind that you'll climb to the top of this hill at the two mile mark." He pointed to the top. "So be smart – keep the pace easy." He nodded at the portable toilets. "If anyone needs one stop in now and then we'll get started." Becky jogged in that direction carrying a roll of toilet paper.

The dirt trail snaked through groves of maples, cottonwoods, and ash trees, conversation lively as we approached a small stream, flat rocks placed strategically so we could traverse it without getting wet. At least theoretically.

Joanne led the way, her long legs easily navigating the improvised crossing, the rest of us following behind in single file, Janelle slipping off the last stone into ankle-deep water, her hands muddied as she landed on the far slope. I was surprised she was the only one. Most distance runners are klutzes.

"Shit. Shit. Shit." It was impossible for us not to laugh at Janelle. "Wait. I gotta wring out my sock."

We resumed running after Janelle re-tied her shoe, ten minutes later the team discovering the climb up to the top was at hand. Initially the slope was easy, but after the first switchback the hill got steeper, everyone's breaths much deeper, our strides no longer than a yardstick.

After a torturous minute I looked up with hopeful thoughts, but the hill continued, another switchback only prolonging the agony. I have no idea how much longer we climbed, my mind numbed by tired legs, and rapid respiration, the trail finally leveling out at a clearing. *Thank God.*

The rest of the six miles was filled with small ups and downs, in many areas glacial rocks embedded in the dirt trail dictating we keep eyes on the ground. I was so relieved when we finally arrived back at the sledding hill, my t-shirt soaked in sweat, and eyelids crusty with salt. From the looks on faces, my teammates were just as happy to be done. I checked my Timex watch as I drank a cup of water. We started sixty-eight minutes ago.

"Okay ladies. One trip up the stairs." Coach pointed. "And we're done." We all moaned.

Twenty minutes later the eight of us were relaxing in the water of a Northwestern alum's backyard pool, Coach O'Shea talking with Mr. Brennan as they grilled hamburgers, the cool water the most wonderful feeling in the world. If I was to die at this moment, nothing would have left me more at peace than this blissful sensation – well, except a cheeseburger, some potato salad, and slices of watermelon. Oh, and a cherry popsicle. I had that and more.

I slept all the way back to campus.

Beginning with the Monday of Labor Day, we spent the rest of the week just over the Wisconsin border at a Girl Scout camp, putting in miles on the Ice Age Trails in the mornings, some days getting our intervals in on quiet county roads, cows staring at us as we ran back and forth on each repetition. It was amusing to watch heads follow us, many of the girls making faces at them as we passed by.

The next day we did twelve 400m repeats from point to point, coach riding alongside us on a girl's bicycle he found at camp, shouting encouragement as we ran, his presence like a persistent fly. By the eighth one my breathing was ragged, sweat dripping down my temples at a steady pace, dry areas on bras outlining the spots where we weren't yet drenched.

I did the nineth and tenth ones as though on autopilot, simply following the girls without thought of my fatigue, the eleventh one eliciting the first affirmation. *C'mon Sarah. You can do it. Be tough.* I don't know how I kept the jog going between intervals – but I did, the challenges from teammates a wonderful motivation. We were side by side on the last one, eight bodies filling both lanes of the county road as our distance to the cone disappeared.

I was so glad to be done.

It was clear we had a good team. The talent level of these girls far exceeded that of my high school teammates. In fact, even in the state of Iowa. Nothing less than my best effort would keep me abreast of them, their daily efforts on the hard workouts a welcome challenge – what I was looking forward to when I arrived at college.

It was weird not being the team leader, the one all the girls looked to for direction each day. But to be honest, it was wonderful to let someone else take charge. To leave all the leadership to the juniors. We spent afternoons swimming in the small pond at the Girl Scout camp, playing shuffleboard, badminton, and croquet, some of the girls playing cribbage or euchre for a change of pace.

Each evening finished with the team sitting on chairs around a campfire making s'mores. I always took charge of building the fire, getting Jennifer to help me find sticks to hold everyone's marshmallows.

"Sarah Crockett over there." Anita nodded at me with a big grin. "Plans on catching a raccoon tonight and skinning it, so we can grill it for lunch tomorrow."

"I get dibs on the coonskin cap." Janelle smirked as she raised her hand.

"You seemed to like the blueberries and strawberries I found in the woods." I smiled. "So, I thought you'd like to try something new. Being the city girl you are, the only place *you* could find a blueberry is at a grocery store." Everyone burst into laughter.

The rest of the week went by so quickly, comfort with my new teammates growing day by day.

We still hadn't had a class before our first meet at UW-Parkside on September 11th, the hilly course one I was quite familiar with. It's where I qualified for my first Kinney Championship in San Diego. Where I ran 17:50 as a sophomore at East High. One that always gave me comfort.

I stared out the van window from the seat behind coach as we drove northward on I-94 towards Wisconsin, lazily watching the sites and scenes. A roller coaster climbing the rails at Great America, hands going up as riders crested the initial hill, a few minutes later Coach O'Shea tossing change into the tollway basket near the Wisconsin border. "Hey look." Anita pointed out the sign as we crossed into Wisconsin, laughing at the words "Bong State Recreation Area" before we turned off the highway towards the Kenosha course.

I wanted so badly to make this first race a memorable one, a performance that would set the stage for an illustrious career. Get me off to a good start. Too many good high school runners had succumbed to factors they were unprepared for or unaware of when they started college. Returned home with a hangdog look that aged their faces.

They didn't acknowledge real issues - the "freshmen fifteen" gained in the dining hall, dorms which were so loud it was impossible to fall asleep before midnight, or the foolish investment in campus social life (aka a boyfriend or sororities) that conflicted with success. I didn't want to be another one of those failures.

And then there was school. Last summer dad spoke with me about the importance of study habits while we sat on the patio, waiting for the grill to heat up for the burgers.

"Think of it like you do training. Only a fool would practice three days a week and skip the others. I guarantee that plan would fail. It's the same with studies. Two to three hours six days a week will get you further than two all-nighters. Be consistent. Do a little bit often." I cut in.

"Yeah, but I'm worried about how smart everyone is." I sighed. "I mean, 100 percent of the students were in the National Honor Society…more than likely all of them valedictorians. So, I'm just another face." Dad could hear my exasperation. He held up his hand.

"Honey, mom and I will love you no matter how you do…even if the semester yields a 1.50." He smiled. "But please keep it a little higher." His grin was much bigger. "I think a reasonable goal is to focus on a 3.00. I know you are capable of A's in English, history, and psychology, but I also know you're challenged in sciences. If you get two A's, one B, and a C in science you still have a 3.25." He leaned over and gave me a hug. "Mom and I will be happy with that."

I felt better but knew at that moment it was all talk. As my high school coach always said. "The proof's in the pudding." Right now, I did know if I was ready to try it.

Eight of us warmed up for the 5K race at Parkside in gray Northwestern t-shirts and purple nylon shorts over bun-huggers, temperatures warm enough that anything more would be too uncomfortable. I was still in a bit of shock. When Coach O'Shea handed out competition briefs that covered no more than a bikini bottom the whites of my eyes doubled in size. *Holy shit! He expects me to wear this?*

Anita cornered Jennifer and I that day after the workout.

"Well girls. No more granny panties!" She burst out laughing. "Looks like you two will be shopping at Casual Corner this afternoon!"

My first college race. I was nervous, but less so because Coach O'Shea wanted everyone to stay together, to make sure we all passed the two-mile mark in a cluster. Dad's advice from my first race here as a sophomore in high school was stuck in my head.

"Whatever you run the first mile, double it and it should be your two mile split."

Eight of us stood in box 15, glancing despondently at the steep hill only a quarter mile ahead, anxious to get the race underway. *I hate this wait. I gotta pee. Let's go. Let's go.* For as nervous as I was, after the tiny cannon fired, I remembered almost nothing of the competition. Only Becky's gold necklace bouncing up and down as we climbed the initial hill and Anita's arm over my shoulder as we shuffled through the first finish chute.

Coach O'Shea was ecstatic as we circled at the back of the chutes, patting each of us on the back, pleased with the twelve second split between our #1 and #6. A pigtailed runner from Drake beating Joanne, Becky, and Janelle into the line, a second Bulldog runner separating Anita and me from our teammates, Jennifer's meager kick leaving her five seconds behind our front five.

We won the meet with twenty-two points, Joanne toting the championship trophy back to the van, everyone thrilled to get the season underway with such a good start. My college career was off to a good start.

———

The following weekend, I dropped a dime-sized token in the slot on the turnstile at the Davis Street station and climbed the stairs, worried this was the outbound platform and not the one towards Chicago. We had an open weekend without a meet, and I was going to take advantage of the break.

I stared at the train on the other tracks, still uncertain if I was on the right platform, the adventure to Lincoln Park already beginning to frazzle my nerves. Annette and I were meeting for lunch at the DePaul campus, the first time we had been together in at least a month. My pre-season cross country camp and Annette's August gigs had kept us apart, our last meeting for ice cream at Dane's Dairy in Iowa City.

Annette and I had shared so many ups and downs in life, my best friend since junior high, inseparable throughout all those years. We had so many happy memories I would always treasure, the thought of her making me smile. I could picture Annette playing the guitar alongside Marie on the Wheel Room stage, her earrings glittering in the spotlight, the fourteen-year-old pair playing with such poise in front of the college crowd at the open mic.

Memories of Marie still made me sad.

After I changed trains at Howard Street, I stared out the L window trying to recall how long ago she had died. Four years. My freshman year at East High. I wondered what Marie would be doing if she was still alive. Going to college? Off to California? Playing at cabarets in Paris? Yeah, that's what she would be doing. Something off-beat. Something crazy. The thought made me smile.

The conductor broke through my reverie, his mumbled delivery hard to understand.

"Next stop..." I couldn't tell what he said after that. "Doors open..." Fullerton flashed by on the station sign.

I jumped to my feet, holding the overhead strap in a vice-like grip, apologizing as I bumped into another rider when the train screeched to a halt. Everyone turned to the right, so I followed, shuffling down the stairs into a busy Chicago street scene, eyes peeled for the Demon Dogs stand. Annette said the food shack was right below the station. I shouted and waved when I spotted her sitting at the picnic table, rushing over with arms spread wide.

"Annette!"

A grin filled my face, the scent of Baby Soft a welcome memory as we embraced. I was so happy, suddenly aware I was more homesick than I realized. We rocked side to side in the hug, both of us savoring the moment, sitting hip to hip on the wooden bench as words burst from my mouth.

"God, it's *so* good to see you. I couldn't wait for practice to finish so I could come down." I smirked. "And I didn't even get lost!" I hugged her again.

"C'mon. I'll show you my dorm room." Annette smiled. "Then we're going to get a burger at Chances Are." Annette clapped her hands together in front of her face. "Do you remember?"

"Of course. We ate there the weekend you sang at Earl of Old Town."

She grabbed my hand, and we skipped down the sidewalk like ten-year-olds, carefree smiles spreading from ear to ear, both of us glancing up at a cardinal chortling high in an evergreen tree on the edge of campus. The rest of the day was just as idyllic – shopping in Old Town, that afternoon going to "The World According to Garp" at the Biograph Theatre, later in the evening listening to a bluegrass music session at the Old Town School of Music.

It was after midnight when I fell asleep on her dorm room floor, Sunday morning munching on bagels and slurping coffee at a diner near campus, walking to Oz Park after and sitting in the grass by a field, sneaking peaks at boys playing flag football while we talked. The scene brought back a bittersweet memory. In junior high the three of us laid on Annette's bed and talked about boys. And how we were going to make it big when we got older.

At noon we returned to her room, and I changed into training clothes so I could run back to the Northwestern campus. *Sigh.* I hadn't even left but I already missed her. I dropped my chin and then looked up with a smile as we huddled in front of her dormitory before I took off.

"Next time you have to come to Evanston. "

I gave her a long hug, smiling through teary eyes, turning to jog down Fullerton towards the lake, taking the gravel running path near the zoo for the nine mile trek back to the Northwestern campus. There was no way I could navigate city streets back to Evanston.

Chapter 2
September 20, 1982

My workouts had been good, but Monday's 5 x 1000m on the track was a great one. One that opened my eyes to times I might run. It gave me goosebumps. Coach O'Shea called the session escalation intervals – each thousand meter run faster than the last. Joanne was up first.

She nodded at coach and then led us through the initial one thousand, grabbing Anita's sleeveless NU t-shirt as we rounded the first corner, spitting out "follow me" as she ran down the backstretch of the track. There were still marshmallows on the tartan surface in Dyche Stadium after Saturday's football loss to Miami of Ohio, each of us trying to avoid the sticky white pillows of goo that had melted in today's heat. *What a dumb tradition*.

Coach O'Shea gave us the eight-hundred-meter split on the first interval "2:38…2:39…2:40" sprinting diagonally across the track to get over to the 1000 meter mark on time as we continued to circle the track. I stayed with the pack, responding to Joanne's steady surge on the backstretch, coach yelling "3:18…3:19…3:20" as we crossed the line.

"Great job ladies…go right into the jog. Don't stop." He was shuffling beside us. "I'll meet you at the starting line. Becky, you've got the next one. We're looking for sub 3:18."

I stared at the hickey on Janelle's neck during our two hundred meter jog, taking a deep breath as we neared the line for the second one, our group of eight still in a swarm. From five yards out Becky picked up the tempo, everyone hitting the starting line inches apart. This one almost felt easier, as though my body was finally loose, my stride relaxed and powerful.

"2:35…2:36…2:37…that-a-way girls." Becky took us around the corner and down the backstretch, coach shouting so we could hear times above our breathing. "3:15…3:16…3:17. Excellent job. Excellent." I may not have been tired when I started this interval, but I definitely was now. The two hundred meter jog was a little slower, proof everyone was feeling the effort.

"Anita, you take number three." Coach smiled at her.

This one was going to be tough. Like jumping into the cold water of Lake Michigan. I had to steel myself to make the leap. *Let's go Sarah. Get it done.* We took off. Joanne helped to control Anita's tempo, although I knew Anita was tired enough that it was easier to keep the pace reasonable. As we ran down the homestretch on the second lap I prayed the next words from coach's mouth started with two-thirty-something. I was so tired I thought it might be two-forty...

"2:34...2:35...2:36." *Yes.*

The pack began to separate on the backstretch, four of us joining Anita and Becky as we crossed the thousand meter mark – Alice and Terri dropping from my peripheral vision.

"3:14...3:15...3:16. Great job ladies. You gotta dig deep on this next one. Don't get lazy."

Now I was tired. Real tired. How we ran 3:15 on the next one...I'll never know. But six of us did, the marshmallows laying in lanes one and two having zero effect on where our foot strikes landed.

One to go. Janelle led it. I was almost too tired to care how much this one hurt – almost.

The tempo felt like I was running an eight hundred meter race, my breathing already rapid when we entered the initial backstretch. *Yikes!* At this tempo I knew the time after two laps had to be close to 2:33 or we wouldn't hit the goal. *C'mon. Stay with them Sarah. You can do it.*

"2:32...2:33...2:34..."

I peeled out into lane two as we entered the last backstretch, Becky and Joanne on the inside, the sound of Anita's breathing just off my shoulder, Jennifer's loping foot strikes right on my heels. Five of us finished at the same moment, Janelle a split second later. It was hard to hear Coach O'Shea's words over my breathing.

"3:12...3:13...3:14." After that all I felt was pain.

I slowed to a stop, bent over with hands on knees, staring at a marshmallow flattened on the track. *I'm so glad it's over.* Someone patted me on the back, my rapid breaths beginning to slow, pain ebbing like the evening tide. *Whoa doggie. That hurt.*

"Nice job Becky…Joanne." Coach put out his hand to slap. "Excellent Janelle. Very good Anita. I'm impressed Jennifer. Good Sarah." He went around to the rest and slapped hands or patted them on the back. Finally, everyone stood tall and shuffled over to get water. Coach O'Shea approached after we all got liquid.

"Ladies, this was an excellent workout today. The type of tempo we'll need to run at the big meets down the road." He paused. "Classes begin Thursday and the stress will amp up another notch. So, call me if you have any issues. You are all good students, but I want to remind you to pace yourselves. Be consistent about studying."

He looked over the squad and continued.

"I know how tough it is here." He smiled. "Heck, I doubt I could have gotten into Northwestern. But ask for help if you need it. Work with the professors and I know you will do fine. Okay, a fifteen minute cool down and then we have weights."

———

Phillip Sanka joined us at Anita's apartment on Friday night for our weekly session of "Dallas," the only male on the men's team interested in watching the show. The rest of them were probably out drinking after their poor team performance at the Notre Dame meet a few hours ago. Jennifer and Janelle were staring at the screen, leaning against a chair while they shared a bowl of popcorn, engrossed in the dialogue between Sue Ellen and JR.

"JR is such a slimeball." Phillip was exasperated. "I mean, I can't believe he slept with Holly. She is such a slut. It should have been JR in the crash...not her."

"I can't believe Sue Ellen decided to marry JR again." Anita booed at the screen. "What was she thinking? If I ever do something that stupid, please shoot me."

"Now Bobby..." Becky smiled. "I don't think there is anything he could do that would make me want to kick him out of bed." She started laughing.

"You wish." I replied. "He'd see those hairy legs and you'd be out in a second." I snapped my fingers. Everyone broke out in laughter, Becky throwing a kernel of popcorn at me.

"A girl can dream, can't she?"

We all talked after the show was over, mentioning to the team that tomorrow night I was going to the Metro to meet a friend from Iowa City for the R.E.M. concert. Phillip indicated he was headed down that direction also and suggested we ride together. I was all for it. We arranged to meet at the Davis Street stop tomorrow at 7:30pm.

As the clock neared 10pm, yawns were abundant, my look at Jennifer met with a slight nod. She joined me in our goodbyes.

"We're going back to the dorms. We'll see you at nine tomorrow morning for practice."

As we walked home, we talked.

"It was cool to run 17:18 today but to finish 39th!" I shook my head. "Wow, I was surprised. I know the Notre Dame course is flat but..."

"Yeah, when we went through the mile at 5:15 and I couldn't even see the front pack...well, I knew I'd be happy to be in the top fifty. Who won anyway?"

"I think it was Connie Jo Robinson...of North Carolina State. She ran something crazy like 16:22."

We walked quietly in thought.

"After practice tomorrow morning I need to start reading "The Canterbury Tales." I have a paper due in three weeks – four to five pages. I'm not looking forward to it." Jennifer held the door for me. "How are your classes?"

"I'm not worried about anything but chemistry." I turned to Jennifer with my hands together. She was majoring in Chemical Engineering. "You gotta to help me. Please. My professor is the worst. I have *no* idea what he is saying in class. I'm writing so fast I don't have time to listen to his explanations." My head moved side to side. "But as long as I get a C, that will be enough to keep me happy."

The following evening Phillip rode the L with me from campus down to Belmont Ave, talking about next weekend's meet at Illinois and a little about classes, my seatmate asking to join us when he learned Annette and I were going to shop at The Alley. He never really said what his plans were.

The Wrigley Field scoreboard loomed to the west as we stood when the doors closed at Addison, both of us anticipating the next stop. The Objects were opening for R.E.M. at the Metro, Annette raving about the Georgia group whenever we talked about music. This was so exciting, like nothing in Iowa City.

She promised to meet us outside by the south exit. The station was a madhouse of activity, people rushing up and down the stairs like there was a fire, on the sidewalk outside the doors a panhandler asking for change, high school kids in Goth clothing hanging on the fringe trying to look cool. I gave Annette a tap on the shoulder and an enthusiastic hug, turning to Phillip to introduce him.

Annette pointed to the right, following Phillip's eyes as he glanced across the street at the Berlin nightclub, indicating The Alley was the other way.

"I want to shop to get some new ideas for an outfit on stage. Something unique…something that makes a statement." Phillip jumped in.

"You should check out Alcala's over on Chicago Ave. They have great Western stuff. And there's a thrift shop around the corner." He pointed. "On Clark Street that you can find 60's clothing…but let's look for accessories at The Alley – you know, scarves, belt buckles, jewelry, and such."

I'd never seen Phillip so animated…except when he watched "Dallas."

She tried on various clothing, including a pair of Doc Martin boots, and then we split up, Phillip going east to some vague destination; Annette and I west on Belmont and around the corner to the Metro. The concert was awesome, R.E.M. playing two encores before the lights came up, Annette taking puffs on marijuana passed through the crowd, never bothering to hand me the joint. She knew I wouldn't smoke.

After the show we caught the L to the Fullerton stop, arriving at Annette's dorm room just after 1am, exhausted from three hours on my feet. Her roommate was gone so I had a bed to sleep in, wearing a pair of Annette's pajamas that were a size too big. As I laid my head on the pillow, I couldn't get over her claim that Phillip was gay, the certainty in her words reluctantly removing my doubt. *Phillip...gay?* I mean, he did dress a little bit different, and didn't hang around with the guys on the team but... Whatever.

———————

Although Thorsten and I talked each week, it seemed the bloom had disappeared in our relationship. It was still easy to exchange gossip, and I enjoyed his updates, but conversations were more polite than intimate, like I was speaking with my cousin instead of a guy I'd been dating for over two years. He was the best thing that ever happened to me in high school, but mom was right. A long-distance relationship was tough to sustain. I just didn't want to admit it.

I began using birth control after mom's discussion in June, but did so for the regular periods, reasoning the pill would reduce my cramps and make everything easier. It was convenient to use this explanation to her, but if truth be told, if Thorsten and I had ever found the right time, there is no question I would have taken advantage. I cared about him that much, would have done it without reservation – yet in hindsight, I was glad we hadn't. The world was bigger than Iowa City.

Many mornings while I got dressed for classes I stared at myself in the full length mirror, happy that I didn't have a flabby stomach or hips so big that, as my brother always put it, "looked like the backend of a hay wagon." But when I stood sideways it was hard to think my chest would attract the attention of any boys – even with a flat stomach. Sigh.

Would I ever meet another guy?

Since the fall quarter began, I had started including extra exercise each morning, riding the stationary bike in the Blomquist Center for thirty minutes, the two block walk to the recreation building making it easy to get in a workout before my first class. The Big Ten Meet was in Iowa City at the end of October and there was no way I could do anything but run well. My parents, high school coaches, and friends would be there to cheer me on. I couldn't let them down.

But what is my goal? How high can I finish?

My constant thoughts of the meet made it tough to fall asleep as September turned to October. It was a worry that wouldn't go away – because I didn't know anything about the competition. Could I be top ten? But the Big Ten had great runners. I had already discovered four of them were All-Americans at the 1981 NCAA Championships. So maybe a top ten finish was a little too big of a reach. A dream that would only set me up for failure. It was difficult to produce a goal.

Each week I scanned the results Coach O'Shea posted in his office, memorizing names and times of the conference veterans, following their performances like they were in a soap opera. Cathy Branta, Katie Ishmael, and Rose Thompson of Wisconsin had consistently run well no matter how big the meet. There was little reason to think they wouldn't do the same in Iowa City. And Nan Doak of Iowa was 10th at the DI National meet last year and would be on her home course. There was no way I could race with her.

The Spartan's Karen Campbell had turned in fast times, two of Michigan runners impressing me with their consistency, and Becky Cotta of Purdue was undefeated, winning every race by large margins – especially on hilly courses. She was good enough to win it all. Would a top fifteen goal be smarter? Yet even that made me nervous. Might be too big of a stretch. How about somewhere between fifteen and twenty? It sounded a bit more reasonable.

The truth was that I really didn't have a clue.

On Wednesday morning, of the second week of classes, I push open the outside door of our dormitory for Jennifer, a heavy backpack over my shoulders as we discussed the Tylenol story in the *Daily Northwestern* newspaper, waving goodbye as she turned towards the Tech Institute, while I walked to Kresge Hall for English.

It was strange to think of myself as a college student, even though we'd been in classes for five days. The routine of pre-season cross country camp had changed, my morning regime now beginning with a 7am ride on an exercise bicycle, cereal and coffee with my roommate in the dining hall, and then classes from 9am – 2:30pm, with a one hour break for lunch at 11am. It was unusual to be eating so early, but it was my only opportunity.

In English class I already had a thick book which needed to be completed by Friday, five chapters for the Early American History quiz tomorrow, and my daily assignments in Calculus II – which I dreaded. But chemistry class was another story. I could barely understand what the professor was saying, his lectures filling my brain with fog instead of fact, shuffling out of class each day very discouraged. Initially I thought I could get a C, but I was beginning to wonder.

At least practices were going smoothly, my confidence growing as I proved to myself and my teammates that I was worthy of their respect. Yesterday on the two ten minute runs I held my own, the 5:45 pace challenging but doable, finishing among the girls on each session. I would need the confidence in Wisconsin this weekend.

It was interesting to discover the strengths of my teammates – the stamina of Janelle, Joanne, and Jennifer – the footspeed of Anita, Becky, and myself. The 3-J's, as I called them, hated speed sessions and loved anything which involved endurance, while my group was just the opposite, thriving on short intervals, relishing anything that required speed.

But I always recognized the importance of being a well-rounded runner. My high school coach, Mr. Raffensperger, preached to me that even though my speed was an asset, a lack of endurance could be an anchor – holding me back from

29

running with the best. That's why I biked in the mornings. To improve my aerobic fitness.

On Friday afternoon, Coach O'Shea drove us up to Madison for the Wisconsin Invitational. We did a run-through on the Yahara Hills course when we arrived, excited to race against the nationally ranked teams – but a little worried about the reality. As we followed the white line around the golf course Anita turned to me.

"Did I ever tell you about the time I beat Cathy Branta?" Anita had a small smile.

"Wow, really?" My eyebrows went up. It was hard to believe anyone could beat Cathy.

"Yeah…because I didn't. In fact, I couldn't beat her if you gave me a stick." Anita burst into laughter.

Saturday morning was unusually warm, the lush golf course releasing moisture from the grass as the sun found a foothold on temperatures, the discomfort ahead nothing to look forward to. Waiting for the race to begin I was drenched in sweat, leaning forward from the back row of our team as the starter blew a whistle, eleven other teams matching our poses.

BOOM.

I followed Anita as she shot from our box – to our side the Iowa State team in red and yellow matching our efforts as we skirted a kidney shaped pond and ran past the first green. Up front was the entire Wisconsin squad, Rose Thomson and Cathy Branta leading their charge, individuals from Kansas State, Texas, and BYU tailgating the Badger squad.

Joanne, Becky, and Anita led our Wildcats, Coach O'Shea shouting, "Good job ladies" as we approached the second green. "Maintain your position. Work together." The red and white of Wisconsin held their team lead as runners circled the second green like horses on a merry-go-round, the burnt orange of Texas, and royal blue of BYU mixed in with the Iowa State harriers.

Anita checked over her shoulder as we made a right turn, tapped her left hip and motioned for me to run at her side, the first mile just past the U-turn on the north end of the course. I pulled up on her hip as we leaned into the corner, just ahead, an official shouting out times.

"5:11…5:12…5:13…5:14."

Joanne, Becky, Anita, and I worked as a foursome, Coach O'Shea pointing out a cluster of runners as we headed back to the club house the first time.

"Good job ladies. Work on that group of Longhorns." He pointed as he shuffled alongside. "They'll come back."

My teammates followed his directive, their eyes tracking the three Texas runners only fifteen yards in front. Joanne pointed and we stepped up the tempo, steadily reducing the gap as we neared the halfway point near the club house, the four of us finally close enough that we could hear the girls breathing. We followed in their wake as we made a giant U-turn, Becky taking a deep breath before we surged towards the Longhorns.

In a matter of twenty-five yards all of us were around them, coach suddenly appearing along the white line to give us more advice.

"Excellent ladies. Excellent." He pointed again. "K-State…the girls in purple."

This time I had to search my soul to find the courage, but I did, following my teammates past the runners in purple, the official shouting two mile times only background noise, my breathing so loud I couldn't hear anything else. We passed the pair before we made the loop around the green at the north end of the Yahara Hills course, one kilometer remaining before we crossed the line. The first negative thoughts crossed my mind.

I'm not going to make it. I can't stay with them.

"C'mon. One more girl in purple." Coach O'Shea's pleas broke through my fatigue. "Just one more."

Like obedient soldiers we pushed after the K-State runner, Anita and Becky catching her before the line, Joanne and me coming up a few steps short. As I slowed to a stop my thighs felt like they had been beaten with a sock full of quarters, breaths so fast it made me squeeze my eyes closed. I couldn't remember ever being so tired. I draped an arm around Joanne's shoulders in the chute, collapsing to the ground when we exited the back.

I'm dead. I am so dead.

The Wildcats finished fourth out of the eleven teams, losing to Wisconsin, Iowa State, and Brigham Young.

Our men's and women's teams flew to Minneapolis for the Minnesota Invitational the middle of October, the last meet before the conference championships, our men's and women's squads tagging along with the football team for their contest against the Gophers Saturday afternoon. Becky was my seatmate on the flight, both of us taking a break after forty minutes of reading. I smiled and leaned towards her.

"I'm worried about putting on weight, you know, eating too much in the dining hall." I buried my head like a scared turtle. "Do you have any suggestions to…?" My words faded.

"Sarah." She had such a serious look. I was suddenly nervous. "Sarah." Becky locked her eyes on mine.

"I just want to say one word to you…just one word." I was waiting for her to smile but she didn't. It was freaking me out. "Are you listening?"

I nodded, trying to guess why she was so serious. *Did I do something wrong?*

"Baggies." *What?*

Becky's face went from earnest to laughter in a split second, my faint response to her giggles half-hearted. *What in the hell is going on?* She finally stopped laughing.

"Didn't you see 'The Graduate?' You know the graduation party scene where some guy pulls Dustin Hoffman aside to tell him the future?"

"Kinda."

Becky smiled and shook her head.

"Anyway, what I'm trying to tell you is, always bring healthy snacks in your backpack. You know, baggies with carrots, nuts, pretzels...apples, oranges, bananas…so you have something good to munch on." Becky patted my hand. "Otherwise, you'll be getting Doritos and Ding Dongs from the vending machines." She laughed. "And definitely skip lunch in the dining hall…too much fattening food."

It was chilly when we got off the chartered plane, the leaves on trees filled with more color than those in Evanston, the skies cloudy and portending rain.

That afternoon we did a run-through on the Bolstad Golf Course marveling at the constant undulations, the hills on this tough course a great tune-up for the Big Ten meet in two weeks. Stacey Bant, my roommate at the Kinney Championships in San Diego two years ago was a sophomore on the Minnesota team, a cast encasing her lower leg, a crutch under each arm. I waved and rushed over to give her an awkward hug, stepping back when we released.

"What happened? Is it broken?" She nodded.

"Stress fracture. Right behind my little toe." Stacey grimaced. "So now I have to use these medieval torture sticks." She indicated the crutches. "For two more weeks. No Big Ten meet for me."

"Bummer. Will you be able to redshirt?"

"Yep." Stacey nodded. A horn honked in the background. "Well, I gotta go. It's my ride. See you tomorrow."

Knowing the course is hilly and running a hilly course are two different things. It was quite apparent the Bolstad GC was filled with ups and downs but the reality of glancing at a hill that never seemed to end was tough to absorb. Although I hung with teammates throughout the race, my success today was more a battle of attrition than a triumphant performance.

From the gun we had seven in a tight pack up front, the squads from Minnesota and South Dakota State with equal representation, a runner from UW-La Crosse charging to the front as we crested the gradual slope four hundred meters from the starting line. Anita, Joanne, and Becky were shoulder to shoulder with the La Crosse athlete leading the race, Jennifer, Janelle, and me half a step back.

We had already climbed two challenging ridges by the time we approached the mile, an official calling "5:25…5:26…5:27" as we passed. *Whoa doggie. This race is going to hurt.*

The big hill on the back side of the course loomed ahead, the thought of it as exciting as shaving my legs with a dull razor. "C'mon girls" was all Becky could spit out, six of us charging up the long slope, breathing so loud it was tough to hear anything but the air racing in and out of my mouth. At the top of the hill there was a spectator waving a big sign back and forth like a carnival barker, repeatedly shouting.

"Go Tori Go!"

I stared at the cardboard poster twenty yards above us, Joanne falling behind as I continued to respond to challenges from Becky and Anita near the crest of the hill. The effort hurt so badly I wanted to cry out. All I felt was pain. *I'm dying.* I passed the two mile but times from the official didn't register in my brain, the last hill at the northeast corner of the Bolstad course a huge obstacle between me and the finish line.

When I made that turn towards the finish I was half-past dead, uncertain how I would ever get to the line, the needle on my gas gauge far into the red. Anita and Becky pulled away from me as we entered the long last straight, Alm from Minnesota passing me with two hundred meters remaining, my resistance fading like a dying comet. I couldn't have been going at more than a jog when I crossed the chalked white line, stopping at the mouth of the chute to put hands on my knees, an official grabbing my arm to pull me forward.

Fifth place. *Not bad.*

Anita was lying on the grass at the back of the chutes, her eyes closed, Becky bent over beside her, glancing up at me. "Nice job girls." I patted Becky lightly on the back and tapped Anita on the forehead. We turned to see Joanne halfway down the chutes with one Minnesota runner in front and another trailing, Jennifer two runners behind that cluster in ninth place. I turned to Anita and Becky.

"We won." We had five before the Gopher's number four.

"Way to go ladies!" Coach O'Shea lifted a hand to slap mine, waiting for me to open my palm. "Nice job Sarah. You were tough."

He waited until everyone's breathing slowed, some teammates standing, others sitting in the grass.

34

"I liked what I saw today. An aggressive start, strong pack running, and a good response to the hills. We'll continue to do work on Mt. Trashmore each week, but I'm sure you can see how important the hills will be in team success at the Big Ten meet."

He paused as a flock of geese passed overhead, their load honks overwhelming his voice, resuming with a smile.

"We beat Minnesota today so we've shown our team can be in the top five at the conference meet. Wisconsin, Michigan, and Iowa are tough, but after them it's up for grabs. So, if we do our job – run as a pack and challenge the other schools on the hills, well…"

We cheered on the boys' team while doing our cool down, Coach Nalley happy with Tim and Bob in the top two spots on the 8K course, Phillip only four places behind them. Their squad was also victorious.

Later that afternoon, while the boys team went to the football game with our coaches, Phillip joined us in Dinkytown for a late breakfast on the Minnesota campus, eight of us spreading out at two tables in Tony's Diner. I was happy coach let us shower so we could remove the grime and get into regular clothes.

"I can't believe the number is up to seven…people who died from the Tylenol capsules." Anita took a bite of the bagel. "Did you read the article in the *Daily* yesterday? They said the capsules were tampered with when they were on the shelves."

"Yeah, my mom was freaking out." I bit off a piece of bacon. "Can you imagine if it happened in Evanston? I mean, Arlington Heights and Elk Grove are only fifteen miles away."

"It's weird that they still don't know who did it." Jennifer continued. "I had some capsules, so I exchanged them…but I'm still uncomfortable."

"Thank God I use Midol!" Anita smiled.

I wish our football team had lost because the plane was crazy on the way home. At least I was pleased with the 17:51. There would have been nothing worse than a happy gridiron team alongside a poor cross country performance.

Coach dropped us off at the dorms after the flight from Minneapolis, Jennifer and I were looking forward to a long nap before we did a little homework. She was such a great roommate. We were both serious students, consistent about putting in study time at the library, and most importantly, getting to bed by 11pm. We needed regular sleep, our room at the end of the hall making it easier because it was away from traffic noise on Sheridan Road, and the obnoxious girls yelling up and down hallways on weekends.

In spite of the school's academic reputation, our dormitory had far too many who went out on Thursday and Friday nights, more than likely sorority pledges, coming home drunk well after midnight, Jennifer and I making a point to pound on their doors early the next morning. The first time I did this Jennifer thought I was crazy, but she quickly took to the payback, laughing at her own brazenness.

After Becky's talk on the plane Jennifer and I began carrying baggies of carrots, grapes, strawberries, and pretzels; including an apple, orange, or banana in backpacks as we trudged towards campus each morning. It was the best advice I'd gotten from a teammate – a simple way to control our intake. Wearing bun-huggers accented my worries about putting on weight, and this simple act kept concerns at bay. Mostly.

Initial thoughts that college was easy had quickly changed, workloads piling up like dirty laundry in the hamper, the assignments never done. I was getting A's in the history and English classes, but in chemistry I felt like a drowning swimmer, struggling every day just to stay afloat. With Jennifer's help I kept my head above water – although I rarely felt ready for the next day's class. Calculus was challenging, never allowing me to coast, but if I put in a steady effort, things would be okay.

Chapter 3

October 30, 1982

It was exciting to be back in Iowa City…but nerve-racking to know why.

The 1982 Big Ten Cross Country Championships. Mom and dad stopped by our hotel Friday after the team dinner, sitting on either side of me in the lobby, planning out the rest of the weekend, meeting my teammates for the first time as they checked out guys from other teams. I was planning to stay after the race, mom promising to drive me back to Evanston Sunday afternoon.

Danny, my older brother, would be in town to watch me run the Saturday morning race, excited to watch me compete – the first time in three years. He had always been my biggest supporter when I was little, encouraging me to try every sport the boys did, patient with me when all the neighborhood kids were anything but, teaching me the ins and outs of everything – how to shoot a free throw or a tip on the correct hitting stance. I begged him to come watch, wanting to make him proud. To let him know he was a big part of the reason I got to this point.

Although the racecourse was on Upper Finkbine, at breakfast the next morning I asked the girls if we could warm up on Lower Finkbine, worried I would get too many well-wishers bothering me before the competition. I was far too nervous and their good intentions would only make the pressure worse.

As always, Anita had something to say.

"No problem Sarah…but I was sorta thinking maybe we should set up a receiving line after the race." She grinned like the Cheshire Cat. "At the back of the chutes. You know, where your fans could come up and say hi…like a wedding reception line." She laughed. "I'll arrange the fees for autographs and if they want a picture with you, it will cost them...a buck."

Anita burst out laughing, all of us joining in.

I did a fifteen minute jog with the girls and then met dad over by the Letterman's Club patio twenty minutes before the race, using the bathroom in the building that he somehow got me into. When I returned, he began.

"Okay, lay on your back, hands on your stomach. Close your eyes." He paused. "In through your nose...two...three...four...five. And out one...two...three...four...five." He repeated this pattern for three minutes and then let me breathe at my own tempo. When I appeared relaxed, he continued.

"How many state titles in cross country did you win?" Dad waited for my response.

"Two."

"And how many state titles did you win in track?"

"Seven."

"Good. And who is the best father in the world?" He chuckled.

"You!"

"You better believe it." Dad grinned. "Today's prediction. Seventeenth! It's my lucky number."

I gave him a big hug and jogged to the starting line.

There is no sporting event more colorful than the starting line of a cross country race on a crisp fall morning, the cool air sharpening the hues. The setting was resplendent with color, leaves awash in red, yellow, and brown; the green grass brilliant against the fluffy white clouds and bright blue sky; athletes in multicolored uniforms of navy and orange, blue and yellow, black and gold; others in single colors of green and purple and red.

Runners did strides to burn off nervous energy, shooting from the starting line like crayons flying from a fallen box, tension filling the air as others nervously shuffled side to side, repeatedly running fingers over ears to put hair in place. There was a long whistle and then dead silence, only the soft sounds of breathing from teammates as we waited for the starter.

"Runner's set." Everyone leaned forward at the command. "BOOM!" And we were off.

It was easy to spot Nan Doak sprinting to the front, her blond ponytail bobbing side to side like a happy dog's tail, the entire Wisconsin team hot on her heels, Purdue's Becky Cotta weaving through the Iowa squad to get beside the leading Hawkeye. Our team got out well, positioned in front of the bell-shaped curve, riding it as though pushed by a wave, all of us praying we'd finish the race as a top five team.

Coach O'Shea was at the turn three hundred yards from the start, shouting through cupped hands.

"Remember to ride the hill. Stay relaxed."

The downhill must have been 250-300 yards long, ninety-two runners moving at a pace that would have been crazy on the flat, each of us anything but relaxed despite his entreaties. Coach claimed the initial 800 meters would be fast, somewhere between 2:20-2:25 because much of it downhill.

At the turn around the 14th green I had no doubt his estimate was pretty close, all of us leaning hard into the corner as though we were running on an indoor track, colors flashing by like wooden ponies on a carousel. Behind us I could hear a loud "oof" and someone stumble. *Bummer*.

Anita, Joanne, and I were twenty-five meters behind Nan Doak and Becky Cotta, the pair charging up the hill side by side, Rose Thomson and Cathy Branta leading the Wisconsin squad, every one of them oblivious to the incline. As runners neared the top of the long hill I recalled Coach O'Shea's words after yesterday's run-through.

"Remember, no one is going to fade up the first hill. Don't be worried. Expect to hold your position. But you'll begin to see cracks in their armor the second hill so take advantage of it, and on the third one I want you push hard and improve your position."

The course worked its way back towards the clubhouse, spectators on either side of the white line shouting through cupped hands, the wall of sound pushing us ahead.

"Go Sarah. You can do it." "Great job Sarah." "Go get 'em Sarah." I recognized the voices of my high school teammates as I ran the gauntlet.

"You can do it Sarah. At-a-way." It was my aunt. "Whoo hoo, let's go Sarah."

"Eyes up." I knew it was dad. "I want you to get three up the next hill." He pointed at the trio.

"Great job Sarah." It was Danny. "Awesome."

I glanced over at Anita and Joanne, the three of us turning in unison down the hill into the second loop. It made me nervous to not see the others, but I didn't have time to look for them. As we galloped down the slope I tried to count the number of runners in front, Iowa's Doak leading the field. *Twenty-three?*

Our feet slapped the grass on the downhill like wet cardboard hitting cement, gravity pushing runners almost faster than legs could tolerate, a Michigan State Spartan just ahead stumbling when the load got too heavy. We curled around the 2nd green, and I turned to see if I could spot teammates just as my high school coach shouted through cupped hands when we leaned into the corner.

"That-a-way Sarah." It was Coach Raffensperger – my high school coach. "You're doing great. Keep it going."

A pair of Purdue runners with white bows in their hair and a redhead from Michigan State were only ten yards ahead. We slid by one of the Boilermakers halfway up the hill, her teammate glancing over when we went by seconds later, the redhead succumbing to our efforts a few yards from the top of the long slope. *Twentieth.*

Coach O'Shea shuffled alongside us as we skirted the clubhouse, fans shouting from every direction.

"C'mon girls. Last loop. Dig deep. Keep it going."

Ten seconds later I heard dad's voice again.

"Awesome Wildcats. Awesome. You got three back there." He pointed ahead. "Now get four more. Next hill."

From my peripheral vision it was clear Anita and Joanne were moving their arms in bigger arcs, fatigue stealing strength from legs with a mile remaining. I'm certain my arms looked the same as theirs. *I'm so dead. I don't know if I can do it anymore.*

A left turn and we were racing down the initial descent a last time, my legs crying out for relief from the relentless

40

pounding, everyone's speed significantly slower this time through. We pulled up on a Michigan runner as the 14th green neared, the three of us hanging back until we came out of the turn. *Here goes nothing.*

Six hundred meters remained, two hundred fifty meters of it uphill. I glanced at my teammate's faces, their eyes pinched tight like they were running through a cloud of dust, only blank stares as we went around the Wolverine. Runners from Illinois, Iowa, and Indiana were just ahead as we suffered the long climb, Joanne slipping behind as Anita and I pushed after the trio just in front. I didn't know how much longer I could last. *I'm dying.*

We passed the Hawkeye and then the Hoosier two seconds later, the Illini runner fighting us tooth and nail as the apex of the hill approached. I had nothing in the tank, my mental toughness gone, Anita slipping away with every step.

"*C'mon darling. You can do it.*" At first, I thought I imagined it, but she said it again. "*C'mon darling. Keep fighting. I know you can.*"

It was Marie – my fallen friend.

Off the top of the hill I fought to pull back even with Anita, both of us going by the Illinois runner with one hundred meters remaining, Anita beating me to the finish line by a step. *Seventeenth. Just as dad predicted.*

I squeezed my eyes closed, the pain racking my body as I ran hands along the pennants in the chute to keep me walking straight, breaths blasting from lungs in a steady beat. Reaching out, I put hands on Anita's shoulders, and leaned forward into her.

"Thanks." I paused. "You were a godsend." I took a deep breath. "I couldn't have…done it without you."

Dad and Danny rushed up to me at the back of the chutes, my father squeezing me in a bearhug, smiling as he said.

"Seventeenth. Just like I predicted."

My brother enveloped me in his arms, the first hug I could ever remember him ever giving me.

"You did good Sarah. Real good." He smiled and patted me on the head.

My high school coach approached.

"Impressive Sarah. Very impressive." He grimaced, uncertain whether to continue. "Did you know that your teammates get knocked over on the turn at the bottom of the first downhill." I shook my head, my eyebrows going up. "Someone caught a heel…the blond-headed runner on your team, and she fell into two of your teammates, the three of them flat on the ground as the pack pulled away. One of them didn't finish and the other two never worked their way back into position. So it's not good…teamwise."

My head dropped. That's why Becky and Jennifer still hadn't come out of the chutes.

Ten minutes later we learned the team was ninth. *Damnit!* If those two had finished in the top thirty – a realistic performance, our team would have been fourth. We were quiet on the cool down, a rain cloud hanging over every head. We had no chance of running in the NCAA Regional with this performance.

I sighed. Being a college runner was harder than I guessed.

Just a year ago my only strategy in cross country was to run to the front and make sure no one passed me. I was happy with seventeenth at the conference meet, grateful for a fifth in any of our triangulars, never seriously thinking I could win any of the races. Now I was one of those invisible athletes sprinting towards the chutes, spectators paying little attention to my time or place, thinking of me as just another unknown runner.

Weird.

It was fun to spend time with mom on the drive to Evanston after the weekend in Iowa City, the four hour trip filled with stories about her college years and the fun she had. We were going to meet Annette for dinner in Old Town and then mom would turn around and head home. I didn't envy her, but the fourth grade students at Hoover Elementary expected to see mom bright and early Monday morning.

When we arrived at the scheduled time Sunday afternoon Annette was sitting on a bench outside her DePaul dorm, a feigned smile and unenthusiastic wave leaving me a bit unsettled. She wasn't dressed to go out. I jumped out of the passenger seat and rushed over, her eyes red and watery.

"What's wrong?" I wasn't sure I wanted to know. She gave me a quick hug and then held my hand, motioning for mom to come over, holding me in a hug until mom approached.

"Let's sit down on the bench." She pointed. Mom glanced at me with a worried look, putting an arm around my shoulders as we sat. Annette took a deep breath and looked at me.

"Your dad called about two hours ago." Tears rolled down her cheeks. She wiped them away with a sleeve. "Danny was in a car crash on the way back to Luther…just outside of Waterloo. He…he…is alive but in critical condition."

I began to sob, falling sideways into mom's embrace. *This can't be true.* It made me think of Marie's death four years ago. *Please God. Please let Danny be okay.* Annette wiped her eyes and continued. It was hard to hear Annette's words over my weeping.

"Your father said he'll meet you at Mercy Hospital in Waterloo." Annette looked at mom, handing her the number for the hospital. "He said you can try to reach him there, but to leave a message if you can't…so…so he knows you're on the way."

Mom stood up, holding her arms out to give Annette a hug.

"Thank you." She kissed Annette's temple and then held her shoulders at arm's length. "I know how hard that was. I'm sorry you had to be the bearer of bad news." Mom leaned in and gave her another hug. "Take us to a phone so I can call."

Mom hugged me tightly and then held my hand as we followed Annette to the public phones in the lobby of the dorm.

My brother looked so fragile in the bed. I just stared, afraid to approach him, both of his eyes swollen shut. A heart monitor with wires snaking to his chest beeped quietly, the gentle rise and fall of his chest the only thing that let me know he was alive. Mom went over and kissed him on the forehead, whispering something in his ear. I didn't know what to do, fighting to stop the tears. Dad grabbed my hand.

"Let's go over to the lounge so we can talk."

I was numb, following my father like a little child. Mom and I sat hip to hip on the couch, dad pulling a desk chair over so he could face us. He washed a hand across his haggard face, took a deep breath, and then leaned forward.

"Danny's in a coma right now. They don't know when he'll wake...but the emergency room doctor said his vital signs are good. That if he wasn't wearing his seat belt..." Dad dropped his head. "But he was." He paused to compose himself.

"He must have hit his head on the steering wheel...his left leg and three ribs are broken." Dad pursed his lips together. "But the doctor said that right now there is no reason he won't recover. That he can come out of this okay." He wiped tears from his eyes.

"I got us a room at the Holiday Inn across the street...so we'll stay there tonight..." His words faded. "For two or three days and then we'll make a decision...on how long we'll be here."

This was all so depressing, guilt settling on my shoulders like a heavy fog. My big brother...who was such a big presence in my life was struggling to stay alive.

Dad insisted I go for a run the next morning, promising to join me so I wouldn't get lost. We drove over to the Northern Iowa campus in Cedar Falls, borrowing a bicycle from a college buddy, heading over to the George Wyth State Park only blocks from the residence. We talked as I ran on the dirt trail while I ran at an easy pace, the forest floor covered with yellow, orange, and red leaves from maple trees. It was so peaceful.

"I get along well with Jennifer, she's saved me in chemistry, but Anita is the life of the team. She's a blast. Anita is the girl I met at the second Kinney Cross Country meet – the one back in San Diego when I traveled by myself."

"She did a great job at the Big Ten meet." Dad smiled. "I'll bet she places at the conference indoor meet. Where's it at?"

"I think Madison…in late February."

"That's great!" He smiled. "I'll be able to come up and watch you run." The thought made me happy.

We finished the eight mile loop in just over an hour, dad discussing plans for the rest of our day while I stretched, driving me to Perkins for breakfast. I showered at the hotel while he walked over to the hospital, arriving fifteen minutes later to see mom and dad speaking with a doctor just outside Danny's room. They looked up as I approached, heads nodding as the doctor finished, waving over his shoulder as he walked away.

"Well, that was good news." Dad began. "Dr. Lee said Danny has shown positive neurological improvement…he claimed it's good news." He smiled and then looked at mom. "Anyway. So, your mother and I are going down to the cafeteria for coffee. Why don't you sit with Danny while we're gone." They started to turn but mom stopped.

"Steve left Drake early this morning and said he'd be here before lunch so he might show up before we get back."

Mom leaned over and kissed me on the temple, then walked down the hallway towards the elevators beside dad. I sighed and reluctantly entered the room. Danny looked exactly the same. I sat down in the chair by the bed. I didn't know what to do.

"Hi Danny. It's Sarah." I grinned." You know, your favorite sister." I was at a loss for words but continued.

"This morning dad joined me on the bike for an eight mile run in some park a couple of miles from here." It was weird talking to someone who didn't respond but it still seemed like the right thing. "The trail was a nice loop and leaves covered the ground. It was really beautiful. I had a good time."

My thoughtlessness was disconcerting. Here I'm talking about having fun and he's in a coma. *What an asshole.* I was suddenly sad, my eyes filling with tears, my heart drowning in guilt.

"Danny, I hope you'll forgive me for badgering you about coming down to watch me at the Big Ten meet." My body suddenly shuttered, only a deep breath allowing me to

45

continue. "You missed the homecoming game with your girlfriend. And then…then you got in an accident because of me. I'm sorry. Please forgive me."

Tears rolled down my cheeks in a steady stream, only rustling at the door interrupting my sadness. It was Steve. I jumped up and smothered my brother in a big hug, trying to decide if the shocked look on his face was from my hug or his older sibling lying motionless in bed. Steve stared at Danny and took a deep breath, settling softly in the chair beside me.

He listened as I told him the latest news, quiet when I finished, finally looking up.

"God, I was so scared." He whispered. "I was afraid he'd die before I got here."

Chapter 4
November 5, 1982

It was hard to readjust to college life in Evanston after a week away, but mom insisted there was nothing more I could do, pleased that I was at least able to see my brother wake from his coma on Tuesday morning. For the most part, Danny slept, but the lucid moments increased in length until he was able to recognize all of us, though unable to remember anything about the accident.

Saturday morning, we had followed the ambulance to Iowa City, getting him settled in a room at the university hospital, our daily updates on his improvement very reassuring, only the surgery on the broken leg hanging over our heads. Dad drove me back to Chicago on Sunday.

The ride to Northwestern was much different than it had been just a week before.

Monday morning, we awoke to the first snowfall of the year, a November snow turning to rain by the time practice began, my toes frozen after trudging through the slop on our sixty minute run. After the seven miles Coach O'Shea had us finish with sprints up the zig-zag ramps of Dyche Stadium, then over to the weight room – a facility which had once been an ice rink warming house.

"Okay ladies, while you stretch listen up." He stared at Anita and she smiled, twisting a hand over her mouth like she was locking a door.

"I want three sets of ten reps on the bench press, leg press, upright rows, and leg curls. We'll do sit-ups and lunges after." He paused. "Challenge yourselves. The Big Ten meet is in two months and those girls from Wisconsin and Michigan think they can kick your butts so we're going to have to outwork them if we're to beat them indoors. Okay. Partner up." I nodded at Jennifer.

We struggled to our feet, bodies stiff from the miserable run, shuffling over to the Universal Gym. Anita raced over to the bench press station like we were playing musical chairs, a smile filling her face as she leaned back on the red bench, calling out the rhyme in coordination with the press.

"I must…I must…I must build up my bust. I must…I must…"

Our first indoor meet on January 7th was a low-key affair at the University of Chicago, with foursomes in the Distance Medley and 4x800, Becky, Jennifer, and Janelle running an open 3K. Even though many colleges hadn't begun classes, the field house was packed – men's and women's teams from Chicago Circle, DePaul, Elmhurst, North Central, Chicago State, Morton CC, and Wheaton College filling every bit of empty space. I was running the third leg on the 4x800 and the lead-off on the distance medley relay.

Anita and Joanne warmed up with me on the first floor of the Crown Center Field House, footsteps above pounding around the track, a cluster of boys huddled by the Heisman Trophy display case partially blocking our pathway. Somewhere in the back of my mind I seemed to remember that the first recipient of the award was from this school.

I stood at the curved line in position seven, a white-haired Irishman wearing an old University of Chicago letter jacket arranging us, winking at me as he whispered that I had the lucky spot.

"Ladies. You have six laps…just remember to turn left." He smiled and then raised the gun. "Runners set…BOOM."

I sprinted out hard, the lead-off from North Central going even faster, forcing me into lane two as we entered the backstretch on the narrow 200m track. "32…33." It was quicker than I wanted for the first lap, but I needed to get away from the crowd. I took the lead after two laps, the Cardinal slowing when she heard the timer shouting a sixty-eight second split, footsteps fading as I entered the homestretch going into the halfway point.

"That-a-way Sarah." Coach shouted through cupped hands. "Smooth and steady."

I was suddenly tired, the easy tempo much harder than it had been the lap before. My fatigue reminded me of my first year of cross country as a seventh grade student – back when I overestimated my conditioning and underestimated the pain. My last two laps were torture, the dry air making it feel like a scrub brush was going up and down my throat, the only thought to just endure. If not for the lapped runners I'm not sure I would have gotten through.

"See I told you." My hands were on knees after slowing to a stop, breaths still fast and deep as I stared at my spikes. Turning my head I saw it was the starter. "Seven *was* lucky." The U of Chicago coach smiled, then turned to put second leg runners in order.

The three of us cooled down outside, dirty snow in two foot high piles lining the edge of sidewalks, the cool air wonderful after the heat inside. Joanne pointed at the sign for the Rosenstein Library as we ran by the most modern building on campus.

"Coach said we could study in the library as long as we're back by 4pm." Joanne sighed. "We've only been in class five days, and I already have a ton of homework." She was a straight A student in Mechanical Engineering and was destined for a great career.

"Oh my God." Anita's voice was tired. "I'm not looking forward to the 4 x 8. It felt like I was sprinting the whole way on my 800m leg."

"Well, no wonder. You went out in thirty-one." I smirked. "Were you planning on running a 2:05?"

"Hey. How's your brother doing?" Joanne nodded to turn right.

"Good. But it's hard for him to get around. He's on crutches and the icy sidewalks are not a good combination." I sighed. "He still gets headaches, but dad said his mind is clear…so we're happy."

But I wasn't happy, still feeling responsible for his accident. The burden was heavy.

It was wonderful to have seven other girls to run with every day at practice but I missed doing Sunday runs with dad. He made it so much fun, driving me out to City Park on the one mile loop, buying me a big breakfast after, sharing stories over coffee during our father-daughter time. It wasn't that I didn't enjoy Sunday runs with my Northwestern teammates, because I did, but I was nostalgic for those moments spent with dad. A time when life seemed so simple.

The two week Christmas break hadn't been enough. I was homesick. And still guilt stricken.

The grind of second quarter classes and training in the cold were both so daunting, most days getting out the door for practices a huge effort. On these runs the cold and fatigue set in after forty minutes, conversation slowing to a halt because we were chilled to the bone, clouds of dread hovering overhead, my thoughts always turning to Danny.

Most of his time over Christmas was spent in bed, on the couch, or in the wheelchair, his attempts at simple tasks like brushing teeth or eating a meal resembling that of a four-year-old. It was so depressing to watch him struggle, my parents' constant reassurances doing little to assuage my guilt.

Danny was a three year letterman in baseball at Luther College, the starting shortstop on a 27-8 team, an athlete who could have been on their basketball or golf teams if he wanted. Now he wore an immobilizer on his leg that wouldn't be off until early February, his planned June graduation on hold. *If only I hadn't asked him to watch me run.* The thought gnawed on my heart every day.

And then there was my high school boyfriend.

When Thorsten and I got together after Christmas I was more nervous that thrilled at our reunion, his greeting hug and brief kiss keeping my hopes alive that there was a chance our relationship could survive – but that early optimism was dashed as the night went on. When he dropped me off at ten thirty, it was clear the passion was gone, my eyes filling with tears as I turned and smiled before I shut the car door, walking towards the house with chin on chest, my heart as empty as a paper sack. *Well, it's officially over.*

At least my grade report was good. The official results arrived in the mail just before the new year with two A's, a B, and a C. The 3.25 made me confident I could handle the classwork at Northwestern – although the good grades came with a massive effort – at a huge cost.

I reminded myself no one is tired on the first half of a ten mile run. That it's the last three miles which kill you. I still had two quarters remaining. To get the A's in English and history last fall I had to work my butt off, the expectations of college professors far exceeding the demands of high school.

Then there was our interval work each week. Not having an indoor facility made it tough to prepare for the indoor season, forcing us to face the cold each day – whether it was nine degrees or twenty-nine. Clearing two lanes of the Dyche Stadium track helped, but there was always an icy residue that could be dangerous if we weren't careful. Basically, training sucked, but what we had was better than nothing.

On these days I had to wear two long-sleeved t-shirts and mittens, the running tights not remotely enough to keep my body warm as we jogged between intervals on days with wind – which was every day. To face these workouts it took herculean efforts, the relentless cold wearing me down like an old whetstone.

Tuesday's intervals in the first week of February was my breaking point. When I knew things were slipping away. On these days Joanne's face always got especially red in the frigid air, her nose running like a leaky faucet, Anita joking that she must be related to Rudolph the Reindeer. Normally I would have laughed at her wit, but today I was too tired to even make a feeble attempt. I felt so empty.

The girls ran the ten 400m repeats between 66 and 67 seconds but I was always the last one across the line, my sixth one a seventy-one, thoughts of four more almost impossible to grasp. The two hundred meter jog in between did nothing to generate body heat, my toes succumbing to the frigid temperature. I was tired and cold, by the tenth one barely getting through the circuit.

Coach sent us to St. James Park for a cool down, the thirty minute trek continuing to drain my over-extended battery. When we turned around it was only the shouts and laughter which made us aware of a group of boys across the field as they slid down Mt. Trashmore hill on plastic discs. Becky broke the silence of our squad.

"God, I can't believe the Big Ten meet is only ten days away." She pointed towards Dodge Street, everyone following behind as we jogged back to campus. "Where did the time go?" Her words made me sigh. I didn't know if I would last that long. My heart had become an anchor, dragging me into the depths, blue skies no longer in sight.

———————

"Coach O'Shea, I need to talk with you." I hung my head and sat in the chair beside his desk. "I'm…I'm not ready for the conference meet." He started to say something but then waited.

"I know I'm in good shape. But the meet at Illinois State was a struggle. The last six hundred meters…it was so hard to continue, to push myself." I paused. "Not because I couldn't. But because I didn't want to. I just didn't care. Everything in my head was saying to stop. To step off the track." A tear rolled down my cheek and I brushed it away. "I know how tough it is when you're tired, but this was different. I didn't have the mental energy to push through it. I was willing to quit. And that's not like me."

I wiped tears with my thumb and index finger.

"So, I guess what I'm saying is…is I'm not ready to run at the Big Ten meet. I'm just too worn out from my studies and training in the cold every day and..." I didn't mention the sadness from my brother's accident still hanging overhead. I stared at the carpet in his office. "I'm sorry coach."

My mood had been iffy over Christmas break – what with the guilt I felt, the stress from schoolwork, and even though I saw it coming – the breakup with Thorsten. I needed some relief. A change of pace. A major change of pace.

"How about if I give you three days off." Coach sighed, attempting a smile. "Then let's see how you're feeling on Monday. We'll make a final decision then."

I reluctantly agreed, certain the short break wasn't going to be enough.

"Thanks coach."

I took a nap Friday after classes; the certainty Annette would keep me out late requiring extra rest. I was reinvigorated after a week away from running, no longer tossing and turning through restless sleep. The women's team left Thursday morning for the Big Ten meet. I would have no practice, the plan to stay with Annette all weekend.

I was glad Coach O'Shea conceded to my wishes. There was no doubt that any attempt at racing would have only driven me deeper into despair.

Jumping on the L at Noyes Ave. I was excited about the adventure ahead. I stared out a window on the car, watching a pair of squirrels chasing each other up and down an oak tree in the cemetery, at the Sheridan stop glancing through apartment windows only feet away, the Metro theater sign reminding me of the R.E.M. concert last fall when we pulled into the Belmont station.

The conductor mumbled words, "Next stop is Fuller… DePaul and…" brought me from the reverie. I raced down the stairs and across campus to her dormitory, calling Annette from the lobby phone, five minutes later my best friend burst through the elevator doors, a big grin on her face as she squeezed me in a hug.

"Girl, this is going to be your weekend. We're gonna party hearty!" She grabbed my hand, and we skipped out the door, smiling as she turned to me. "First up…a new hairstyle!"

I couldn't get over my new look, the long hair I'd worn in pigtails as a high school athlete was now gone. I stared in the mirror, running fingers through the layered bob as the stylist stepped away, the new sensation so foreign. Annette came rushing into the back room from the lounge, her smile stretching from ear to ear.

"Let me see. Let me see." Annette cupped my chin to turn my head. "Oh my God. It looks sooo good!"

Her enthusiasm made me feel better.

"I swear girl, the boys are going to be calling you all day long." She smirked. "You'll have to get an unlisted phone number." We both giggled.

I stood in front of the salon window staring at my reflection, the person looking back at me so unfamiliar. She pointed at the Lincoln Avenue bus as it slowed to a stop at the corner, both of us sprinting to catch the "Green Limousine" (as she called it) before it got away. Margie's Candies was our destination. Ice cream was our treat.

Three hours later, after my first experience with Thai food, we walked north on Halsted Avenue towards Harrigan's, passing DePaul students already drunk, Annette's new boyfriend playing a ninety minute set at the narrow bar. Aiden McDermont was drinking a beer at a table up front when we arrived, his lanky 6'2" frame towering over me as we shook hands. He had straight brown hair and a beautiful smile, the length of his locks now longer than mine. *Weird.*

"So, you're the girlfriend Annette has talked so much about. It's wonderful to meet you." He wrapped an arm around her shoulders. "She didn't tell me you were so pretty."

I blushed. I didn't know if Annette had told him to compliment me or not, but it was still wonderful to hear.

"She told me you were there for her first public performance." I grinned and nodded as we squeezed around the tiny table.

"It was at a coffee house in Iowa City. She played with Marie – our third Musketeer." We both sighed. "Up on a 6'x 6' stage in Things & Things & Things, singing 'Tell Me Why' better than Neil Young. And she was all of fourteen years old."

Annette leaned over and kissed me on the temple, turning to Aiden with a smile.

"Sarah was our manager." Annette grinned. "She got ten percent of our pay…which was nothing." We all laughed. Aiden looked over my shoulder.

"Well, I'm getting a nod from Gary, so it's time to go on."

He sat on the stool in the front window of the bar, a six-string in his lap, the spotlight tight on his face as he welcomed the young crowd. Aiden played songs by Van Morrison, The Chieftains, and U2 in homage to the Irish bar, thanking the crowd after he sang "I Don't Like Mondays" by the Boomtown Rats.

"Now I'd like to bring out a beautiful singer who has a beautiful voice. One I know you're going to like. Please welcome…Annette Anderson."

She turned to me and smiled at the shocked look on my face, stepping into the spotlight, everyone in the bar cheering raucously as she thanked the patrons.

I thought Annette was so pretty and always so hip, loving her because she carried off the chic look without trying. I wore lip gloss and occasionally a light touch of peach eye shadow if I had something special, feeling a Plain Jane next to her.

But Annette always looked like a million dollars – wearing mascara and penciled-in brows, her green eyes highlighted with an amethyst eye shadow. Tonight, she wore a hand-painted silk scarf to hold back her long blond hair, acid-washed blue jeans, and a baggy forest green cable-knit sweater. She was the envy of every girl in the audience.

"I want to dedicate this first song to my best friend in the world. She is sitting here in the crowd." Annette nodded at me, her eyes glistening. "It's called 'Tell Me Why' – a song you might know." She grinned. "It's by Neil Young." It was exactly what she said five years ago at her first public performance.

Aiden played the introduction and after the four bass notes she began singing, nothing but the guitar and her powerful voice filling the small bar.

"Sailing heart ships through…broken harbors out on the waves in the night…"

Annette sang with Aiden for forty-five minutes, the pair harmonizing so beautifully it brought tears to my eyes. I was astonished by their performance.

I wasn't in bed until well after midnight both nights, the days filled with adventure and surprise, the Saturday highlight meeting a random guy at the party who captured my heart – even without being drunk. Annette and I got home at 1:30am, my girlfriend ready for more but aware I was exhausted by the late hour.

After a late breakfast on Sunday Annette pulled out a card Danny had sent her earlier in the week. She held my hand while we drank coffee after the meal, softly reading his words.

"Dear Annette, I know you two are thick as thieves, so I wanted to make sure you pass this on to my #1 sister." She looked at me and smiled. "Remind Sarah how much I love her and that I wouldn't have gotten through this tough time without her support. She is the best sibling in the world! But Sarah can be a devil at times, so you have my permission to spank her if she doesn't keep smiling. Thanks. Danny."

I rode the L all the way back to Evanston with a smile plastered on my face, staring at my new reflection in the window.

Chapter 5
March 28, 1983

I finished the second quarter with a 3.25, the B- in chemistry courtesy of Jennifer's unfailing assistance, her explanations finally finding a foothold in my brain. Over spring break much of my free time was spent in Iowa City with Danny, playing HORSE at Hoover Elementary on the eight foot basket, every afternoon riding tandem with him on a borrowed bicycle dad got from a friend. The track team was in Florida, but I didn't mind. I wanted to spend time with Danny, finding ways to keep him active, the stubbornness we both possessed an asset in his rehabilitation.

My support was as much a service to me as it was to him.

Since the weekend with Annette my joy for life improved, running my butt off to make up for lost time, her support and Danny's letter recharging a dying battery. Before that point I worried the end of my time at Northwestern was at hand. That I would have to return to Iowa City with tail between my legs – defeated by Big Ten running and my stab at a prestigious school.

I'd never experienced such a low period, not even after Marie's suicide, the relentless demands of school and running pushing me to the edge, challenging me to get out of bed to face each new day. Though the rest of the team spent their break in Gainesville, FL I was more than happy to forgo the trip, the time spent with family was the last piece of the puzzle in my recovery.

At my initial workout on the track March 28th, I was unbeatable, first in every one of the 1K repeats, my average for the five 3:11 – enough proof to believe a 16:20 in the 5K was in the cards. On April 2nd I ran 9:41 for a 3K at North Central College, passing the 1600 at 5:03, my win over Joanne, Becky, and Anita hard to fathom. I was in heaven, besting my high school PR by eight seconds and establishing a new school record.

We cooled down around the small campus, the reality of what I'd accomplished still hard to comprehend. It reminded me of the Drake Relays win in the 800m my sophomore year at East High, the victory that day just as unexpected.

"I tried to stay with you, but when I saw the clock was still in the fours as we were coming up on the 1600…" Joanne shook her head. "You must have some magic potion." I smiled and shook my head.

"Who was the girl in red in our pack?" I looked at Anita. "I didn't recognize her."

"Beats me." Anita grinned. "But I promise she recognizes my ass and elbows because that's all she saw down the final straight!"

I nearly fell over laughing. I was so happy after our cool down I called home, borrowing change from Jennifer and Janelle for the pay phone in the field house lobby. Danny answered on the second ring.

"Hello."

"Is this the Billy Goat Tavern?" I had to stifle my laughter. "I want to order two cheeseburgers."

Danny started laughing, aware it was me. He shouted across the kitchen in a nasal voice.

"Cheezborger, cheezborger." I waited for the next line from his favorite Saturday Night Live skit.

"What you want with that?"

"How about some French fries?"

"Cheeps, no fries." We both giggled like children.

"Guess what I did today?"

"Robbed a bank?"

"No. I broke the school record in the 3K!"

"Awesome. I knew you were in great shape." I could tell Danny was smiling, my heart exploding with joy. "My #1 sister is gonna kick some ass this spring."

"Coach O'Shea said he is going to take me to Stanford on the 21st.

"Sa…weet! I promise that 3K record is going down again."

Cobb Field. The hallowed track at Stanford was surrounded by palm trees and coastal live oaks; in front of us the setting sun streaming around Hoover Tower as I jogged with Anita and Joanne around the Palo Alto campus, the air in the ancestral home of the Muwekma Ohlone Indians beginning to cool as stadium lights took over for our solar system's star. Keith and Craig were lined up for the first heat of the 5K, but we had to get ready, so we didn't have time to cheer them on.

"Last year Ceci Hopp ran an 8:57 in the 3K at this meet. That's so insane." Anita sighed. "I still remember I was in the middle of the backstretch when she crossed the finish line. How embarrassing."

"Well, at least you broke the school record." Joanne continued. "And you beat me by eight seconds."

"Yeah, I remember shaking Ceci's hand after the race thinking…she beat me by almost a minute." Anita smiled at me. "And now, a year later, some hick farmer from Iowa." Anita smiled at me. "Broke my school record."

There must have been forty runners between the two waterfall lines, an announcer going quickly through the field while we waited for the starter to get us underway. Coach O'Shea expected a sub five minute pace from us for the first mile, asking for seventy-four second laps. *Whoa.* It was hard to get my mind around a sub-5 pace in a 3K.

As uncomfortable as I had been wearing the purple bun-huggers at my first cross country meet, looking across the line at the fifteen girls on my waterfall, it would have been embarrassing to be the only one with the running shorts I wore in high school. It was as if this new clothing proved I belonged in an elite group – like the green sport coat given to the Master's Champions.

A redhead from a school I'd never heard of was in the position next to me, fine hair on her cheeks illuminated in the stadium lights, the rail-thin legs giving me the creeps. I tried to look away but even with a glance couldn't help noticing how skinny her neck was, the tank top hanging loosely off her shoulders like rags on a scarecrow. The sight made me so uncomfortable. She needed help.

"Runners set." We all leaned forward at the 3K starting line on the backstretch. "BOOM."

Runners were pushing and shoving like riders trying to get on a rush-hour L, desperately seeking a spot up front, three Stanford runners from my row cutting to the curb at the break line on the homestretch, moving at a pace that appeared as if they were in an 800m. I had no idea what place I was in, my only concern was staying on my feet, and avoiding being trampled in the stampede.

From the press box the announcer called out the frontrunners.

"In that lead group is Stanford's Ceci Hopp, PattiSue Plummer, and freshman Alison Wiley, the trio going after a sub-9:00 in the 3000 meters tonight. In their pack is Nan Doak of Iowa...Margaret Davis of Iowa State, and in the black and gold...that's Sabrina Dornhoffer of Missouri."

I had no idea what my initial split was, the clerk's voice unrecognizable, only Coach O'Shea's reassuring words helping me relax.

"You're good Sarah, you're good."

I didn't know if I should try to get into lane one, but coach didn't say anything, so I held my position. Individual runners constantly charged by, passing me from lane three. It seemed crazy to put in surges so early in the race. Especially because the ones who sprinted up to the lead pack were eventually shuttled to the rear as others overtook them and cut in front. The effect reminded me of an Indian File workout.

I contented myself with staying in lane two as I navigated the backstretch for the third time, happy to be in the front half of the race and running at a steady pace. The surges of those fools were only going to tire them later on. When I heard "3:40" at the twelve hundred meters all I could think was I ran a 3:36 on the leadoff of the DMR at the University of Chicago in January. *Holy shit!* I still had over a mile to go.

I ran even with the runner on my inside, her ponytail swinging side to side, the Chloe perfume she wore reminding me of a high school opponent - who was it? *Sandra something?* I had no idea what place I was in as we approached the 1600 mark – *15th? 20th?*

"4:53…4:54…4:55."

On the corner I spotted Becky Cotta about forty yards ahead, the Purdue runner who finished fourth at last fall's Big Ten meet in Iowa City. *C'mon Sarah.* The anorexic redhead was just in front of me. *Go get her first…then I can worry about Becky.*

I managed to overtake the redhead, but it seemed every time I got around, she passed me back, my herculean efforts going unrewarded. It nearly broke me. I was dead, coach's shout of "a 1000 meters Sarah" met with little response. Only a certainty that at this point the two-and-a-half laps would be no easier than two-and-a-half miles.

Like a quail shot from the sky, legs slowed as my neuromuscular system revolted, a kick nearly impossible in this exhausted state, only a vigorous arm drive getting me across the white line. I collapsed to the track after I finished, pain racking my body, the breaths finally slowing after a few seconds.

I rose to my feet with the help of an official, looking across the bodies littering the track like dead soldiers. I staggered over to Joanne, pulling her up with both hands, surprised to see Anita standing at the fence by Coach O'Shea. It was clear she was crying.

"What happened?" I nodded at the two.

"Anita fell on the cut-in and must not have finished." Joanne took a deep breath. "I saw her go down…but there was nothing I could do. I feel so guilty."

I reached over and put an arm over her shoulder.

"Joanne, there is nothing you could have done. Don't beat yourself up." I gave her a hug. "Let's talk with Anita. She's going to need us."

Later that evening the three of sat in the stands with arms around a teary-eyed Anita and watched Becky and my roommate in the 5000 meters, cheering Becky to a 16:29 and Jennifer to 16:41. Afterward we walked towards campus for ice cream at the Axe and Palm. I was ecstatic about running a 9:35 today, but didn't want to act a braggart, Anita starting to get back to her normal self after our TLC.

As we licked the cones and gabbed, Anita perked up when a tall blonde sat at a table nearby, my impetuous decision surprising me. I immediately stood and walked over to him, my back to the girls.

"Hey. Can you do me a favor?" He looked at me with cautious eyes. "We run for Northwestern and are here for the Cardinal Classic...over at Cobb." He wrinkled his eyebrows. I knew Anita loved blonds. "See the girl in the purple sweater behind me?" I whispered. He looked over my shoulder and nodded.

"Anita had a shitty race today and is bummed. So...can you come over and cheer her up?" The blond beefcake shrugged his shoulders and nodded, a grin filling his face.

"Sure. I'm Graham." We shook hands.

"I'm Sarah. I'll get her to stand and then..." My head dropped into my shoulders, afraid to say the next words. "Can you give her a hug?"

He laughed, towering above as he followed me over. Anita and Joanne were eyeing Graham as we approached.

"Joanne. Anita. This is Graham." He smiled.

"Graham has something for you." I looked at Anita. "But you have to stand up." I had a devilish grin plastered on my face.

She looked at me with a "this better be good or I'll kill you" stare, doing as I instructed. Graham stepped forward and leaned in, giving her a long hug, whispering something in her ear, a smile filling her face.

"Anita." Graham grabbed her hand before they separated. "Everyone has a bad day, but very few girls get a hug from the best-looking guy on the Stanford campus...so smile and consider this a red-letter day."

We shrieked with laughter. Graham was amused by our response, waving as he walked away. Once he was out of earshot I turned to Anita.

"So…what did Graham whisper." I leaned into Anita. "I wanna know."

She pulled a zipper across her mouth, her first real smile since the tumble in the race. Anita hugged me and then we laughed like lunatics.

———✳———

My first Big Ten track championship.

Because of traffic the bus trip from Evanston to West Lafayette took three hours, the men's and women's Wildcat squad spread around the bus in quiet clusters, Jennifer helping me with chemistry homework, a copy of "The Color Purple" in my backpack saved for the long days at the meet on Friday, Saturday, and Sunday.

I glanced out the bus window at fields of soybeans and corn filling the scenery to the side of I-65, smiling at a memory from the Drake Relays two weeks ago. Of late the girls on the team began calling me Dandy, after announcer Jim Duncan described me while I waited at the line for the start of the Invitational 1500 meters.

"In position eleven, that's Northwestern's Sarah Tucker. She was a seven-time Iowa state champion in track for East High School, the freshman in purple and white now running for the Wildcats, her best a 4:23.11. Folks, keep an eye on her. She's a dandy!"

Just in front of me I could hear Phillip and Anita, the pair talking about last week's episode of "Dallas," segueing into clothing and MTV videos as I continued to work. I was half listening while Jennifer showed me how to do an equation.

"Do you know Sarah's friend Annette? She's a great singer." Phillip continued. "I'm trying to get her in an outfit a bit like Pat Benatar or Debbie Harry – you know, lots of jewelry, eye shadow, and something exotic…like a leopard mini-skirt…or even a crinoline ballerina skirt. A little more edgy. With her beautiful voice and the clothes…she would steal any show."

"I gotta hear her sometime. Sarah said she's amazing." Anita put in her two cents. "Have you seen Madonna's video? 'Burning Up'…she's got it, she's going to be a star. I swear. You'll see."

"What do you think of the Culture Club? I mean, Boy George is hot!" Phillip was emphatic. "Did you see the outfit? The braided hair, eyeshadow, and lipstick."

I could picture the look on his face, certain Phillip was gay.

It was strange to run a prelim in the 1500 meters on Friday afternoon at Purdue. In high school we only had a final at the state meet, sixteen runners competing in each class. I was thirteenth on the Big Ten list, the 4:21.77 I ran at the Drake Relays three seconds faster than my state record, but nothing to write home about – not in this competition. These girls were better. Much better.

Wisconsin's Cathy Branta ran a 4:13 at Stanford two weeks ago and Sue Foster of Michigan won the conference indoor mile with a 4:40.57. *Holy shit!* Fortunately, I didn't have to race either today – although the Badger's Rose Thomson and Minnesota's Jody Eder would be in my third heat, neither a slouch. Their 4:14 PRs were far superior to my best.

I stood in the shade of the clerking tent, watching the first two heats. At the team meeting yesterday Coach O'Shea went over the qualifiers – the first two in each section automatically making the final, the eight fastest times getting at-large spots. Both of the initial heats were "sit and kick" so I could guess that's what I would see today. The same thing at the AAU meet in Knoxville when I raced Kim Gallagher a couple years back.

I stood at the waterfall line next to Jody Eder, nervously shifting weight from one foot to the other, running thumbs back and forth along the waistband of my bun-huggers, taking a deep breath as I reminded myself to be ready to kick when I heard the bell. From the stands I could hear Anita.

"Go get 'em Sarah." The starter raised his arm. "Wahoo!"

"Runners set." Everyone leaned forward and posed. "BOOM."

Eder sprinted down the backstretch like a banshee, doubts creeping into my mind about the race plan. Now I knew how a squirrel feels crossing the street. *Should I chase her? Or will everyone slow when we circle the first corner? Shit. Shit. Shit. What should I do?* As we came out the far corner the pace dropped like a cannonball hitting water, Eder cutting the throttle, her tempo slowing to a crawl.

"That's Minnesota's Jody Eder leading, Thomson of Wisconsin, and Lantis of Illinois in the top three spots. They're approaching the first split...1:18...1:19...1:20."

Oh my God! Way too slow. Four seconds slower than the initial splits of the slowest heat.

"Too slow. Get out Sarah, take the pace." It was Coach O'Shea leaning over the fence on the backstretch.

I looked at the water tower high on the hill across the street as I slid out to the lane three line, my rhythm increasing with every step. By the time we were in the corner I was leading, focused on running a seventy second lap. *What am I doing?*

Someone was breathing just off my shoulder, the runner behind clipping my heels as I crossed the finish line with two laps remaining. *Back off!* I wanted to turn around and punch her, but knew I had to maintain my tempo. Coach O'Shea shouted encouragement as I flew by a second time.

"At-a-way Sarah. Smooth and steady."

The first niggling doubt crept into my mind as I passed over the "1" on the backstretch with 600 meters remaining. *Whew, I'm really getting tired.* I knew it was too early to be using my arms so vigorously but had no choice, my legs heavier with each step. Around the corner and down the homestretch in front of the fans all I could think of was my fatigue. And that I had one more lap.

BOOM!

I rounded the penultimate corner and entered the final backstretch, my eyes horizontal slits, pain pounding on my body, too tired to care about coach's admonitions. Jody Eder was the first to go by, Wisconsin's Rose Thomson right on her heels. I fought to hold off the next runner before I got to the "1" but it was to no avail, my gallant efforts feeling so pathetic. *C'mon Sarah. Don't quit. Keep pushing.*

When I exited the last corner and entered the homestretch, I was in fourth place, a quick glance telling me three athletes were right there. *Drive your arms! C'mon Sarah! Drive your arms!* Halfway down the final straight my rhythm stuttered and the three overtook me, my body unable to respond to their speed, another athlete edging by inches before the white line. *Damnit!*

I stumbled face-first to the track, skidding on palms, the race number ripped from my chest as my torso dropped. I was too tired to move.

"Let me help you up." I turned my head and squinted into the sun. I could tell by the curly hair it was Jody Eder. I rolled over on my back and she reached out. "Give me your hands." I stood and took a deep breath.

"Thanks."

"No, thank you." She smiled. "You were the courageous one. Not me. In fact, this entire heat should be thanking you. Four made the final because you pushed the tempo." I gave her a weak smile and she patted me on the back. "Good luck the rest of the weekend."

Fourteen made the final. I was fifteenth.

Saturday's 3000 meter race didn't go much better, my 9:42 enough for tenth place, Michigan's Sue Foster taking her first title of the weekend with a 9:32.92. Sigh.

This meet was so humbling – as were the meets all year. I had improved all my PR's yet had nothing to show for the efforts, only a single victory at a small meet in Naperville. This talent level was far beyond my initial guesses last fall. Dad always claimed that if we knew how challenging the road ahead was, most would not have even started. That naivete could often be an asset. It was hard to disagree with his assessment.

The women at the Big Ten meet were truly athletes, possessing the same fierceness and dedication as their male counterparts, willing to dive at the line in order to win, gladly digging deep into the well of courage when challenged. We were equals in every way. Guys who came in with a disdain for women's athletes quickly changed it to respect when they saw how tough we were.

Title IX was the difference. The first athletic scholarships Northwestern gave for track – just three years ago, the impact noticeable in today's impressive performances, the depth in each event a testament. Ten years ago, only a handful of females in the Midwest could break five minutes in the mile, yet three months ago at the Big Ten Indoor Championships, seventeen girls did over two days.

Four weeks after the Big Ten meet I finished my first year at Northwestern, scarred from the battles yet wiser for the experience, the tough times making me appreciate the resilience I possessed. I was determined to work even harder in the months ahead – willing to do anything to be good.

Chapter 6
June 13, 1983

The first day back in Iowa City I rode over to the cemetery, skies threatening rain as I walked the bicycle to Marie's headstone. I sat cross-legged in the grass, staring at the inscription.

Marie Rose Munson
October 28, 1963 – October 28, 1978

"I'm back in town so I thought we could talk. I was here over spring break but..." Tears rolled down my cheeks. "I had a good outdoor season – didn't do anything too dorky." I wiped my tears and smiled at the granite. "Although I did fall at the Big Ten meet." Marie was always such a spaz. "But it was because I dove at the line to beat a girl…although I know you still would have laughed at me."

I used the back of my hand to wipe my eyes.

"Annette and I get together a lot. We always have such a good time." I smiled. "I took the Northwestern girls to one of her performances. They were *so* impressed. Annette always looks so cool – lots of bracelets and the signature scarf in her hair. Just like she wore when you played alongside her." I took a deep breath. "I can still hear your voice whenever Annette sings…and I know she does too. You would be so proud of her. She carries the torch for you."

I sat quietly, staring at the grass, pulling up memories.

"Well, I gotta go. But I'll stop by again." I kissed my hand and placed it on the stone. "See ya."

I rode home humming the song Annette wrote for Marie, the words playing in my head as I coasted down Dodge Street hill.

"Where did you go my dear old darling, why did you leave us in such pain…"

It felt good to be back on my old training routes – the Jewish Cemetery eight miler, a six-mile trek around Finkbine Golf Course, another of the same distance on the old quarry road along the Iowa River, the mile loop around City Park for my faster tempo days. But my favorite by far was the DQ route on days when I did two workouts, the hot fudge shake halfway through the run reward for my extra effort.

I met Stacey Hersh there one evening for ice cream, the girl from West High who beat me at the state cross country meet my junior year – a low point in my high school career. One that almost made me quit running. At the time I had no idea what anorexia was, only that she kicked my butt every time we raced – no matter how hard I trained. The first time we competed her skeletal frame shocked me; legs skinny from ankles to hips, collar bones jutting out horizontally from her shoulders like bushy eyebrows on an old man. It was spooky.

Stacey arrived two minutes after me, a smile filling her face as she shut the car door. Her frame looked normal. *Thank God.*

"It's so good to see you." Stacey gave me a hug. "You look so good. I really like your hair…it's such a fresh look."

"Thanks." I pointed to the line at a window. "I tried to reach you when we were at Stanford…in April but your roommate said you were out of town. I was so bummed."

"Yeah, I was in San Francisco for a Talking Heads concert – David Byrne is awesome. We had a blast. He came on stage by himself with this cassette deck and a gray over-sized suit…like he had borrowed it from an NFL lineman. It was humorous. But he's great."

"Cool. How is school at Stanford?" I shook my head. "Northwestern is tough." Stacey nodded.

"Yeah. My freshman year was *so* hard. But this past year was much easier. I guess I discovered how much time to invest in studies and how much time to invest in me."

We sat at a bench along the river and talked for forty-five minutes, hugging each other before leaving. It made me sad to recall all she went through with the anorexia. There were girls in the Big Ten who had the same issue – whether it was the coach's fault or the mistaken belief that "thin is good" – I

69

couldn't say. But I knew it would never produce long-term success – her hospitalized eighty-nine-pound emaciated body all the proof I needed.

Coach O'Shea gave us a plan for the summer training, but it was Danny who helped me implement it. We did the hill work on the four block climb up Dodge and Governor Streets, my brother encouraging me as I neared the top of the four hundred meter incline, riding alongside as I jogged back to East High for leg presses on the Universal Weight machine and twenty-five yard lunge walks on the football practice field.

We did double workouts of four miles on Tuesdays and Thursdays, my older brother riding beside me mornings and afternoons in heat, humidity, and rain, timing the tempo runs on Friday through City Park. On Sunday dad found dirt trails to do my long runs, joining me on Danny's bike, the conversations lively as I did my long miles at an easy pace.

But as hard as I worked, I never did more than fifty miles a week, unable to fathom that some girls might be doing more.

Danny was much stronger now, his limp mostly gone after the accident last October, dad working with him at the East High baseball diamond each morning after my run. My brother was determined to return and play his fifth year at Luther College, finishing his career on a high note. I sighed whenever I thought about the car accident, my guilt lessening as his conditioning improved...but it was still there. *Does time really heal all wounds?*

Thorsten and I ran into each other after the 4th of July fireworks, Danny and my parents hanging back while we hugged under a streetlight and then exchanged inane pleasantries, his friends speaking in muffled voices as they huddled awkwardly behind, my ex-boyfriend looking at his buddies, and then back at me when conversation faded.

"Well...it was great to see you Sarah." He forced a smile. "Good luck this fall in cross country."

I sighed and rejoined my family, Danny wrapping an arm over my shoulders as we walked to the car.

70

The following weekend mom drove me into Chicago so we could spend time with Annette. I hadn't seen her all summer, only aware that the new band she and Aiden put together practiced in the DePaul studio each day. Mom and I stayed at the Hotel Lincoln, the same place as two years ago, Annette subletting an apartment with her boyfriend just south of Oz Park.

We arrived mid-afternoon in light rain, mom deciding to take a nap while I went for a run in Lincoln Park, the path now familiar after so many Sunday runs back to campus from DePaul. As it was Friday, my workout was the four mile tempo. After a ten minute warm-up I stopped at the mile marker by the water trough to stretch, my hamstrings tight after four hours of sitting in a car. The crack of a golf ball at the driving range caught my attention when I was doing the leg swings leaning against a locust tree, finishing the routine with carioca beside the trail.

I smiled. It was wonderful to be back in Chicago.

I jogged to the Mile 14 marker, the running path so empty it felt like it was all mine, bending over to check my laces. Then I leaned forward at an imaginary line and took off. Under Lake Shore Drive at Belmont Harbor I continued along the docks at a six minute pace, metal lanyards clanging against boat masts in the gentle breeze, my stride still relaxed as I passed the Mile 15 sign, splitting a 6:02 on the Timex watch.

It felt easy so I stepped up the pace, a glance at Mile 16 showing the second mile at 5:47. *Awesome*. Making a small loop I reset the watch at Cricket Hill, reminded of the great view of downtown on top as I jogged back to the Mile 16 marker, immediately at my tempo as I headed south towards the hotel.

Navigating the muddy Montrose underpass I continued down the lakefront path, staring at a sailboat far out on Lake Michigan, occasionally glancing to my right to make sure I didn't get hit by an errant tee shot on the 9-hole Waveland course. *This is so fun.* Past the Addison clock tower and around the small grove of trees I smiled when I looked at the third split, my breathing steady despite the 5:44 pace. *Yeah baby*.

It was hard to control myself the last mile knowing a 5:20 would have been possible – but I did. My final split was 5:44, the breathing relaxed and controlled despite the challenging pace. I slowed to a stop and walked with hands interlocked behind my head, smiling at a middle-aged jogger as she came towards me, figuring the average pace in my head – 5:49, equivalent to a 18:06 5K. *Wow*.

Two hours later we met Annette at Chances R in Old Town, my girlfriend squeezing us in hugs, mom commenting on how nice Annette looked as she held her at arm's length. She was right. The confidence Annette gained performing the past year made her more attractive.

"God, you don't know how much I missed you two." Annette smiled and put the Ray-Bans in her purse. "The days this week went by so slowly. I thought this evening would never arrive."

Mom held up three fingers and the hostess escorted us to a table.

"I can't believe it's been..." Mom was counting the months in her head as we sat. "Ten months since I saw you last. It's like twelve dog years." We all laughed. "But going out with a mom can't be all that exciting."

"Mrs. Tucker. Are you kidding?" Annette held mom's hand. "I love being with you. There is no way I'd miss this for a million dollars!"

"So when do we get to meet Aiden?" Mom grinned. Annette looked at me from one eye.

"What did you expect?" I shrugged my shoulders, sporting a devilish grin. "It was a four hour drive."

"Well, Aiden is going to join us at The Old Town School of Music tonight…he got tickets to a Nancy Griffin show." Mom's eyes lit up. "I thought you'd like her."

"Did you know that at the age of fourteen she played her first gig?" Mom nodded her head.

"No way." I was shocked at the revelation. It was same age as Annette and Marie when they played at the coffeehouse.

72

The concert was wonderful, Annette inviting us to her apartment after the show for wine. We talked until midnight, feeling so worldly as we hailed a cab on Lincoln Ave. for the mile ride back to our hotel.

Saturday morning, I got up at 8:30, running six miles on the Lincoln Park trails, the path much busier than it was yesterday, yuppies jogging at a ten and twelve minute pace in the most fashionable of running attire, their $60 training shoes like putting lipstick on a pig. I loved flying by all of them, especially the cocky guys who thought they could match my pace. *Eat my dust you losers!*

After my shower we took the Clark St. bus to Andersonville for a late breakfast at Svea, a small Scandinavian restaurant where they served pancakes with lingonberries and Swedish sausage. Mom claimed to have read about it in the paper, but I suspected there was more to the story than she was telling.

Afterward, we shopped in the Andersonville stores and then took the green limousine back to the hotel, both of us getting a nap before we met Annette for an early dinner up on the hotel rooftop, the view of the lake breathtaking with the sun at our backs.

"Okay. Aiden and I are playing at 10pm." Annette was afraid mom wouldn't be happy with the late hour, surprised when she eagerly smiled.

"Wonderful."

"We'll reserve a table for you two." Annette grinned. "So, you won't have to worry about a good place to watch."

We sat about twenty feet from the stage at Fitzgerald's in Berwyn, thrilled when the spotlights came up, listening to Aiden and Annette as they harmonized on the first song. Mom closed her eyes and enjoyed the moment, a smile filling her face as they sang. Annette looked so cool, dressed in a gold lamé halter top, leopard print mini-skirt, and black ankle boots, five or six bracelets encircling her left wrist.

After the fourth song the applause was longer, a roar filling the 150-seat venue, Annette staying at the microphone while Aiden changed guitars.

"I wrote this next song a couple weeks ago. It's called 'Anything' and is dedicated to my second mother…Mrs. Tucker, the woman who always encouraged me to reach for the moon." The spotlight was tight on Annette's face, her hoop earrings glittering as she gently rocked side to side while a slide guitar played in the background – Aiden's guitar, the drums, and a piano joining in as the upbeat rhythm unfolded. She began on the fourth beat, her voice soft and sweet.

"Running from the teenage blues, tired of all the crazy rules, feeling something like a…fool.

Reaching for the baited stick, thinking that it's all a trick, wondering if I'd ever be…cool.

Clutching at my debris, you were always there for me, led me to the…moon."

The power in her voice was astounding as she sang the refrain for the first time.

"So I…I would do anything…anything…in the world."

"I…I would do anything…anything…in the world…for you."

She finished the fourth stanza and the audience jumped up as the slide guitar and horns faded, their enthusiastic applause continuing unabated, Annette bowing with a hand over her heart. It was hard to believe she was nineteen – only two months younger than me.

The mid-summer blahs hit me after the trip to Chicago, the relentless routine and steady miles wearing down my mind and body. Impulsively I signed up for the July 24th Iowa City MS Half Marathon, the same event I ran before my freshman year of high school. I finished second in that inaugural 13.1-mile race, somehow remembering the time was 1:40:40 – a 7:40 pace. Could I break 1:30 in 1983? Sub seven minute pace. I hoped so.

I wore my '79 Kinney tank top and an old pair of nylon shorts, scanning the starting area as race time neared. There were twice as many runners as the last time I competed, Gilbert

Street filled from the Recreation Center to the police station. It didn't take more than two or three seconds to spot a girl doing strides on the College Street bridge, the power in her relaxed rhythm unmistakable. *Who is she?*

She lined up on the front row, some males wishing her good luck, others showing looks of distain – as though they thought she didn't belong. I smirked. I was certain that by the end of the race every single one of that group would find themselves sadly mistaken. Snaking through the crowd I lined up two rows behind the brunette, her ponytail pulled back with a hair tie, the lime green tank top easy to spot. It was humid despite the 7:30am start but at least it was cloudy, though rain was not supposed to fall this morning.

BOOM!

It felt good to release the tension in my body, to feel a rhythm in my stride. A cluster of males got out extremely fast – most too fast, the dense crowd at the starting line quickly dispersed, everyone finding their own niche as we chased the police car down Gilbert Street. I was about twenty-five yards behind the girl in lime green, two guys on my right hip saying something to each other as we passed the first mile at 6:47. Their tempo felt good, so I ran alongside the two biding my time, children sitting at the curb waving and shouting that I was the second girl.

My breathing was steady as I neared the six mile – an early promise that sub 1:30 was realistic today. The real race, the one that would determine my final time, would begin in about ten minutes, at a point where fatigue would tell me yea or nay. I was grateful the course was flat, this tempo too fast if I had to navigate hills. The lime green tank top was no longer visible in the distance, my initial dream of running with her gone. She was as good as I suspected.

Large traffic cones were located down the middle of the street once we passed the six mile marker, blue lights on the leading police car flashing as it approached from the opposite direction. Just behind two guys were racing side by side, another stocky runner located ten paces back, three more males trailing by one hundred yards. I stared ahead until I could see the lime green tank top running along the cones from a block away, three guys to the side, her rhythm relaxed and steady.

Dang, she must be five minutes ahead of me.

The distance between us closed rapidly, a smile flashing on her face from forty yards away, a thumb going up as she neared. She looked right at me as we passed each other.

"Go girl!" And then she was gone. *Cool.*

Another minute and I made the U-turn, an official shouting my split.

"43:29." *I'm finally heading home.*

For the first time one of the guys spoke to me. It was the tall one.

"Stick with us." He paused to breathe. "We want to break ninety."

I was too tired to talk so I gave him a thumbs up.

The next five miles were a test of my toughness and tenacity, the pace a notch faster than I wanted. *Dang it. Wasn't this supposed to be fun?* Pain came and went like my monthly cramps, the tall opponent providing words of encouragement as we passed the nine mile marker. Part of me wanted to slow down, to take it easy – but I couldn't.

It was at times like this that I wondered why I chose to be a runner. I hated that I was so competitive, unwilling to relax when I could have taken it easy. I was exhausted, dancing at the edge of a cliff, yet I continued to push well beyond my comfort zone, knowing the suffering would go on for at least another twenty minutes. *I must be an idiot.*

At eleven miles my partner pointed at a guy about forty yards ahead and glanced at me.

"Let's get him." He took a deep breath, obviously as tired as I was. "That's the dude." Another deep breath. "Said no girl…was going to beat him."

His words lit a fire in my belly. There was always one guy who had to be an asshole. By the twelve mile mark we were ten yards behind my new rival, the effort to get closer nearly killing me. I didn't know if I could continue, my breathing fast and furious, pain overwhelming a tired body, willpower fading rapidly. My tall partner turned to me again.

"Make it big."

I knew what he meant. Don't dilly dally. Go by with a strong effort. I didn't know if I could do it. From one step behind he struggled to get the word out a last time.

"Big."

I went by with a surge, the early morning heat and humidity overwhelming me, my body screaming to stop, spots dancing in front of eyes as I continued the fast pace. The only thing keeping me going was the guy I'd just passed and the sight of the MS Half Marathon banner flapping in the gentle breeze. As I got closer, I stared at the digits on the clock, "1:28:24…1:28:25…1:28.26…1:28.27" and then I had finished, eyes squeezed shut as I staggered through the chute, letting the pennants slip through cupped hands.

As soon as I was out the back I leaned forward with hands on knees, sweat dripping off my nose in a steady stream, the tank top plastered against my body. *I am so dead.*

"Here." It was the tall guy. He handed me a cup of water. "You were amazing. Congratulations."

"Thanks for your help." I gave him a weak smile and he waved.

"See ya."

I grabbed another cup of water and walked over to a grassy hill to lay down, pouring half of it on my forehead, drinking the rest. I must have dozed, suddenly aware of someone talking.

"Congratulations." I didn't recognize the voice, squinting as I opened my eyes. "Impressive performance. What's your name?"

"Sarah Tucker." She extended her hand. It was the girl in the lime green tank top.

"Katie…Katie Schilly." What? My eyes were as big as frisbees.

"*You're* Katie Schilly." I was incredulous. She nodded and smiled. I jumped to my feet, suddenly unaware of the fatigue. "The Katie Schilly…from Central Square High School?"

Katie nodded, eyebrows climbing. She was shocked, not expecting to hear such a trivial fact from someone she had never met. She waited for me to explain.

"Oh my God! I wrote a paper on you when I was in high school!" She thought I was pulling her leg. "No, really. You and your mom sued the State of New York Education Department so you could run on the boys' team…because the girls didn't have a team. You were a cross country co-captain your senior year. And you even got hate mail."

"Wow." She chuckled. "I never would have guessed."

"Why are you here?" I rubbed salt out of my eyelids with the tank top strap.

"I live in Ames and am training for a fall marathon. I wanted to use this as a tune-up." She backed up slightly. "To check my fitness."

"Well." I suspected she wanted to go. "It's so cool to meet you." I reached out to shake her hand.

"No. Wait." She smiled. "Come cool down with me." *Oh my God.*

We jogged for ten minutes, Katie mentioning the award ceremony wasn't until 9:45 so we had lots of time to gab. She was going to graduate school at Iowa State and hoping to qualify for the US Marathon Trials at a November race in California, and then get one of the three spots on the US team for the '84 Olympic Games in Los Angeles.

I mentioned racing against Margaret Davis and Suzanne Youngberg at the Stanford meet, two of the current ISU runners on the Cyclone squad, Katy asking my times in the 1500 and 3K, predicting I would be in the top ten at the Big Ten meet this fall. It made me so happy to hear her words.

We talked about our favorite races – Katie's the 1976 AIAW Cross Country championship in Madison where Iowa State won the team title by forty-eight points.

"The weather sucked. I froze my butt off – even in a stocking hat, gloves, and long johns." She started giggling. "I remember sitting in a portable toilet and peeing ten minutes before the race, thinking ice cubes would come out." We both burst out laughing. "But I finished 8th so it could have been zero and I still would have been happy."

For me it was my love for the Drake track – meeting Olympian Cindy Bremser there, winning seven state titles on the blue oval, all moments I would forever hold dear. A sudden thought hit Katie when I mentioned Drake, her eyebrows lifting again.

"Are you the girl who won the high school 800m at the Drake Relays?" I grinned and nodded. "I watched you…it was…1977. I remember because you and the other girl almost fell as you leaned at the line…Jim Duncan said you broke the state record."

Katie segued into her college experience, describing what running was like at Iowa State.

"Sarah, you don't understand the impact of Title IX." She looked up at the golden dome on the Old Capitol as we jogged up Iowa Avenue. "We always traveled to cross country meets in a station wagon while the boys were able to rent vans…I mean, we had eight girls. Coach Murray drove six and seven hours through rain and snow while the boys had a chartered a bus."

Katie sighed.

"And we always slept four to a room, usually eating dinner at McDonald's or Hardees to save money." She laughed. "I remember we had cereal for breakfast…*in our room*…before the national championships in Wisconsin. Breakfast in bed!" She looked at me, laughing at the memory.

"God, I miss those days."

We exchanged addresses at her car after the award ceremony, Katie giving me a hug and a *Kangaroo* t-shirt like the one she wore on the stage – apparently a new shoe company she was sponsored by. I walked over to Iowa Ave to catch a bus home. Mom was never going to believe this!

The days passed and July became August, the start of my second year just around the corner. I was looking forward to the cross country camp before classes began, Coach O'Shea describing the Mt. Olympus Resort in his letter to the team, the park only ten mile from the Wisconsin Dells, promising the area was filled with miles of dirt trails and lush woods.

We had good freshmen class arriving for the 1983 season – Sue Simon and Alena Palmer finalists at the Kinney Cross

Country meet in San Diego last fall, Deena Albright the Ohio State champion in the eight hundred meters. The disappointment of last October's nineth place finish at the Big Ten meet still bothered me, some the angst from Danny's accident the same weekend. Everyone knew we had enough to finish fourth last fall, but as dad always barked, "they don't give out awards for potential – only results."

I knew the others felt just like me, that we just had some bad luck, willing to put the race behind. But I swore to God it would never happen again. We all believed we could be one of the best cross country teams in the conference this fall and would do whatever it took to achieve that goal.

Success is motivating but sometimes failure can light a fire in your belly just as bright. I sure hoped it did this year.

Chapter 7
August 23, 1983

We had a great time training on trails thirty miles northwest of Madison WI, the boys team joining us for the two week boot camp at the resort. After morning workouts, we raced go-carts around the quarter-mile track, dying to beat the boys, discovering who was most courageous on the amusement rides. The water park filled most of our free time the first week, Anita burning to a crisp after three days, most evenings the teams sitting around the campfire and making s'mores, some nights listening to Tim play his six-string guitar as we relaxed by the fire pit.

Anita came up with the idea on one of our easy Tuesday runs at camp.

"They give jocks to the boys…why don't they give running bras to the girls?" Anita wasn't joking…for a change. "I mean, if the boys get tights, we get tights. If the boys have two in a room on the road, we have two. Why should this be any different?"

She had a point.

"Yeah, but what are we going to do?" Becky asked. "Stage a protest? I mean, I'm sure as heck not going to run without a bra." She giggled. "Or burn it."

"Here's what I was thinking." Anita grinned. "How about if we set up an appointment with Barbara Sandy, she's the Associate AD, and let her know our beef? Explain to her what Title IX is all about." Everyone agreed.

It sounded so good on the Wisconsin trail, but when Anita convinced me to join her at the meeting with Barbara, I was a little less confident. I wore navy slacks, a white blouse, and clogs, Anita – as always, a little more flamboyant, her purple silk blouse and black skirt making a much bigger statement.

After the pleasantries Anita began.

"We know you are a big supporter of Title IX – of providing equal opportunities for women. To make sure women are treated fairly." Anita paused. "And yet there are things that still aren't equal. For example – the Athletic Department provides jocks for the men but doesn't even think about buying sports bras for the women? I mean, what's that? I shouldn't have to pay for my own workout gear…bras are expensive."

Anita paused again, hoping for a response. I could tell Ms. Sandy was a little surprised, probably wondering if we were joking, so I cut into the awkward silence.

"And why don't we have tampons and napkins in the women's locker room? I shouldn't have to borrow one from a teammate." Anita looked at me and smiled. "I'd hate having to quit halfway through a workout because my period started."

"You know. I never really thought about it." She was finally engaged, snapping out of her surprise. "But you two are one hundred percent correct. I'm glad you brought that to my attention." She thought for a second. "I'm going to call Bill Jarvis right now to look into your first issue."

We listened as she asked the equipment manager to find out prices for sports bras, Anita and I looking at each other in disbelief, amazed this was turning out so well. She hung up the phone and turned to us.

"He said he'll get back with prices this afternoon." She looked at her daily planner. "I have a meeting with facilities this afternoon. I'm going to talk with them about installing free dispensers."

"Along that line." Anita grinned. "When you talk with them, how about looking into replacing the urinals in our locker room with toilets." Anita covered the smile with her hand. "It's embarrassing, shows a lack of respect for women's sports." Barbara grimaced as she nodded. "I mean, you wouldn't leave a tampon dispenser in the football locker room, would you?"

Fortunately, Ms. Sandy grinned so Anita continued.

"Right now, the girls only have four toilets. That's for tennis, softball, and cross country/track – about fifty women. We need more."

"It will be done." She looked at her watch. "Anything else?"

"One last thing." Anita smiled, turning on her charm. "Can I call you Barbara?" She nodded. "Barbara, we finished 9th place last year at the Big Ten meet." The Associate AD's smile faded. "Well, that's never going to happen again." Anita had a resolute look on her face. "We're going to finish third…maybe second at the conference meet this fall." We both nodded. "You can count on it."

We stood and shook hands, leaving Barbara with a smile on her face.

———✦———

Jennifer and I settled into our 1-bedroom apartment on Sherman Avenue, grateful to have peace and quiet each evening, my ridiculous notion that the Northwestern students would be quieter than those at state schools not remotely true. We were over the moon at the change even though we had to cook our own food, biking two miles to the store for groceries, plastic milk cartons strapped on our rear carriers with bungee cords, a backpack over shoulders barely providing space for everything else.

Fortunately, our classes hadn't started.

The trip to Durham in early September for the Duke Triangular took us two days – seven hours of driving in vans on Wednesday and six hours on Thursday – Coach O'Shea and Coach Nalley looked like they could use time for a nap when we arrived on campus.

The Saturday meet was on the Blue Devil golf course, host Duke and neighboring University of North Carolina the only competition at our first meet of the 1983 season. It had been hot when we left Evanston but the humidity in Durham was brutal Saturday morning, temperatures already in the upper 70's, sweat rolling off brows before we even began a warmup.

Coach O'Shea caught us before we started the jog.

"Get a drink of water before you go." He waved and smiled at Coach Buehler. "Expect to start a little slower today – 5:30…maybe even 5:40. The girls from Duke and UNC are accustomed to this weather but we aren't. So be patient."

After the gun it felt like we were racing through the gates of hell, the 10am sun already relentless, none of the course providing a bit of shade. At least it was flat. We bid our time the first half of the race, patiently trailing the lead pack, passing the mile at 5:32 and two miles at 11:12. On the last loop our squad slipped past tired runners until there were five of us in the top ten.

A pair of Tar Heels beat me to the finish line with a better final four hundred meters, my 18:02 slower than any 5K I ran in high school. What did I expect in this heat? Yet the fact that today's winner, Joan Nesbit of the Tar Heels, was 37th at last year's cross country championship gave me hope, finishing only ten seconds behind her. The dream that I might get to nationals gave me goose bumps.

Bodies littered the grass behind the finish line chutes, trainers draping cold towels over prone bodies, Coach O'Shea encouraging our team to drink, everyone assembling under a tree to get out of the sun. I was glad we didn't have to run an 8K like the boys. Even 5K was too much in this heat and humidity.

We defeated the host school 20-35 and the UNC squad by a score of 25-30, my third place finish along with a 5th-6th-7th-9th by teammates a great way to start the season. Our cool down was done in the shade of tall pines and yellow poplars, all of us unwilling to venture into the sun even though the boy's race had already started.

We watched in shock as Keith went down ten feet past the finish line, landing on the ground like a ton of bricks, all of us rushing over as athletic trainers loaded him on a golf cart, his breathing rapid and skin grayish, ice bags resting on his forehead, chest, and groin as they drove him towards the swimming pool.

Coach Nalley tossed wet towels over shoulders and guided the team over to the water table, Craig and Phillip bent forward with hands on knees, Paul lying in the grass with a forearm over his eyes. We quickly grabbed cups of water and dispensed it to the boys, some taking sips, others pouring it over their heads. It was scary to watch the reactions of runners so fit, the heat taking a heavy toll on tired bodies.

I had a huge respect for their efforts. I knew how much it hurt to push to the limit.

Two weeks later we hosted the 1983 "Meeting of Minds" on the UW-Parkside course – Harvard, Stanford, and Marquette joining the Wildcats for the inaugural competition the weekend before classes began. It was fun to meet the teams in a casual setting at the Friday evening picnic outside Anderson Hall, the evening ending on a spectacular note.

As always, Anita thought up the idea, calling it "The Wildcat Gong Show," everyone agreeing to the format for an amateur contest, coaches from each school attempting to display dubious talents. The Harvard staff was selected to go first, the Crimson leaders bowing to the six judges, the head coach emceeing the effort.

"For your viewing pleasure, the coaches from the #1 school in the nation." Everyone booed except the Harvard squad. "Arnie will eat his way around an apple while juggling three tennis balls. My job is to hold the apple so he can take bites." Arnie smiled, juggling the balls with ease as he waited to begin the skit. "To accommodate the difficulty of this task we ask you hold applause until the end."

The head coach nodded, and Arnie resumed the juggling, a rhythmic clap by athletes as he took the first bite and swallowed, juice running unabated down his chin, his third bite nearly resulting in a stumble, the assistant finally completing his way around the apple after two more bites. Everyone applauded wildly for the inspired effort.

Anita banged cymbals together (I have no idea where she got them), the sound reverberating across the field as she turned to the judges.

"Impressive. Very impressive. I bet the Crimson squad is so proud of their coaches." She smirked as the Harvard squad laughed. "Judges, let's see what you think." They held up a number from 1 – 10.

" I see we have two tens, two sevens, one eight, and a six. Forty-eight points for the Harvard duo. Not bad. Congratulations gentlemen." She slammed the cymbals again. "Okay, up next are the Wildcat coaches…O'Shea and Nalley. Let's give them a big hand."

Our team was already laughing, Coach Nalley sitting at a skirted card table, wearing an oversized sweatshirt, our coach kneeling behind and sliding under the back of the sweatshirt so he was out of sight. It had to be claustrophobic to be stuck inside there. On the card table was a pair of shoes, a brush, plastic razor and a can of shaving cream, a tube of toothpaste sitting beside the purple toothbrush.

Coach Nalley slipped arms out of the sleeves and then under the hem of his sweatshirt, putting hands into running shoes and – voila, his arms were now legs. With the sleeves of the sweatshirt now empty, from behind Coach O'Shea slipped his arms in. Coach Nalley looked like he was seated on the card table and two feet tall. Everyone roared at the effect.

Coach Nalley rolled his eyes and began.

"My athletes always tell me I am such a stud and wonder how I do it." Cautious laughter. "I tell them, boys…it's all in the preparation. I wasn't born this good looking." More laughter as he clicked the shoes together like Dorothy in the Wizard of Oz. "So, after my shower in the morning the first thing I do is comb my hair just right."

Anita located the brush for the phantom hand attached to our coach, Coach Nalley leaning forward as it was raised overhead, the brush raking across the thinning hair in a slipshod action. Now all the laughter was full-throated, Coach Nalley's grimace at the rough brushing quite real.

"Sometimes you have to suffer to look good." He grinned. "Next, I shave." His eyes followed the phantom hands search for the shaving cream. "Women love a smooth face."

Our coach found the shaving cream right away and filled the other hand with far too much lather, blindly slathering it all over Coach Nalley's face, half of it in his mouth, the excess spit out like he was a contestant propelling watermelon seeds. Our boys' team was rolling in the grass, shaking with laughter, the other coaches cracking up at the absurd scene.

Anita put the razor in the phantom's hand, the orange-handled Bic shaver going up and down Coach Nalley's face in a haphazard fashion, Anita wiping lather from his eyes.

"And lastly, I brush these pearly whites." He grinned, crossing his eyes.

Anita helped again, putting the toothpaste and brush in the phantom hands, a huge dollop squeezed on the toothbrush, Coach Nalley moving his head side to side like he was watching an irritated fly. The toothbrush finally found his mouth, teams roaring in laughter at the toothpaste on his nose and cheek. He had to turn to the side and spit before he could continue the monologue.

"Well kids, it's that simple. Look at this mug." He gave us a profile. "Beautiful…isn't it." Coach Nalley used one of the shoes to wipe a blob of toothpaste off his nose. "So, if you want to look as good as I do this is all it takes. Thanks for listening."

Coach Nalley tipped his head forward in a bow, all the athletes jumping to their feet, a grin filling his face as he stood to the applause, Coach O'Shea popping out from the back of the sweatshirt with hair all over the place, admiring the havoc he created.

Northwestern won the Gong Show.

The next day our women's team lost to Stanford 32-38 but defeated the Harvard and Marquette squads – not too bad when you considered the Cardinals were second in the nation at last year's NCAA Championships. Coach O'Shea was thrilled with our team performance, handing out hugs like he was handing out candy. Becky was on fire today, finishing in third place, only two seconds behind Harvard's Kate Wiley and nine behind Regina Jacobs – last year's NCAA runner-up from Stanford.

Joanne was 6th and I was seventh, both of us nipping the Cardinal's Allison Wiley just before the finish chute, Anita grabbing 10th, frosh Alena 12th, and senior Janelle 15th – our other freshman Sue Kennedy finishing thirty-first. I turned in a PR on the tough Parkside course, my 17:22 twenty-one seconds faster than my time from last year.

Wait until dad hears this.

All I could think of on our cool down was that Allison Wiley finished ninth a year ago at the NCAA meet. Today I beat her by one second. Wow. I was so happy, smiling like a two-year-old with a lollipop. Yet I had to temper my enthusiasm, appreciating the randomness of today's finish – and collegiate results in general. Just because I beat Allison by two seconds, there was no reason to think she couldn't beat me by twenty tomorrow. Or the next day by thirty.

Performances weren't etched in stone like in high school. My last three years at East High I was 1st, 2nd, and 1st at state, any notion that I might finish twenty-second, or even eighth a ludicrous thought. But finishes in college varied so much. It was feast one day and famine the next.

As we loaded up the van after the race Coach O'Shea pulled me aside.

"Sarah. Great job today. You're good enough to qualify for the NCAA Championship…but that doesn't mean you will." He smiled. "So just keep focus on your training and I guarantee the odds will improve."

———

The next weekend we scored eighteen points at the Chicagoland Championship and then the middle of October won the Michigan Invitational on a tough course, scoring twenty-two points, and defeating Big Ten rivals Michigan, Purdue, Michigan State, and Minnesota, setting us up for an epic battle at the Big Ten meet. Five of us were in the top ten that Saturday in Ann Arbor. I was #3 for the Wildcats, running an 18:11, grabbing the fifth spot overall, Becky ten feet in front of me at the finish line. Our split for the top six was only twelve seconds.

We were on fire.

Although I continued to get together every other Sunday with Annette at JK Sweets – my favorite restaurant in Evanston; life was studies, running, traveling to meets, and getting eight hours of sleep, each day rolling by like a treadmill. My social life was non-existent, the daily training intensity always tough, getting together to study with teammates the only thing close to excitement.

After the meeting last August, Barbara Sandy put Anita and I on the Wildcat Women's Sport Council (WWSC), captains for the six other teams joining us to represent their sports. I enjoyed the monthly 7am meetings because we got a catered breakfast at the student union – fancy omelets, fresh squeezed OJ, and delicious pastries – instead of the cold cereal and bad coffee at the apartment.

After eating we examined various issues – ways to increase attendance at women's events, inequities between the male and female programs, the volleyball captain begging Ms. Sandy to hire female trainers – her teammates complaining about inappropriate treatment by the all-male staff. Anita and I walked to class after the meeting, heading towards Kresge Hall.

"I can't believe the equipment guy was such a pushover."

"What are you talking about?" I scrunched my face.

"I made Bill Jarvis a batch of brownies and he was in heaven." Anita laughed. "How do you think the cross country team got the oversized towels instead of those postage stamps the other teams get?"

"No way!" All Anita did was laugh and nod.

———

At the Wisconsin Invitational on the 22nd we finished third out of twelve teams – defeating nationally ranked BYU, Kansas State, and Texas. As good as we were, the Badgers were even better, the Wisconsin squad prevailing, Iowa State's women second on the Yahara Hills course in Madison. ISU's Margaret Davis and Suzanne Youngberg were only twenty yards in front of me...oh so close. Last spring at Stanford, they beat me by over twenty seconds.

The 1983 Big Ten championships were at the University of Illinois on Oct. 29th, the Savoy course flat and fast – one that would normally make me quite happy. But today there was a problem. Thousands of years ago glaciers rolled across the Prairie State depositing the richest soil in the northern hemisphere as they melted. But these glaciers also left flat farmland which wouldn't stop the wind which blew in from Missouri. It certainly didn't today.

To say we were confident going into the race would have been an understatement. After the team performances in September and October we knew a second place finish was realistic – that we were capable of going from ninth to second in one year. And even better if we were lucky. As coach always said, "Even the best teams have bad days."

We did our last strides out from Box 6, huddling a hundred yards from the line with an arm extended into the center, Anita leading the cheer. "Wildcats on three…one…two…three…WILDCATS!"

In those moments before a big race thoughts ricochet through your brain like a ping pong ball on cocaine, none of them locating a firm foothold, the only certainty that a good team finished would have to be earned. We jogged back to our box and pulled off sweats. Clad in the bun-huggers, it was the first time I'd noticed Sue Simon had put on some weight.

A long whistle and everyone leaned forward, wind ruffling my jersey as I waited for the gun to fire.

"BOOM."

We got out as we had all year, charging to the front, a quick glance left showing the usual suspects to the side – eight Badgers led by Cathy Branta, Doak and Spangler in front of the Iowa squad, to the right most of the Minnesota team, and a runner in red from Ohio State. *Cogan?*

The first big turn was around the third green on the far side of the course, runners crowded together like mall shoppers at Christmas, twenty to twenty-five athletes packed in the amorphous blob up front. Jennifer and Alena were to my right, Joanne, Anita, Becky, and Janelle just in front, Deena trailing in our slipstream, cheers louder as we neared the club house for a first time, the initial mile marker fifty yards away. Sue was not in our pack.

"That-a-way ladies…nice job…stay together." Coach O'Shea's voice was hard to hear over the wind.

Up ahead the timer shouted "5:15…5:16…5:17…5:18" and then we were past, heading back into the wind on the second mile loop, the front pack thinning – Doak and the dark-haired Spangler holding spots to the side of Wisconsin, Minnesota mirroring the image of our five. About three hundred yards into the second loop Deena fell off our pack, the strong headwinds stealing her resolve. *That's the way it is.*

I glanced at our three juniors to my side; blank stares etched on each face, eyes squinting from the effort as we face the onslaught of wind. By the time we circled around the eleventh green Alena was still nearby, Janelle and Jennifer succumbing to the relentless gusts. Heading towards the club house the resistance was now at our backs, but we didn't ease efforts, Joanne digging deep into her well to keep close as we neared the second mile.

Times didn't register in my brain as we passed the two mile mark and headed back into the gale for the final loop, Wisconsin with five in front of our team, three Gophers holding positions just steps in front of our four. I glanced behind as we made a gentle turn, the #4 and #5 Minnesota runners well behind Alena. We still had a chance at second.

Joanne was struggling mightily to stay with us, dropping back an inch at a time as we navigated the U-turn at the far end of the course and headed for home. Three of us worked side by side on the long straight into the finish, the features of the clubhouse growing as we neared the orange banner, the strong wind threatening to knock it down. Becky and I sprinted hard, desperate to overtake the Minnesota runners just ahead, passing Wisconsin's #4 and #5, but unable to close on the Gophers.

I was angry with myself as I walked through the finish chute. *That's how you lose team titles.*

Ten minutes later we heard the results. *Damnit!*

1. Wisconsin – 35   2. Minnesota – 77   3. Northwestern – 83

It was hard to be disappointed with third – but after beating Minnesota in Madison last weekend it seemed reasonable to do it again today. Becky got me by a step at the line, my 11th place six spots better than last year. Though we didn't get any team award, we earned a measure of respect from our Big Ten opponents, Cathy Branta shaking my hand after the award ceremony, praising our squad for the performance.

"Good job ladies." Today's champion smiled. "The Wildcats went from the outhouse to the penthouse in a year." I laughed.

"Well, maybe the sub penthouse."

Coach O'Shea's "Big Ten Coach of the Year" award was a nice consolation, but we all would have been happier with second.

Chapter 8
November 12, 1983

Our season ended two weeks later at the Region IV Qualifier: Wisconsin and Minnesota, the two teams which qualified for the NCAA Championships in Pennsylvania. We didn't even get an individual selection for the national meet at Lehigh; Iowa's Nan Doak and Jenny Spangler, along with Maureen Cogan of Ohio State grabbing the coveted spots. Joanne and Becky were close...but no cigar.

It was easy to convince myself that our third place finish was fine, but it felt like racing down the platform watching the day's last train pull away, our uninspired effort costing us a trip to the NCAA Championship. I desperately wanted to be there. *Damnit.* You don't have many chances in college, and this was another opportunity gone by. If I didn't work harder, it would continue to happen.

Coach O'Shea gave us two weeks off for rest and recovery. I was grateful to have more time for studies and a modicum of social life, planning an overnight with Annette...and hopefully meeting another boy. So far, I'd come up empty. Anita laughingly called me the Virgin Mary when she found out my middle name was that very same – Mary.

Anita and I had talked about our disappointing discovery all the way back from the regional meet at Bradley, deciding to broach the subject with Barbara Sandy at the WWSC breakfast on November 15th. I'll have to say I was surprised to discover this fact. That morning Anita took charge.

"Most of you probably don't know." Anita looked around the round table. "But we finished 3rd at the NCAA Regional meet last weekend, missing a trip to the NCAAs by one spot – nine measly points." She paused.

"It would be easy to say that's the way the cookies crumble but for one thing...women only get *two* teams to nationals...the men have *three*." Anita paused and looked

93

around the table. "Does that sound fair to you?" Barbara's painted eyebrows went up.

"I didn't know that." She thought a moment and then spoke. "Is anyone else aware of a similar disparity in your sport?" Kathy raised her hand.

"In basketball only forty teams qualify for the women's tournament…for the men, well next year it's going to be sixty-four teams."

"We're on to something." Barbara head shook side to side, her lips pursed. "I'm going to look into this and get back with you at our December meeting." She wrote herself a note. "What else?"

I raised my hand.

"Last month we talked about getting more fans to the women's games…and by the way, our cross country team will be at the basketball game Friday night and the volleyball game on Sunday." I paused, Anita staring, with no idea about what I was going to say.

"But anyway, I was thinking we should put on some 'Learn by Doing' clinics for girls 10-14 years old…like an hour before the game." Ms. Sandy was nodding her head and encouraging me. "We could get athletes from other sports, ones that played it in high school…you know, so they could show the girls how to do a volleyball serve, or the correct shooting technique, or whatever."

"Excellent idea Sarah." She smiled as she wrote. "I really like it."

Phillip rode the train with me from the Noyes station, talking about the indoor season as we found seats near the front of the car, excited to be competing in the 800m and mile – distances much better suited to his talent. It amazed me how well he performed on the small tracks despite our lack of an indoor facility.

"I love running down in Gainesville on their track, and at the Bally Invitational on the board surface…Coach Nalley said we would run a 4 x 800 there." He looked at me and smiled. "I'm going to get Tom Bach's 1:51.0 record in February…even

94

if it kills me." Phillip was a senior so this was his last shot. I grinned and he continued.

"What do you have on tap with Annette?"

"She is taking me to Kingston Mines to listen to Koko Taylor...it's that Blues nightclub on Halsted. Annette has a cassette of her...gosh I really like her style. It's so powerful." I stared out the window as the L pulled into the Wilson station. "Then she talked about some party Saturday night."

I debated asking the next question, afraid how Phillip would respond. He never talked about why he came down – what he did.

"How about you?" Phillip's eyes were evasive. "Not much...I have a friend down here...we just hang out."

I took a deep breath and plunged forward.

"Phillip...I want you to know..." I spoke softly so no one would overhear. "I...I know you are gay..." His eyes suddenly watered and chin dropped. I grabbed his hand and leaned in, interlocking our fingers. "It's okay. I think you're fine. Don't worry. You're a wonderful person."

He wouldn't look at me, staring into his lap with a hand cupped over his eyes, not responding to my grip. *God, that was so stupid. I shouldn't have said anything.* I admonished myself for the foolish decision, convinced he would never speak to me again. I racked my brain for the words to say, but nothing sprung to mind. I sighed.

"I'm sorry if I hurt you, but I will never tell anyone...ever." Hoping to add levity, I included. "Well, maybe my mom."

He smiled for the first time, taking the offered Kleenex and wiping tears, knowing mom was my sole confidant. I leaned in and gave him a hug.

"I'm here for you." I gave him a sad smile.

I felt better but I'm not sure he did. He stood as the Belmont stop approached, waving to me with a halfhearted smile as he exited the doors to the platform. *I hope what I said wasn't a mistake.*

It was wonderful to be back in the comfort of my home over Christmas break, Danny looking fit as a fiddle and on schedule to graduate from Luther College in May, Steve wearing fifteen pounds of muscle like a chiseled statue, last fall the starting quarterback on the Drake football team.

Dad and mom were in heaven, the presence of their children the greatest medicine a body could receive. Mom asked about Annette and how things were going at DePaul. I mentioned her latest gig at Harrigan's.

"You should have seen. The place was packed with college students." I smiled at the recollection. "Annette and Aiden played for ninety minutes, and the crowd begged them for even more. She's really getting a following."

Each day over Christmas break I ran five or six miles through the snow and freezing temperatures, using East High's weight room for strength training, my tempo days at the City Park the only fast work in preparation for our indoor season.

Coach O'Shea had talked with the distance runners before finals in mid-December, suggesting we begin competition at the Harvard Invitational on the last weekend in January. No one disagreed. I guess he could tell we were as disappointed as he was after the hard-fought cross country season. And probably sense our frustration with the regional meet. Only time would rekindle our enthusiasm.

Harvard's meet on January 28th was our inaugural race on boards, the girls laughing as I zoomed around the track on Friday evening with arms wide, a goofy grin plastered on my face. On Saturday, Kate Wiley won the 3000 meters, her 9:14 quite a bit faster than my fourth place 9:34.8. Though I was relaxed before the race, thoughts that I was an imposter zipped in and out of my brain, attempts to feel confident a fruitless endeavor.

Intuitively I knew that the tempo and intensity would be much faster than cross country, and it was, but I wasn't prepared for all the pushing and shoving, or the challenge of trying to pass on such a small oval. It was definitely a learning experience. And a humbling one at that.

Phillip sat with me after we were finished for the day, whether the fact he won the 800 and broke the school record or that he believed I was sincere about being supportive, I really couldn't say. I was just grateful the curtain between us had dropped. He needed all the support he could get, reports in the local and national newspapers grim. The AIDS epidemic was spreading through Chicago's gay community and I'm certain catching the disease worried him. It certainly worried me.

The first weekend of February our team flew to Gainesville for the Florida Invitational, the cool, cloudy weather nice, but still a disappointment. All the girls laughed that Anita brought her swimsuit, expecting it to be blue skies and eighty. We couldn't get on the track Friday afternoon, so we ran down to the outdoor facility, marveling at the massive oak and cypress trees all around, a bell ringing from the tall tower as we jogged through campus, everyone talking about where we were eating tonight.

The indoor track was the strangest set up I'd ever seen, the six-lane, 200m located on the second level of the basketball arena, the shape better described as round rather than oval. I was excited to run the mile rather than the 3K, thinking the wide turns would produce faster times. Anita and Alena joined me for the eight-lap race, Coach O'Shea asking us to be under 2:30 at the 800 meters, from there seeing what we could come up with.

The past three weeks we had been doing faster repetitions – 200's, 300's and 400's, last Tuesday three sets of 2 x 400 at seventy-three seconds, a one minute rest between the pairs, and two minutes between sets. That day it was twenty-six degrees when we started the initial interval, the entire track shaded from the setting sun, ice beginning to form in spots where there were once puddles on the oval. Everyone shivered before we took off, heads shaking at the absurdity of the moment. *This really sucks.*

Anita, Alena, and I got through the first set fine, turning in a pair of seventy-threes, the one minute break in between feeling like fifteen seconds. The second set was no easier, a 73 and 74, the two splits seeming much tougher than the first. How we got through the last set…I'll never know. But we were able to produce a 72 and 71, Coach O'Shea smiling from ear to ear.

Saturday morning, I stood at the waterfall line, glancing to my left, sliding fingers under the hem of my bun-huggers. A runner from Georgia, another from Virginia, and a pair of Gators our main competition in the mile, Bulldog Linda Detlefsen the fastest in this field. After the gun Anita charged after the Georgia athlete clad in red and black, the pair taking the field through a thirty-five and seventy-one, Alena and I more conservative in the sixth and seventh spots.

After passing the halfway mark at 2:22, Detlefsen took the lead by herself; Alena and I in fourth and fifth at 2:24, Anita slipping to the spot just in front of us as we passed the thousand meter mark.

"3:01…3:02…3:03."

We went around Anita with two laps remaining, Detlefsen almost thirty yards ahead and out of reach, so our focus went to catching the Virginia runner in navy and orange as the gun fired for the last lap. I cut the gap to five yards but was unable to overtake her, crossing the line in third, my heart beating like a jackhammer as I bent over to catch my breath. I walked towards the winner to shake her hand, patting the Cavalier's Haworth on the back, then over to Anita and Alena standing next to Coach O'Shea.

"Way to go ladies." He recalled the splits on his stopwatch. "Sarah 4:51.3…Alena 4:53.5, and Anita 4:54.1. Very good. I'm pleased with your efforts."

"This is the weirdest track." I wiped sweat off my brow with the shoulder strap of my jersey. "There's no place for spectators so people are watching from all over the place."

"Coach, what did Detlefsen run?" Alena was curious.

"4:45.5." He tipped his head and continued. "She was third in the 1500 last year at nationals…so she's the real deal."

A week later we were running at the University of Illinois on their 262-yard track, the oversized facility making for unique lap counts. My mile race was six and two-thirds circuits. *Strange.*

Victories in college are not as common as those in high school, but I somehow did today, taking the mile with a 4:50.2, outkicking the Illini's Julie Lantis on the final straight. It was cool to hear applause from the hometown crowd fade when I slipped past her, grinning to myself as I caught the U of I runner unaware just ten yards from the line.

Sue Simon, our freshman finishing second to last, tears rolling down her cheeks after the race. I put an arm around her shoulders. The freshman fifteen had her in its grips. She leaned into me, wiping moisture from her face with the strap of her tank top.

"I've really worked hard to eat better since we got back from Christmas." Her head dropped. "But it doesn't seem to do any good. I eat tons of apples, oranges, and bananas…and lots of salads." The tears resumed so I reached around to give her a hug, stepping back but keeping hands on her shoulders as I spoke. I waited until she looked me in the eyes.

"Sue, I know you're doing your best." I pursed my lips in a sad smile. "Just keep trying. I know you can do it. We'll keep meeting in the mornings to ride the exercise bike…and I bet by March you'll be as in good shape." I smiled.

She gave a half-hearted smile but didn't look convinced.

For the final meet before the Big Ten championships we ran at Illinois State, Coach O'Shea sticking me in the 800 and 4 x 400 to work on closing speed. I surprised myself in the open eight hundred, although coach claimed it only served to give him a few gray hairs. The initial pace was quick, so I was content to sit in last place, staring at the asses and elbows of the entire field, wondering if the decision to run this race was a mistake. *Gosh, I used to be fast.*

On the second lap I passed two and was in seventh, getting one more on the backstretch of the third lap, wondering if I could catch three or four more before the line. When I heard the gun for the final lap I was twenty-five yards behind the leader, certain waiting to kick would not be a good choice. *I gotta get my ass in gear.*

Moving into fifth place coming around the penultimate corner I gave it everything in my arsenal, charging down the backstretch, catching two more "dying quails" as I moved into third, the runners from Illinois State and Western Illinois only ten yards in front of me. *C'mon Sarah. You can get 'em.* I shot off the final corner and gunned down the last straight with arms pumping as hard as I could, passing the Redbird almost immediately, the WIU runner in purple and yellow only five yards in front. I out-leaned her at the line.

The smile on my face said it all. If you had told me I had to choose between a month of free ice cream or this victory, I would have chosen the victory. It tasted better than all those delicious treats.

We were back at Illinois for the 1984 Big Ten meet, the boys competing in Iowa City for their championship. This was going to be a busy weekend for me. I was the first leg on Friday's 4 x 800, teaming with Anita, Alena, and Deena, later Friday evening running a prelim for the mile – and hopefully the final on Saturday. Coach talked about putting me in the 4 x 400 on Saturday but said we'd cross that stream when we got to it.

With only eight teams in the 3200 relay the start wasn't too crazy – although the exchange zones were all over the place on their 262-yard track. I waited on the outside waterfall for the race to start, listening to the thud of the 4-kilo shot as it landed on the infield surface nearby, banging loudly into a wooden backstop, the starter finally blowing his whistle.

Leading my waterfall group around the corner, I cut towards the curb as I passed the last cone, the rapid rhythm of this pace dissipating my nervousness. I must have been going fast, no one challenging my lead as I completed the first lap, Coach O'Shea cupping hands as he shouted from the second corner.

"Perfect Sarah…keep it going."

With two laps remaining Anita cheered for me from her position on the outside of the first exchange zone, a Purdue runner challenging me before the next turn, my surge holding her off – barely. *Oh man, that hurt.*

"Good job Sarah. Nice." Coach was clapping his hands.

As I went by Anita on my last lap the clerk was beginning to put the runners in order. The Purdue runner surged again on the backstretch, but I refused to let her get past my shoulder, the effort to hold her off nearly killing me. *C'mon, c'mon, c'mon.* Into the last turn the Boilermaker dropped back, choosing not to go wide and run extra yards around the corner.

The exchange was thirty yards ahead, Anita wiping her left hand on the jersey strap as she waited, nervously bouncing up and down, sliding down the track as I approached. *Not so fast. Wait. Wait.* "WAIT!" I shouted. She hesitated and I put the baton in her hand a split second before the Purdue team, Anita taking off like she was shot from a cannon.

I slowed to a stop on the inside of the track, pain hitting me in a cascade of waves, locking hands atop my head as I watched Anita's lead increase on the backstretch. *At-a-way Anita. Man, that hurt.*

Coach O'Shea circled his arm like a third base coach as she flew past him on the corner, her lead now ten yards. She looked strong until her final lap, handing the baton to Deena with a two yard lead, our freshman taking off with a determined look on her face.

We were in third when Deena made the exchange, the Michigan and Purdue legs passing her on the last lap, on our anchor Alena gamely charging after the Wolverine who was almost twenty yards ahead. The Boilermaker squad had a huge lead because of a great third leg, Becky Cotta anchoring them to the easy win, waving appreciatively to the crowd as the Purdue runner crossed the line.

I rushed over to Alena after she finished, coach patting her on the back as he looked up at me.

"We crushed the school record by fifteen seconds…9:01" He held out a palm so I could slap it. "Way to go Sarah…your split was 2:12."

Three hours later I kicked hard on the last lap and turned in a 4:53 to qualify for Saturday's final in the mile, grateful the early splits were at a snail's pace. I stayed around to watch Iowa's Nan Doak win the last event of the evening, her 9:38 in the 3K a bit slow because most were coming back in the 3-mile

101

tomorrow. I don't know how she found the courage to try that double.

Sue Simon was nearly lapped by the Hawkeye winner, my teammate walking off the track as the last finisher with her head down. I hustled down the bleachers, jogging over to the 3K start, sitting alongside her as she changed shoes. Tears were running down her cheeks. I didn't know what to say.

"You looked good early…the 5:29 was a good split…" Sue cut me off.

"Yeah, but I had nothing left the last half of the race." She just stared at the ground. "I've tried so hard to lose weight but…" The rest of the sentence faded away.

"I'll get my sweats and we can cool down outside." Sue didn't respond. "Just wait here. I'll be right back." Neither of us said a word on the ten minute jog.

Saturday afternoon I didn't know what tactics to expect, the large field quite possibly forcing a fast tempo from the gun. But then again…you never knew. It could just as easily be a jog. This may have been the deepest and best field at the Big Ten meet – Wisconsin's Cathy Branta, Michigan's Sue Foster, the Gopher's Jody Eder, Boilermakers' Becky Cotta, and Illinois' Julie Lantis all national caliber, each having turned in sub 4:40 this indoor season.

My best was 4:49…and that was outdoors.

Sue Foster, last year's indoor champion, was determined to control the pace after the gun fired, sprinting to the front, our initial two hundred at 33 seconds, the four hundred split at 1:10. I was in 7th halfway through the race, my 2:25 only steps behind Foster's 2:23.

With two laps remaining heads in front of me pivoted like that on a ventriloquist's dummy, everyone preparing for what was just ahead – a dramatic tempo change. *It's going to be on the backstretch.* We all knew it.

Cathy Branta shot to the lead at that point, Foster unable to hold off the burst of speed despite her obvious effort, Eder closely following the Badger and pulling behind her into lane one. With two laps remaining the field spread out like a lonely strand of spaghetti, the effort it took showing on every face. I was in sixth place behind Branta, Eder, Foster, Lantis, and Cotta, the Big Ten veterans sprinting at a breakneck speed as the bell rang.

It took all my willpower to stick with them as we entered the backstretch, the hometown crowd cheering as Lantis pulled into second place with 250 yards remaining. Everything told me her early move had been a fatal mistake, that the strong effort was much too early…but only time would tell.

The announcer called out the order. "It's Branta, Landis, Eder, Foster, Cotta, Tucker." The speed these women possessed was incredible, certainly a thirty second tempo going into the final two hundred, my brain on autopilot with no thought of doubt or fatigue – only a primeval response to the competitor's efforts.

At this point in the race I always looked for signs of tiredness, locking in on Landis – something telling me she was the one. Two-thirds of the way down the last backstretch I spotted the hiccup in her stride, the rhythm slowing, heels dropping lower on each recovery, the big swing of arms trying to make up for the leg's fatigue.

Although the others were less than ten meters ahead, they looked so strong I knew I wouldn't catch them. *C'mon Sarah. Focus on Lantis.* Seventy-five meters remained and Lantis faded to fourth, sixty meters left, and she dropped to fifth, both of us charging down the homestretch in lanes two and three as we neared the line.

C'mon Sarah, get her.

Thirty meters to go and she was so close I could have touched her shoulder. Ten meters to the line and I was by her, somehow managing to stay erect as I crossed the white stripe in lane three. *Oh my God. I did it! I did it!* I slowed to a stop, pleasure rather than pain filling my body, breaths as rapid as a bedroom alarm clock.

Anita rushed up and gave me a hug, Coach O'Shea as happy as a bee in a field of flowers. He patted me on the back and smiled.

"Gosh Sarah. Jim Duncan was right." The grin filled his face. "You are a dandy."

Cathy Branta won with a 4:38.31, my fifth place time a 4:43.81. I called home from the lobby of the ancient facility, mom answering on the first ring.

"Mom, I got fifth in the mile and our 4 x 800 was third. We broke the school record...9:02." I was so happy with my performances.

"That's wonderful honey." I laughed to myself. Mom wouldn't know a good time if it bit her. "Hold on." She covered the mouthpiece and shouted upstairs, dad joining us on the bedroom extension.

"Dad, I ran a 4:43.8." I could hear his surprise by the inhale. "I was five seconds from first...Cathy Branta. Becky Cotta only beat me by one step."

"Whoa. She's an All-American." I could tell he was proud. "A big PR...and it's only the indoor season. Excellent."

"I'll find out if I qualified for the NCAA meet next Sunday." I smiled. "So, keep your fingers crossed. Well, I gotta get my cool down in...love you. I just wanted to let you know. Bye."

Chapter 9
March 4, 1984

The 1984 NCAA Indoor championship was March 16-17 in Syracuse University's Carrier Dome on a banked ten lap to the mile board track. Unfortunately, I wasn't going to be there. Though my time in the mile at the conference meet was good, it still wasn't fast enough to qualify. It was so disheartening to think a time I would have killed for in high school didn't make the cut.

At East High I always expected to qualify for state…and even to place. But racing in college was a different story. Adjectives like good or great didn't begin to describe the collegiate talent level. More like astounding or astonishing. I ran my last 800 in 2:17 at the Big Ten meet, and the final 400 in 1:05 – and still got my butt kicked. These girls are…good.

In some ways I didn't mind staying home. It seemed like there was never a chance to relax. We had one more week of classes in March and then second quarter finals on March 12-17 – our spring break in Arizona the following week. I could definitely use the change of pace. I was tired of the constant cold.

Monday morning, I stepped out of the bathroom before my first final, a towel wrapped around me, trying to decide what to wear to class. My wardrobe was pretty boring. Other than a nice sweater, it was hard to make a clothing statement when the weather sucked. Jeans and hiking boots were the only practical things with cold temperatures and sidewalks strewn with rock salt. I listened to the radio in the background, hoping they would give me today's forecast.

"…weeks ago I heard the voice of an angel singing in Harrigan's Pub." I perked up when I heard the male DJ on WXRT mention that bar. "Who sang a medley of songs in her ninety minute set…I know this is one you are going to like. It's called 'Anything' and the angel who sang it is Annette Anderson." *Oh my God! They're playing her song on the radio.*

I sat on my bed and turned up the clock-radio so Jennifer could hear it in the kitchen, a slide guitar playing soulfully before the rest of the band converged, Annette joining them as their rhythm built. I sat motionless until her song was over, laughing at the DJ as he prepared to cut away for commercial.

"A little bit of heaven to start your day…from your best friend in the world." *If he only knew.*

It was 10:53am on Sunday. *This must be heaven.* We rushed down the long escalator and through the sliding glass doors of Sky Harbor airport to soak up the wonderful warmth of Phoenix, Anita pointing at a cactus on the rocky slope across the terminal traffic, so enamored of these temperatures that she claimed to be willing to give the spiny plant a hug.

When Coach O'Shea pulled up in the van we filled the 15-passenger vehicle with bags, Becky rolling down the window to savor temperatures, everyone pointing out the red soil and varieties of cactus, enjoying the aromas of red bougainvillea as we flew across Hwy 202, the boy's van following closely behind. It was my first time in Arizona.

"Ladies, here's the plan for today." He had to shout over the wind rushing through open windows. "We'll be at the hotel in five minutes. Middle distance and distance. I'll give you fifteen minutes to change into running gear and then we'll run for sixty minutes. You can do your unpacking later."

From somewhere behind Anita shouted.

"Mike, when are we going to the casino?"

He smiled, shaking his head as he continued.

"Coach Dahlquist is taking sprinters and field events to the ASU track at noon, so you'll have a bit more time. But be dressed and ready to go."

We waited outside the hotel lobby for Becky and Joanne to show up, everyone's shirt sleeves rolled up over their shoulders. Coach led us down Scottsdale Blvd, crossing the

106

busy street at the light, jogging the two blocks to Papago Park. *This is so cool. I can't believe it's eighty-one degrees.* He waited by the water fountain until we circled around.

"Okay ladies. As I said in the van, we're going to run 30 minutes north on the canal path at an easy tempo – although no slower than eight minute pace…and then return to the park. We'll have 20 minutes of circuits followed by..." Anita raised her hand.

"When you say *we'll*, does that mean you'll be doing the circuits with us?" Coach rolled his eyes.

"No…and then *you'll* do ten strides on the grass."

The canal trail was a blast – flat as a pancake, an asphalt bike path with a wider area of crushed red stone to the sides. Jennifer pointed at a mountain goat high on the red sandstone formations as we jogged by a pond, the unidentified floral aroma in the air wonderful. We talked the entire sixty minutes, time evaporating as rapidly as our sweat.

Coach was waiting for us by a circle of picnic tables under the shade of trees, a cup of McDonald's coffee in hand.

"Ladies, listen up. I put a sign at each station…but let me explain. There are ten stations – pushups, sit-ups, bench dips, right leg step-ups, left leg step-ups, jumping jacks, back arches, right leg squats, left leg squats, and burpees. We move clockwise between stations. Twenty seconds on, ten seconds to get to the next spot. Four complete circuits." He pulled a whistle out from under his t-shirt. "Pick your station and we'll…*you'll* start." He smiled.

I wasn't sweating but was definitely hot, the early afternoon sun beating down on bodies as the minutes circled by. Becky and Anita were the first to tuck tank tops into the bottom of sports bras, so stomachs were exposed, all of us imitating the style as faces got redder from the heat. A last long whistle and we were finally done.

"Okay, get some water." He pointed. "Then take off your shoes…I want the strides barefoot."

Sixty minutes later we were at the pool, everyone wearing bikinis tops and running shorts, Anita clad in a skimpy black two-piece ensemble, the scent of bougainvillea and sunscreen filling the air. Eight chaise loungers were in a neat line on the north edge of the turquoise water.

"This is the life." I smiled at Alena through my Ray-Bans, someone's cassette deck playing on the far side of the pool. "It's eighty-five degrees…we're done with finals…time to celebrate girls!"

Anita turned up the music, dancing at the side of the pool in her bikini with hands overhead, singing along with Cyndi Lauper at the top of her lungs.

"I come home, in the mornin' light." We all joined in. *"My mother says, When you gonna live your life right? Oh momma dear, we're not the fortunate ones. And girls, they wanna have fun. Oh girls just wanna have fun."*

Around four everyone gravitated to rooms for a Sunday afternoon siesta, the early morning wakeup call and our mid-day workout running down batteries. At 5pm we met for a dinner excursion, vans filled with talkative athletes and too much perfume, Anita and Janelle dressed like they were going out on the town.

Monday through Thursday was the same routine – 8am practice, 11am breakfast/lunch, at noon the pool or a spring training baseball game, 5pm dinner, coaches dropping us in downtown Tempe at 7pm and picking us up at 9:30pm, the boys acting as if it were a contest to see how fast they could get drunk.

I was grateful that we didn't have any big drinkers on the girls' team.

Initially I was surprised when Anita mentioned she never touched a drop, but discovered her father was an alcoholic, the only reason she went to bars was the music...and the boys. The first night Phillip joined her and our female sprinters, along with Janelle and Becky – their group drawn to the businesses with music blasting from the front door. The rest of us decided on "Sixteen Candles" at the Valley Theatre.

Tuesday evening, we stumbled on an Open Mic in the ASU Memorial Union, Deena surprising us by signing up and playing Ragtime music on the piano – the 'Maple Leaf Rag' by Scott Joplin and a classic by Jelly Roll Morton. We were astonished, none of us aware that she could play, her quiet demeanor so different when she performed. It reminded me of the evening with Annette and Marie five years ago, the memory of their duet making made my heart ache.

By Wednesday evening the girls were tired of dancing, joining us at the ASU-Texas baseball game, Anita and I feeling our oats as the night wore on. We sat five rows up, just behind the visitor's dugout, razzing the Longhorn team, knowing they would have nothing to say away from their home field. I was the first one to shout.

"Hey fourteen, is that your IQ or your shoe size?" The girls looked at me in disbelief. I just smirked.

Anita joined in when the next Texan stepped into the batter's box.

"Twenty-two, ten bucks says you strike out."

Now the girls started laughing, hooting at the guy when he struck out, walking towards us with his head down. The bottom of the inning I shouted as the Longhorns trotted on the field.

"Hey, forty-four, you better start throwing righty because your left arm sucks."

Anita and I were quite good at it, both with older brothers who played and taught us the patter. The ASU crowd loved us, their fans laughing at each of the put-downs. Our teammates were quite amused at the boldness.

Two nights later we competed on the ASU track, stadium lights gradually eclipsing the sun as the air began to cool. I loved watching the boys' steeplechase, enamored by their grace over the water jump, and the ease they hurdled barriers which were up to my waist. I know I could have been successful at it if given the opportunity…but we only had an open 3K. *Sigh.* Along with the pole vault, it was just another instance where boys had something we didn't. *It's so unfair.*

That evening I led off the 4 x 800 with a 2:10.3 and our foursome turned in an 8:49.7 to win, a 2:08.11 in the open for second place – a pleasant surprise. I had no expectation going in, simply to hang with the leaders, shocked to see 1:53 on the scoreboard as I entered the final homestretch, a runner from Wake Forest beating to the line by a step.

After the race I cooled down on the track marveling at what I'd just accomplished. That was a lifetime PR in the eight hundred. At a dinky quad in Tempe. It reminded me of high school when I ran a 9:49 3K in Burlington at a nothing meet, on the bus ride home Coach Raffensperger pointing at the HS list in Track & Field News – my time besting the number one mark in the nation. *Wow.*

After a cool down with Deena we sat in the stands and cheered for teammates, but all I could think of was this promised to be an exciting outdoor season.

———————

Early April weather in Evanston sucked – as always. After temperatures in the 80's in Tempe it was hard to suffer the slings and arrows of snow flurries and the frigid NW winds, my tolerance to this weather worn to a frazzle. I prayed we would at least have good temperatures for my favorite meet – the Drake Relays. We did.

"Good luck Sarah." Cindy Bremser reached out to shake my hand, a smile on her face as I waited at the 1500 waterfall line on the blue oval.

"Thanks." It was so cool that she remembered me. "Same to you."

I had run against ten of the eleven in this field, each one so talented the thought made me shiver. It was the first time I'd raced Dawn Lentsch since high school, her presence yet another thing to keep me motivated today. After introductions by Jim Duncan, I took a deep breath, dad's voice clear through the din.

"Let's go Sarah…kick some butt."

"BOOM."

Elbows hit me on both arms, but I gave back as much as I got, experience teaching me victory didn't go to the meek. Bremser took the lead, the pace rapid as we circled the first corner and down the homestretch in front of an appreciative Relays crowd.

"That's Bremser of Wisconsin United in front, followed by Minnesota's Eder, Lantis of Illinois, Cotta, Detlefsen, Iowa State's Dawn Lentsch, and Sarah Tucker of Northwestern."

I knew the pace was honest, so I held my position, a timer shouting "1:05…1:06…1:07" as I flew by the first split in seventh place, filled with a certainty that this race was going to hurt…and soon. I stared at Dawn's necklace bouncing up and down as we rounded the south corner. With seven hundred meters remaining I was still in seventh place, dad's voice providing comfort as I passed the starting line a second time.

"You're good Sarah. You're good."

Down the east side of the stadium, I snuck by Lentsch as we entered the penultimate homestretch, a quick glance showing her eyes squinting from the pain. Illinois' Lantis, the one I beat at Big Ten indoors was next in front, her stride still powerful as the crowd cheered us down the homestretch. *Stay with her Sarah.* I followed on her heels around the corner, both of us going around Cotta on the final backstretch, the finish line only two hundred fifty meters away.

Bremser was twenty-five meters ahead as she entered the last corner, Eder and Detlefsen struggling to maintain contact with the speedy Badger. There was no way I was going to catch Cindy Bremser. I tried to slingshot off Lantis when we came out of the last turn, but she refused to give in, my furious arm drive doing little to close the gap.

Today I was the one who finished half a step behind, after crossing the line both of us leaning forward with hands on thighs, waiting for the pain to dissipate. *Fifth. Not bad.* We both stood tall.

"Nice race Julie." I shook her hand.

We turned to look at results on the scoreboard on the north end of the track. I clenched my fists and shook them in the air when the mark appeared, the 4:20.25 another career best. Dawn Lentsch was still resting hands on her knees, obviously embarrassed with today's performance. She finished last. It was one of the shortcomings of having such a good prep career in Iowa, expectations of fans often unrealistic. I stood beside her and leaned over.

"Dawn, I know today sucked but you are one the greatest competitors I've ever faced." She turned her head and smiled sadly. "C'mon. Let's get some water." I put an arm over her shoulder, and we shuffled into the grass infield, fans applauding as we crept down the slope, remembering us from our great high school battles on this very track.

May 18th. The famed horseshoe stadium in Columbus Ohio. It was the 1984 Big Ten Championships. The 85,000 seat football stadium was massive, making me feel like a tiny gladiator in the Roman Coliseum, lane eight of the Jessie Owens Track butting up against the stands. The size of the facility made me feel a bit claustrophobic.

I'm not sure if Coach O'Shea knew something I didn't, but the only event he had me run at the conference meet was the 1500 meters. I was afraid to ask why, hoping he believed I could get under 4:20 – a time that we both believed might get me to nationals. At least that's what I wanted to think. The thought gave me goosebumps.

We both knew I didn't have enough speed to make the eight hundred meter final, and the quality in the 3K was so deep that a PR still might only get eighth place – a wasted effort. So, I wasn't complaining. All the top girls from other teams had to double, and this move improved my chances of placing higher than I did indoors. But it also put all my chips in one basket. *Hmm.*

Friday afternoon on our warmup Anita and I jogged along the Olentangy River and then over towards campus, skirting Mirror Lake and turning onto the web-like sidewalks between classroom buildings, the beautiful white blossoms on buckeye trees so stark against the green leaves – like a corsage pinned on a prom dress.

Anita was in the first heat with Wisconsin's Cathy Branta, my teammate leading the field through splits of 1:12 and 2:26. I watched from the 1500 meter starting line, cheering for Anita

112

as she crossed the line in fourth place, her 4:26.8 appearing on the big scoreboard for the first prelim.

I was suddenly nervous, aware of my tenuous position. If I got anything but first or second in my heat, I was playing with fire. The first two automatically qualified for the final, but time qualifiers relied on a quick early pace to get one of the eight precious non-automatic spots. That was a risk.

A slow early tempo in my heat could doom chances, and a fast tempo would raise my odds. But did I have the wherewithal to take the lead? I wasn't so sure. *Oh my God. What am I going to do?* I reflected that even though Anita's time was descent, there was still a chance that even it wouldn't be enough to get her into the final. I was so nervous.

I needed to rid myself of the tension, so I sprinted down the backstretch, staring at the ten other girls waiting on the waterfall line as I jogged back into my position. *Shit oh shit oh shit. Don't mess up Sarah.* The clerk backed away from the line, our starter tooting on his whistle.

"Ladies. On your mark." We leaned forward as he raised the gun overhead. "BOOM!"

Jody Eder took off like she was shot from a cannon, and we followed her down the backstretch like obedient ducklings, hanging in her wake as she slowed the initial pace to a crawl. I could hear Coach Wilson shouting on the corner. "Perfect Jody." No one was willing to challenge her tactic – despite its foolishness. Certainly not me.

We crawled down the homestretch, a clock at the finish turning over to one minute as we slipped past the line. *Oh my God. We're running at a 5:20 pace!* I listened to the clerk reading four hundred splits, my breathing so relaxed it was easy to hear.

"1:19…1:20…1:21." *This is insane.*

We diligently followed Jody down the backstretch at the same pace, her tempo as consistent as a metronome, our eight hundred meter split 2:40. I could feel the tension in the air, everyone aware that by the time an official rang the bell it would be a radically different tempo. I kept a spot on the outside of the pack, not concerned about the extra distance, knowing that I had to be ready to respond in the snap of fingers. If not…my season was over. *Be ready.*

In response to Coach Wilson, Jody picked up the pace as we entered the penultimate homestretch, fans greeting us with tepid applause, everyone going into a full sprint as the bell rang for the last lap. I was on Jody's shoulder, knowing it would force runners who might want to pass on the corner navigate it from lane three. And only a tremendous burst of speed would get them by – a fatal mistake this far from the line.

A runner in green pulled up on my outside shoulder, her arms pumping furiously as she ran in lane three, the extra distance keeping her there until we came out of the turn. I stayed on Jody's shoulder, refusing to give into the entreaties from the Spartan, praying that I could hold her off until we entered the final corner. *C'mon Sarah. Dig-dig-dig. C'mon.*

I could feel her resistance fading twenty meters into the turn…but I was so tired I wasn't sure if I had enough to make the distance. Coming out of the corner I was still on the Eder's shoulder, both of us gunning down the straight with all we had. Eighty meters. Eder snuck a peek behind, looking for someone charging after us. I was struggling, too tired to check. Fifty meters. She glanced again; her face filled with a ferocity I'd seen too often when she charged by me. *Shit. Someone's coming.*

There was a dull roar from the crowd. By the din I had to guess it was a runner from Ohio State. Twenty meters. *C'mon Sarah. Don't quit. One step past the line.* Jody and I leaned at the same time, a flash of red flying by after we were across the white stripe. *Oh my God. I'm so dead.* Slowing to a stop I put hands on knees, my chest rising and falling in quick fashion, eyes glued to the red tartan track.

Jody reached over and put a hand on my back.

"Great job Sarah. Congratulations." I was too tired to respond. Both of us looked up at the board as the announcer read the results.

"Our two automatic qualifiers from heat two were Minnesota's Jody Eder with a 4:42.11 and Sarah Tucker from Northwestern with a 4:42.22." He paused. "We'll have to wait

114

for heat three to find the eight, time qualifiers…but these two will be running in the final of the 1500 tomorrow at 2pm."

Cathy Branta won the three thousand meters later that evening with a 9:15.30, ten of the fourteen qualifiers for Saturday's 1500 final, including the three heat winners, choosing to run a second race that day. I was excited for my chances tomorrow.

At 9:18pm I sat beside teammates at Bennigan's restaurant, devouring a cheeseburger, smiling as I dipped a French fry in the glob of catsup.

"Gees Sarah." It was Anita. "I can't believe you ran *sixteen seconds slower* in the 1500 than I did, and you still made the final." She smirked. "I mean…what the hell? My little sister is seventeen and *she* ran faster than 4:42."

"Yeah." I smiled. "But your sister can't run a sixty-three second last lap…so don't waste your money betting on anything but this horse." I grinned, both thumbs pointing at my smile.

Rain. It had to rain. Like competing during my period, it didn't mean I couldn't run as fast. Because I could. It just meant that everything was going to be more miserable. Clothes that were soaked, a uniform clinging to me like a second skin, lane one filled with those annoying puddles – rooster tails of water flying off spikes when you trailed directly behind a runner. Basically, it sucked.

I stood at the waterfall line for the 1500 meters, my bangs so saturated they appeared to be painted on like eyebrows, shifting from one foot to the other, running fingertips over ears to position errant hair, rainwater dripping off my nose and earlobes in a steady stream. At least there was no lightning. The starter pulled out his pistol and wrapped a clear plastic bag around it, sticking his hand inside as he raised his arm overhead.

"Runners set." He looked across the row of fourteen runners. "BOOM!"

Michigan State's Sue Schroeder sprinted to the lead, Anita on her right hip as they entered the first turn, the pace quick as we circled the initial corner. No one wanted to dilly-dally today, the conditions so miserable we just wanted to get the race done. Unlike yesterday, the finish line clock just turned over to fifty seconds as we passed the initial three hundred meters. *Much better*.

At breakfast Coach O'Shea told me to keep Branta, Eder, and Schroeder within striking distance at all times, explaining these were the three that would actually control the race – no matter who was leading. Coming out of the corner rain was landing so hard it bounced off the track, forcing me to squint, the timer under an umbrella shouting over the heavy downfall.

"Sixty-six...sixty-seven...sixty-eight."

Schroeder and Anita continued to lead, Branta and Eder in their wake, the Gopher close enough that rainwater flew off her curly blond hair into my face. The annoyance was just another reminder of how miserable it was to run in the rain. Positions remained the same through two laps but as we entered the homestretch with five hundred meters to go Anita began to fade, the two races yesterday stealing her courage.

As the bell rang Schroeder and Branta went around Anita in tandem, Eder half a step ahead as my teammate disappeared from peripheral vision, my resolve tested as we entered the backstretch a final time. Only their close proximity kept me fighting down the straight, pain wrapping itself around my body like a wet blanket. *C'mon Sarah. Stay tough. You can do it.*

Coming out of the last turn Branta drove her arms hard, pulling away from us with an ease that astounded me. I fought but couldn't catch any of them, the Badger taking her second Big Ten win, Schroeder and Eder finishing in a dead heat just two steps in front of me.

We slowed to a stop and shook hands, everyone looking up at the scoreboard, wiping the rainwater off faces as we stared up at the results.

1.	Branta	Wisc	4:16.47
2.	Schroeder	MSU	4:18.58
3.	Eder	Minn	4:18.62

4. Tucker   NU   4:19.13

———————

It was raining when we landed in Portland Monday afternoon, the two hour drive to Eugene dreary. The weather reminded me of the Big Ten meet in Columbus. I was still amazed that my time qualified me for the NCAA Championship at Oregon on the famous Hayward Field track – one of the lucky few across the nation who could claim such an honor.

Pouring over the list of competitors as we approached the facility I was at ease because my preliminary wasn't until Wednesday evening. A quick glance up as we approached the hallowed track filled with athletes practicing pre-race routines on the track, in the background Spencer Butte visible through rain clouds. I got goosebumps as we stepped onto the track. *This is so cool.*

Only twenty-one runners declared for the 1500 so there were just two heats, the top two finishers in each prelim and the eight best times qualifying for Friday's race. Big Ten rivals Becky Cotta of Purdue and Sue Schroeder of Michigan State were in the first heat on Wednesday, Florida's Gina Procaccio the only one in my section that I'd ever raced against.

I beat Gina indoors in Gainesville and I beat her again today, but a 4:23.17 didn't move me on, my time only 0.14 seconds from making the final. There was no "Q" on the scoreboard after my name. *Damnit.* I had put all my prayers on getting into the final, hoping the field on Friday would pull me to a PR, and that the time would be fast enough to get me a spot on the Olympic Trials 1500m list.

But I never got the chance.

I stared out the window on the flight home, trying to put the race behind. I had my first final on Monday and my second year at Northwestern would be finished by Wednesday. It was hard to be disappointed with my first trip to the NCAA Championship…but I was so close – missing the finals by less than a foot. In this sport inches and hundredths were deal breakers. Game changers. *Sigh.*

Chapter 10
June 16, 1984

Last March before finals I wondered what it would take to make the1984 Olympic Trials in Los Angeles, locating the qualifying time for the 1500 meters in Coach O'Shea's Track and Field News. It was 4:09.00. *Dang. That's just not going to happen.* So, I put that dream behind me, not giving in to false hopes, lamenting that a childhood dream was gone.

But on the last day of the Big Ten meet last May I overheard Julie Lantis and Jody Eder talking about their chances, the Gopher claiming that although they didn't have the 1500 "A" standard, both might qualify for the Trials with mark that was in the top twenty-four – even though at that moment they were uncertain where their times stood in the rankings. Coach O'Shea confirmed their suppositions when I queried him.

As a result, I revitalized the dream, pinning all my hopes on running a sub 4:19 in the NCAA 1500 meter final – guessing it would be a time I needed. But I blew it in my preliminary race. If I had just run a 4:23.02 instead of the 4:23.17 in Eugene, I would have qualified for the championship race and gotten another shot. Now there were no more competitions. No more chances. *Sigh.*

A week later, on the last day of my finals, I learned from Coach O'Shea that they both qualified for the Olympic Trials – Lantis grabbing the 24th (and final) spot with a PR only 1.23 seconds faster than mine. I was crushed, walking towards the apartment with my head hanging, somehow finding myself sitting on the boulders along Lake Michigan, tears rolling unabated down as I pondered my fate.

To think 0.15 seconds faster at the NCAA meet, probably less than one foot, and I would have gotten another chance and possibly been in Los Angeles for the Trials, experiencing the once-in-a-lifetime honor of racing with America's elite. But I didn't turn in that performance. The reality crushed me.

I had sacrificed so much, passed up so many opportunities, and all I got for my efforts were…nothing. Absolutely nothing. Nil. Nada. It just wasn't fair. Most girls had time for parties and boyfriends – a social life – but I had neither, putting all my energy into running. *I must be an idiot.* The emptiness in my heart seemed endless.

So, I lashed out at Jody and Julie, childishly reasoning they were the ones who stole my spot – all my anger directed at them. I was mad because I was heartbroken. That it was all their fault I wasn't in Los Angeles. I was so jealous of their good fortune and wanted it to be mine. *I* wanted to be there. Had sacrificed enough to be there. Deserved to be there.

Though I berated myself for the foolish grudge, this loss hurt so badly I really didn't care.

Jody and Julie had always been nothing but nice to me, praising my performances, always encouraging me whenever I stumbled. The more time I spent alone, the more my emotions spiral downward like an airplane out of control. That was my only shot at the Trials – probably ever. The chances of still running competitively in 1988 were slim and none. My dream was gone. The one I'd first had when I watched the 1976 Olympic Trials as a seventh grader. *Shit.*

I called home, mom answering on the third ring.

"Hi honey. I was downstairs doing laundry." It was comforting to hear her voice after the stress of finals. "Steve is back and brought enough dirty laundry to fill five washers." She laughed. "And naturally, he's out with friends." I sighed.

"I wanna come home this weekend." She could tell by my voice that something was up.

"That would be wonderful." She hesitated. "Do we need to talk?"

"Not right now, but I will this weekend. I'll take the Zephyr tomorrow morning and will be in Mt. Pleasant at 2:30pm. So, if you can pick me up there that would be great."

We talked for fifteen minutes; mom excited about having me home. I needed to be back in the comfort of my family –

120

especially during the Olympic Trials. I couldn't sit in the apartment by myself and stew. Jennifer was home in Noblesville for two weeks, planning to rejoin the team for summer training at the end of the month. From the bottom of my rabbit hole blue skies appeared miles away.

I re-read the note from Katy Schilly on the train as I rode home on the Zephyr. Results from the Olympic Marathon Trials had been in the *Tribune* three weeks ago, her 46th place finish in the May race a shock. Especially when she had a realistic chance of making the 1984 Olympic team. I wanted to console Katy, to let her know how I still held her in high esteem, that one race wouldn't define her career. I smiled at the puppy on the front of the card.

Dear Sarah,

You must be my guardian angel. Thank you for the wonderful letter. It came when I needed it the most. Yes, it crushed me to watch the race get away at the twenty mile mark, dropping from fifth place and a realistic shot at the Olympic team, to twenty-fifth place at twenty-two miles and no chance, the last four miles the most torturous of my life.

I've done a lot of soul searching since then, but you motivated me to continue racing. I'm running the San Francisco Marathon in July, hoping to prove to myself, and my opponents, that I had the talent to make the team. You're my inspiration. Thank you!

Katy

I stared out the train window feeling content, watching the Mississippi flow as we crossed the mighty river into Iowa, the ghosts of Huck Finn and Jim drifting by on their way to Hannibal Missouri. I guessed I wasn't the only one to miss out on an opportunity. I sighed, dad's favorite adage playing in my head.

"Suck it up buttercup."

After hamburgers on the grill for supper, dad and I watched Kim Gallagher win her 800 meter semi-final at the Trials, her 1:59.28 a time I had a hard time getting my head around. By the way she finished, it was clear she would be the one to beat in the final on Tuesday. Three years ago, I had raced her at the TAC Junior Nationals in Knoxville, her 4:19 beating my second place finish by eight seconds. *Was it really only three years ago?*

After Sunday's ABC coverage of the Olympic Trials in Los Angeles I jumped on my bike and rode out to St. Joseph's Cemetery to see Marie, replaying Kim Gallagher's race in my head as I pedaled up the Dodge Street hill. I wondered if Kim would remember me anymore? Slowing to a stop at Marie's gravesite I hopped off the bike, sitting in the grass, speaking to her headstone.

"Hey Marie. It's been too long. I just finished finals on Friday and took the train in Saturday morning." I sighed. "I was kinda bummed all week…two of the girls that I ran against at the indoor Big Ten meet – Julie and Jody…I beat Julie by a step and lost to Jody by less than half a second. Well, they're both at the Olympic Trails…in Los Angeles…right now." I took a deep breath. "And I'm not. Twenty-four qualified and my time was twenty-sixth."

I paused, tracing a finger through her first name etched on the stone.

"But…you know what? Sometimes I can be such a whiny bitch!" I started laughing. "That's exactly what you would have told me." I could hear Marie's laughter in my memory. "I mean…my life has been so good...and I have nothing to complain about. I have a family that loves me and teammates that have been so much fun…and I get to see Annette all the time. So really…my life is good."

I pictured Marie up on the stage with her big hoop earrings, singing in harmony with Annette.

"I just want to say that I love you…and that I hope you are proud of me…I think of you all the time. Oh, and I want to thank you for the encouragement you've given me at races. I wouldn't have done as well without you." I sighed. "Okay. I'm going…but I promise to keep in touch."

I resumed my training while in Iowa City, the two week break slipping by much too quickly.

Dad and I watched the Trials each night after supper, four of the Big Ten runners I'd raced head-to-head competing in the semi-finals and finals at the LA Coliseum, cheering loudly for all of them despite the 1800 miles between us. I hoped they could hear me. They were my motivation on each day's run.

On Friday evening we camped in front of the TV with a bowl of popcorn, listening to Jim McKay and Marty Liquori announcing the women's 1500, Julie Lantis finishing a dismal last in her semi-final, Kim Gallagher winning the second semi with an astonishing 4:10.81. Dad agreed that she was on fire.

Saturday evening Mary Decker, Cindy Bremser, and Joan Hansen made the US team in the 3000 meters, Cathy Branta finishing fourth and missing a spot on the 1984 Olympic team by eight seconds – despite a nine second PR. I felt her pain, knowing how heartbroken she must have been.

When the ABC camera caught a closeup of Cindy Bremser after she finished, I recalled dad's prophetic words at the 1980 Drake Relays, back when I was a sophomore at East High – that one day Cindy would be an Olympian. She finally was. I still had the Drake Relays gold medal she gave me that same weekend when I won the prep 800m, her award hanging upstairs on my bedroom bulletin board.

Sunday morning, we all went to breakfast at Perkins for Danny's 23rd birthday, the first time the family had been together since Christmas. Mom held my hand as we sang Happy Birthday at the restaurant, her beautiful voice a bittersweet memory from our family years of camping, my older brother planning to meet his girlfriend later this afternoon. They were getting serious.

I dropped by Things, Things, and Things throughout the week at random times of the day, hoping I would *accidently* bump into Thorsten, each time riding home on the bus alone, wired on too much coffee, replaying the poignant moments of our first date with a sad smile. He was probably spending the summer in Missouri…with a cool girlfriend. Sigh. *I'm going to die a spinster*.

———•———

I enjoyed being in Iowa City but was ready to prepare for the cross country season, and it was easier to avoid distractions in Evanston. After my failure to qualify for the Olympic Trials, I wanted to leave no stone unturned in training for my junior year, a focus on running the only thing on my plate. No more coulda, woulda, shoulda. I wasn't going to be beaten because I wasn't fast enough, or strong enough, or tough enough. I was going to work my ass off.

In late June I got a letter from Sue Simon, the postmark on the envelope showing the two-page missive was from her home in Spokane, Washington. After news of what she was doing this summer Sue jumped to the reason she wrote – she wasn't coming back to Northwestern. I was shocked by the announcement, hoping no one had driven her away.

"I know none of you were aware, but I struggled with eating issues in high school, my counselor convincing me I was finally ready for the new challenge…but I wasn't. Coach O'Shea was understanding, never pointing out the obvious, and none of the girls were mean-spirited or judgmental, but you…"

I sat the letter down, afraid to read the next words. She *had* put on weight but was diligent about riding the exercise bike with me. And she always seemed to eat well. Was I too over-bearing? Did I not listen enough? I took a deep breath and nervously picked it up, my armpits prickling with sweat.

"were the only reason I survived. You were always there with kind words. Always had my back. Helped me when I struggled. Please tell the girls there are no hard feelings. I enjoyed my time at Northwestern but right now, it's the wrong place for me. I need to be close to my family and support from my counselor. I'm enrolled at Gonzaga University and will continue working towards a degree in Social Work, so I'm excited for the future. Please keep in touch. I value your friendship. Love Sue."

The team got together for the first time on June 25th, everyone meeting at Anita, Becky, and Joanne's apartment on Sherman and Noyes at 8am, all of us exchanging hugs in front of their dark brick building while we waited for Anita. Janelle had graduated and Alena was in Atlanta, none of the freshman expected to be in Evanston. I could feel the excitement in the air, last year's failure to get the team to nationals hanging over heads.

Anita came flying out the door wearing lime green running shorts and a sleeveless white t-shirt, the armholes cut down to the waistline of her shorts, the white sports bra mostly exposed.

"It's a good thing we're out here because the bathroom…" She smiled and waved her hand back and forth in front of her nose. Everyone laughed.

Coach O'Shea set up the summer training program – Sunday our long run; Monday and Friday hill work and 200's, Wednesday a four mile at a 6-6:15 pace, the other days easy six mile runs. We began at a slow pace, jogging down the sidewalk towards Davis Street, our destination James Park.

"Has anyone watched Springsteen's 'Born in the USA'?" Anita was from New Jersey. "If he'd pulled me up on the stage at a concert like he did that girl in the video, I'd do more than just dance with him." Everyone started laughing. "I'd take him backstage and…" She had a huge grin.

"Aw c'mon. No way." I chuckled. "He'd just throw you back into the crowd like a scrawny fish."

"What are you talking about." She placed a hand demurely behind her head as we waited for the light. "He'd be all over this Jersey girl. I'm hot!"

"What class are you taking?" Joanne turned to Jennifer.

"Organic Chem." Jennifer sighed. "I have three lectures and a lab on Thursday afternoon. What a way to spend my summer."

"How about you?"

"I'm doing ME research at Tech every afternoon, Monday through Friday. It's been interesting so far. I'm just glad to have the position. Its great experience."

We approached James Park in southwest Evanston, Mt. Trashmore – the garbage dump turned into a sledding hill looming high above us at the far end of the grassy fields.

"Well girls." I looked around the team. "Just remember our disappointment at Regionals last fall."

Anita glared at me and then smiled.

"As God is my witness." She spoke like Scarlett O'Hara in 'Gone With the Wind' – the back of a hand over her forehead. "I'll never let any Big Ten team beat us again."

We stood in a line five runners wide, heads pivoting left and right, all of us leaning forward and taking off as a group up the hill on our first repetition. We were determined to qualify for nationals. Whatever it took.

———————

My summer job was as a counselor for youth camps at Northwestern, the 10am – 3pm hours providing spending money for my time in Evanston. Dad and mom claimed I saved them so much money by getting the athletic scholarship that they were more than happy to pay the summer rent. My group was girls eight and nine years old; teaching them soccer, basketball, and softball, hoping they discovered the joy of activity and confidence in their bodies.

I also volunteered at a food pantry in Hillside Church one afternoon a week, sorting food that came in from area grocery stores, boxing it up for distribution to those less fortunate. It was humbling to see mothers standing in line with kids trailing behind, the excitement on their faces as they carried the food home like a birthday present. Anita and Jennifer joined me on the Wednesdays, biking two miles there, following me an extra five miles on the way home.

The weekend after the 4th of July I took the girls down to the Aragon Theater in Chicago to listen to Annette and her

126

band open for R.E.M., everyone dressed to the nines, all of looking out of place as we rode the L southward, a drunken group of Loyola students at the other end of the car talking loudly as the Lawrence stop approached.

As always, Anita was the belle of our group – the "girlie girl," wearing a short black dress, black ankle boots, and a jean jacket; her hoop earrings, a variety of necklaces, and the bright red lipstick making her stand out. I tried with my acid-washed jeans, white t-shirt, and a black satin jacket but my effort was a lost cause. Except for Anita, it was so weird for all of us to be dressed up, my teammates more comfortable in running clothes and jeans.

The girls were shocked to be in a complimentary VIP Box for the concert, stunned by Annette's performance in front of a thousand fans, the crowd applauding for over a minute after she sang "Anything." I recognized lots of the songs but there were many I'd never heard, her repertoire growing by leaps and bounds. Watching Anita, I could tell she was jealous of Annette's leopard mini-skirt and gold lamé halter top, the one-inch heels on her ankle boots accenting her long legs, surprised when I told her Phillip put together the outfit.

Annette came back on stage to sing "Don't Go Back to Rockville" with Michael Stipe, my girlfriend holding her own alongside the lead singer from Athens Georgia, their duet capturing the loudest cheers of the night. The backstage passes got us into the dressing rooms after the final R.E.M. encore, Annette rushing up to greet me as I stepped across the threshold, both of us squealing as we embraced.

I introduced her to my teammates, hugging her boyfriend Aiden when he came over, Annette insisting they all have a glass of champaign as everyone toasted their performance. While we talked, Aiden serenaded the girls on his six-string, Anita quite taken by his charm. We left the Aragon at 1:30am, hailing a taxi to take us back to Evanston. I was exhausted. I suspected Annette's evening was just getting underway.

Our training routine continued through the dog days of July, my mileage consistently between forty-five and fifty, the extra biking in the afternoon aiding my aerobic fitness. I thought I was in great shape but recently I noticed three extra pounds on the scale – even though it wasn't around my period. My thoughts went to Stacey Hersh and Sue Kennedy, weight issues leading to their downfall. It made me nervous.

"Hi mom. I got a question for you." I was paying for the call, so I didn't dilly-dally. "I've...I've gained a little weight, maybe three or four pounds...it makes me nervous. I need your input."

She understood my worries, helping Stacey Hersch get through her struggles when she dealt with anorexia. Mom knew zero about running, but she was quite aware of a good diet.

"Have you missed any periods?"

"No, I'm good."

"What about meat. Do you have a serving each day?" I gave her an uh-huh.

"How about fruit and vegetables?"

"Jennifer and I have lots of fruit and we always make a vegetable for dinner."

"What about skim milk?"

"On my cereal and two glasses for dinner."

"How about ice cream?"

"Well." I cringed. "I don't have it as much as I used to...but maybe a cone every other week."

"Well, that's the problem right there...I know it's on the food pyramid somewhere." She laughed at her own joke. "I'm glad you called. You're doing all the right things, eating well, and your body is perfect. Sue Kennedy was doing all the right things too...it was simply that her body was going through a natural rhythm...and it wouldn't let her lose weight. It's unfortunate, but that's reality. So don't let it worry you. Everything's fine."

She paused.

"Honey, remember when you got second at the state meet and were so depressed?" Uh-huh. It was a memory I hated thinking about.

"Well, I'll say the same thing now. I won't love you anymore if you are an average runner or if you are a great runner. I'll always love you. Just do your best and I'll know you're the most wonderful daughter in the world."

"Thanks mom." I sighed. "I love you."

Cross country practice started August 20th. We were champing at the bit.

Chapter 11
September 7, 1984

Our first meet of the season was September 8th at UW-Parkside. One of my favorite courses and a benchmark and where I could see how my summer work was paying off. We won the meet again, our second time, the fifteen points a perfect score against the other eighteen teams. I won the race with a 17:09 – a 5:30 pace, crushing my PR at Parkside by thirteen seconds. *Hot diggity dog!* At the two mile marker I knew I was going to win, my strength up the long hill separating me from teammates and cementing the victory.

On Monday, following the Parkside race our squad was ranked 16th in the nation – the first time a Wildcat team had ever been found in the NCAA standings! We were so pumped when Coach O'Shea broke the news at practice that our one thousand meter repeats on the nearby golf course were the fastest intervals we'd ever done.

A 5K in 16:00 is 3:12 for each kilometer, today's average of our six intervals a second faster than that. Becky led the first one on the freshly mown grass, our 3:10 prompting Coach O'Shea to caution us to save it for the last one. Anita's 3:11 on number two elicited a small smile from coach as we jogged to the starting line for number three, the freshmen trailing a bit behind as fatigue reared its ugly face.

Joanne took the next one, six of us hanging together, our three rookies trailing behind like the string on a balloon, coach shouting "3:11…3:12…3:13…" as we passed. Becky turned as we clustered ten yards past the line.

"Good job girls…keep it going."

Alena led the next one, the veterans hitting the 1K at 3:12, our frosh between 3:15 and 3:17. Coach O'Shea turned to them.

"You three." He pointed at Amy, Jackie, and Mary. "Only one more."

Jennifer took charge of the fifth one, six of us hitting the line at 3:12. Coach nodded at us with a smile on his face.

"Great job ladies. The three freshmen…jog while they do the last one." He turned to us. "Just remember we are a team…do the last one as a group."

I led everyone across the line at 3:10, smiles on every face as we patted backs after the workout. There is nothing as satisfying as a great workout, afterward each of us lost in our own thoughts, savoring the joyous moment. It was as though we had defied odds and defeated Goliath, pride and confidence oozing from every pore. I could feel our hubris in the air.

"Well ladies." Anita grinned; arms extended as though she was greeting the world. "Time to start kicking ass and taking names!"

———✦———

The 2nd Annual Meeting of the Minds was in Boston on September 22nd, host Harvard, along with Rice and Stanford competing with us on the famed Franklin Park course. Boston's largest green space was designed by Frederick Olmstead – the same landscape architect who designed Chicago's 1893 World's Columbian Exposition in Jackson Park. I learned that interesting fact reading a book about Olmstead last summer.

We jogged the course on Friday afternoon, temperatures more pleasant in Boston than in Chicago, the race time high expected to be in the upper 60's on Saturday. That evening there was a banquet for the teams, afterwards the men's and women's Northwestern squads walking in groups along the Charles River, watching the scullers launching boats from the Weld Boathouse.

Saturday morning four teams lined up in Franklin Park – host Harvard in the box next to us, Kate Wiley in a crimson singlet with the white "H" wishing me good luck, her Canadian accent belied by the way she rhymed "out" with "boot" when she encouraged her teammates to accelerate from the starting line.

We were all shuffling back and forth in our box like nervous racehorses, running fingers along the back hem adjusting bun-huggers, thumbs arcing over ears to put phantom strands of hair in place, Becky bending over and discreetly spitting into the grass. *C'mon, let's get this show on the road!* Three toots on a whistle and the starter raised his hand.

"Runners set." He paused. "BOOM!"

We exploded from box four, eight Wildcats together as we sprinted down the initial straight, staccato shouts from fans as we flew by the crowd. Ninety percent of the runners must have been in the lead group, the Cardinal team and our eight, along with Wiley and Stricker of Harvard filling the dusty grass path as we made a gentle right turn. It was early in the season, but the grass was already well-worn, thousands of runners here before us.

Past White Stadium where local high school teams played, we curled around the football facility and back towards the starting area, the course to this point as flat as a pancake. I took a deep breath and glanced to my left, Stanford's Alison Wiley running alongside her sister Kate, Cardinal coach Brooks Johnson shouting through cupped hands at teammates Regina Jacobs, Ellen Lyons, and Ceci Hopp.

As we came out of the long U-turn I glanced behind, Becky, Alena, Jennifer, and Anita looking quite comfortable despite the brisk pace. Behind the starting line spectators shouted encouragement, the field of runners heading back towards the first loop. Just ahead we could hear a timer shouting.

"5:01…5:02…5:03…5:04"

Alongside White Stadium a second time sweat began dripping down my temples, the bright sun and lack of shade beginning to take its toll. I could see the only hill just in front, the gentle climb barely enough for us to break stride as we stepped onto the slope, my breathing getting louder as we continued towards the top.

Coach O'Shea was two-thirds of the way up, encouraging our squad, his pleas to our freshmen a lost cause as they fell behind from the torrid pace. There were still six in our Wildcat pack, the Stanford squad appearing no worse for the wear, the pair from Harvard holding a half step lead on the field.

The downhill was so gradual it was barely noticeable, the fast pace and warmth beginning to take its toll on tired bodies – runners falling behind like seed corn off the back of a pickup truck. By the time we got to the two mile mark the lead group was smaller, six Stanford runners, one from Rice, and five from Northwestern clinging to the Harvard pair.

"10:12…10:13…10:14…10:15"

"That-a-way ladies." Coach shuffled alongside us. "You're doing great. Keep it going. You can do it."

Hoo boy. I was getting tired.

The shade of the trees in the Wilderness Loop was nice but the dusty trails were annoying, puffs of dirt exploding as spikes hit the ground. It reminded me of the Balboa Park course years ago – at least we didn't have the same tough hill. The Harvard duo pushed the pace at two-and-a-quarter miles, four of the Cardinal runners and three Wildcats matching them, Alena and Becky with me, the other runners falling away like booster rockets on the Discovery.

Now we were nine – six of them All-Americans.

The Crimson pair pushed again at two-and-a-half miles and my willpower was nearly broken, the clickity-clack of spikes as we crossed asphalt paths somehow an enjoyable break from the strain on my body. *C'mon Sarah.* Alena joined me and we pulled back on the leaders, my breaths coming fast and furious, four hundred meters between the five of us and the finish line. Kate Wiley continued to push the tempo, stretching me to my limit.

I don't know if I can do it. I'm so dead.

We made a right turn with three hundred meters remaining, both of the Wiley sisters, Regina Jacobs, and myself still in a vague cluster. Behind the starting line and then another right turn, the finish banner was only two hundred meters away. Coach O'Shea was waving his arm in big circles, shouting at the top of his lungs, trying to get me to respond.

"C'mon Sarah. You can do it!"

Kate Wiley and Regina Jacobs took off with a burst of speed I couldn't match, Alison Wiley five yards ahead and refusing to give into my repeated entreaties. I crossed the line two steps behind her, the effort hurting so badly I couldn't open my eyes. I stumbled down the chutes, wobbling like a drunken sailor, too tired to be elated. I didn't think the pain would ever go away.

I stood at the end of the chutes wiping sweat off my face with the back of a hand, counting off teammates as they exited the flagging, our fifth runner only one step behind the Cardinal's number five – a good sign. *Could we have beaten them?*

I shook hands with Regina and then congratulated the Wiley sisters, shuffling over to shake hands with Ellen Lyons. When I was a sophomore in high school she won the Kinney National XC meet, beating me by nearly a minute on the hilly 5K in San Diego. She had joined me on a course run-through at Balbo Park that day, her status as the #1 high school runner in the nation intimidating. Today I beat her by nine seconds. *Whoopie.*

1. Kate Wiley   Harvard
2. Regina Jacobs Stanford
3. Alison Wiley   Stanford
4. Sarah Tucker   NU
5. Jenny Stricker Harvard
6. Alena Palmer   NU
7. Ceci Hopp   Stanford
8. Ellen Lyons   Stanford
9. Becky Beach   NU
10. J. Spevak   NU
11. C. Curtain   Stanford
12. Anita Keller NU

We beat Harvard and Rice, losing to a Stanford team ranked #2 in the nation by a score of 31-41.

I will never forget this race. For the first time in my life, I knew I could qualify for the NCAA championship. It wasn't a wish or a hope. Only a certainty that I was going to be there.

On the outside I looked exactly the same, but on the inside there was a confidence I'd never experienced.

I fought head-to-head with the best runners in the nation – ones that would be in the top ten at the NCAA meet, giving them a run for their money, responding to every challenge they threw at me. It made me think of what Annette said after her performance at the Aragon. I clearly remember her words.

"You know Sarah…I'm a good singer. I have an ability very few people possess." She looked over my shoulder staring at an inanimate object in their dressing room, not bragging or showing off. Just stating a fact. As if she told me she had green eyes. Now I can say the same.

I'm a good runner.

Our Northwestern squad was ranked 13th the following Monday, the impressive performance in Boston jumping us three notches towards the top. Over the next three weekends we had a series of wins in invitationals at Iowa State, Michigan, and the Illinois Inter-collegiates on Eastern Illinois' course, somehow navigating the logjam of teams and moving into 11th after the impressive victories.

Awesome!

Annette and I still got together for lunch every Sunday, alternating between campuses, her latest news that I.R.S. Records was setting up a date so they could record their first album. She was over the moon, excitedly talking about an opportunity to be on a monthly show on MTV, amazed that things were finally falling in place.

"I can't help thinking that none of this would have happened without your mother's support." She sighed. "I mean, to play at the Aragon was out of this world…but singing alongside Michael Stipe...that evening opened doors that I never expected. That's how we got the contract with I.R.S."

"Wow." I leaned over and gave her a hug. "Just remember," I smiled. "I get ten percent!" We both laughed.

"How's your team doing?" Annette took a sip of coffee.

"You won't believe it but last Monday they ranked us #11 in the nation." I grinned. "We're like rock stars." Annette burst out laughing.

We hugged before she left, my clogs making me almost as tall as Annette. Almost.

———————

The Big Ten meet was at Purdue on October 27th, everyone on our squad healthy and ready to challenge Wisconsin's dominance at the meet, confident enough that we believed we had a shot. The Boilermaker's golf course on Northwestern Avenue was the site of the championship, Anita claiming she was going to steal a street sign as a keepsake after we won the meet.

We trudged through light rain on Friday afternoon's run-through, nothing about the course tough or remarkable. It wasn't as flat as the Boston course but certainly not as challenging as Iowa State's. Although we were boisterous at first, the drizzle dampening spirits, conversation petering out as we turned to our own thoughts, Becky chirping in as we slowed to a stop near the chutes.

""My last chance to grab a 1st Team All-conference spot." Becky shook her head. I could hear the disquiet in her voice. "I can't believe I'm a senior."

As always Anita chimed in.

"I can't believe my underwear are riding up my ass."

Everyone burst into laughter.

On the ride back to the hotel from the course all I could think of was that after this weekend I would only have one Big Ten cross country meet remaining. Becky's words freaked me out. Where had all the time gone?

Saturday morning was overcast but rain wasn't predicted, low spots a little sloppy from last night's rain – but in general the course was good. The Hawkeyes were lined up next to us in box three, neither Jenny Spangler nor Nan Doak racing, whether due to injury or what, I didn't know. But I did know it improved my chances of finishing in the top five.

We did one last stride out, circling up one hundred yards out, Joanne the first to speak.

"Focus on the team…do your job." She looked around at the faces. "It been wonderful to have you as teammates." Becky cut in.

"Okay…Wildcats on three. One-two-three…WILDCATS!"

The starter was thirty yards out, a long whistle, and then he raised his hand.

"BOOM."

We charged hard, overtaking the Iowa squad after one hundred yards, to our left the red and white of Wisconsin, on our right the Michigan squad racing down the first fairway, chasing after the golf cart leading the runners. As the rhythm changed from a frantic sprint to a steady tempo, I glanced to the sides looking for the usual suspects.

Six Badgers, Eder and Banta from Minnesota, Sue Schroeder of Michigan were right there, looking for Purdue's Becky Cotta but remembering she graduated last spring. Illinois, a team that we had beaten at the Inter-collegiate meet by four points was nowhere to be seen.

On the far side of the course we settled into a rhythm, tempos slowing a bit on patches of soggy grass, Becky and Joanne staying at my side, their breathing relaxed and steady. I glanced over my shoulder as we made a right turn, Alena, Anita, and Jennifer right there, Deena gamely holding onto the back of our pack. Coach shouted through cupped hands.

"That-a-way Wildcats. Stick together. Work as a team."

Puddled rainwater rooster-tailed off spikes, the muddy water speckling my face and singlet from a position just behind Branta and Ishmael. I was tempted to pull beside them but wanted to maintain contact with my teammates – help them get through the race. At the mile, a timer shouted from beside the breadboard with a "1" as I went by.

"5:14…5:15…5:16…"

We circled behind the starting line and into the second loop, seven Wisconsin runners, five from Northwestern, and pairs from Minnesota, Illinois, and Michigan still with the front group up. A half mile into the second loop the pace slowed a notch, tempos not as rapid as we climbed a short hill, eighteen to twenty runners in the front pack. A gentle turn and we were at the halfway point, Ohio State's Maureen Cogan pulling up on my shoulder. I had wondered where she was.

From up ahead I could hear three sharp whistles, the Wisconsin coach Peter Tegan with a thumb and index finger in his mouth, Branta and Ishmael increasing the pace as though commanded by the sound. *Shit. Shit. Shit. Should I go or should I stay?* With the team in mind, I hung back, Minnesota's Eder and Bant, tagging along with McNee of Illinois to chase after the Badgers. It took all my willpower to stay back but I had to help my teammates.

I could see the 2 mile marker ahead, Coach O'Shea shuffling alongside encouraging Anita and Jennifer, their willpower fading as we turned into the last loop. There were eight runners in front of me, the gap fifty yards and growing larger, desperation beginning to take over my thoughts. *I gotta get up there. I can't wait any longer.*

I looked at my teammates, the squint in their eyes telling me what I needed to know – they were as tired as me. Coach O'Shea appeared from out of nowhere.

"Okay ladies, time to make hay."

I took a deep breath and nodded to Alena and Becky. They glanced at me, knowing the moment was at hand. I charged after the eight, reluctantly leaving Anita and Jennifer to fend for themselves. They understood…but it was still hard to do. Ohio State's Cogan joined me as we circled around a green and back towards the finish line, a quick glance showing Branta and Ishmael another fifty yards ahead of the group I was chasing.

At that moment I knew the best I could do was third place. The Wisconsin pair had too much ground on me, and I wasn't quite their caliber. The gap on the second pack was down thirty meters, and then it was fifteen, suddenly aware that Alena and Becky no longer at my side, a quick glance behind revealing they were twenty meters behind. I finally worked my way up so I was close enough to McNee that I could smell her Dior

Poison perfume, the Illinois runner glancing over as I pulled even, seven of us now in an informal chase pack.

Resting in their slipstream for a moment I looked over my opponents, wondering who had the courage to pick up the pace with six hundred meters remaining. Eder? Christiansen? My guess was yes. McNee? Cogan? Herbst? Bassett? Maybe. There was only one way to find out. I took a deep breath and increased the tempo, Christiansen and Eder responding to my challenge, McNee trying but slipping behind with the others. *I'm so dead.*

When I was overcome with fatigue, and awash in pain, I discovered in high school that counting each time my right foot struck the ground helped distract my mind, the internal dialog a diversion from the fatigue gnawing at my willpower. "*1…2…3*" Past the eighteenth tee box the golf course sign said '482 yards' the finish banner even with the eighteenth green. "*14…15…16.*"

I analyzed my competitors. Eder was faster than me, but she didn't have the speed endurance. Christiansen had the endurance but not the speed, my only hope that I could somehow navigate the treacherous waters between the two opponents. I broke Eder first, the Gopher unable to push the fast pace from so far out, Christiansen remaining on my hip, the Badger relentless.

I was running as hard as I could, hanging on by a thread, one-hundred fifty meters to the line, my tank filled with fumes. *I'm dying.* Christiansen was going to beat me. Suddenly I could hear her voice.

"*C'mon darling. You can do it.*"

It was Marie. With a primeval effort I commanded my legs to go faster, beating my rival to the finish banner by a step, desperately leaning at the chalked white line, falling face-first, and sliding across the wet grass on my chest, the race number ripped from its pins.

I lay there like a Super Woman who had dropped from the sky, flat on the ground with arms extended ahead, too tired to move. Officials reached under my arms and lifted me to my feet, the neckline of the jersey so low my sports bra was exposed. I was too tired to care.

I readjusted the tank top as I staggered through the chute, an official walking beside to make sure I didn't collapse, letting the recorder at the end of the chute know I was third. Cathy and Katie gave me quick hugs, Cathy Branta noticing the green blades staining my chest, joking that instead of using Kleenex to fill my bra I used grass.

I was surprised I wasn't too tired to laugh at her joke.

Becky was tenth or eleventh, Alena trailing her teammate by two spots, each with an Illinois runner just behind them, Joanne and Anita somewhere in the twenties. *Wow, Illinois must have started slowly.* Our battle with the Illini team for second was going to be close. We huddled at the back of the chutes with Coach O'Shea, everyone talking excitedly, steam drifting off each head as we sipped on water.

Coach recounted my dive at the finish line, Anita noticing the green showing through my white tank top. She pulled out the neckline of my jersey and took a peek, laughing at what she saw.

"Oh my God Sarah." Anita covered her smile. "Bill Jarvis is going to be *sooo* pissed when he sees your sports bra is green." We all laughed.

1. Wisconsin   27
2. Illinois   79
   Northwestern 79

Two weeks later we qualified for the 1984 NCAA Championships, the first women's team at Northwestern to compete at this esteemed level.

———————

The Penn State University golf course. It was thirty-four degrees on Monday, the ground still damp from a late-night rain. Coach O'Shea gave me the green light today, indicating that I could run my own race, explaining that team tactics were

140

too difficult at this level of competition – that it wasn't worth the worry. I wore a long-sleeved cotton turtleneck under my singlet, brown work gloves on my hands, impulsively tossing the stocking hat as we waited to get the race underway. It wasn't windy enough to warrant the item.

Villanova was in the box to our right, on the other side a group of individual qualifiers, including Minnesota's Jody Eder, the Illini's Kelly McNee, and Harvard's Jenny Stricker – the others I didn't know. I had beaten each one of these three – although by scant margins. Regardless, it was reassuring to run with people I knew, quality runners I could gauge my efforts against, their presence providing immeasurable relief.

I waited in our box for the starter to get us going, my shoulders shimmying from the cold air and my sweaty body, absorbing the scene I had waited for far too long. Taking a deep breath I turned to my teammates.

"Let's kick some ass!"

I remembered the gun going off, the entire field racing ahead like a cattle stampede, my only sensation that I was exactly where I should be. After that not much. Today's times meant nothing – only the place when I crossed the white line. The top twenty-five US runners were All-Americans and after that you were SOL – shit outta luck. It happened to me at the Olympic Trials, but it wasn't going to happen today.

"Perfect Sarah. Perfect."

Coach was waiting a half mile into the race, counting off positions, his words all I needed to hear. It meant I was in the top thirty. I didn't have to freak out. Jody, Kelly, and Jenny were within a few feet of me, Michigan State's Sue Schroeder joining us just past the initial mile mark.

Five minutes later Coach O'Shea shouted.

"Time to compete Sarah!"

I had waited so long for this moment, taking off like a gust of wind over water.

Eder got me today, but I beat the others to the line, only three Big Ten runners in front of me. Cathy Branta won the race and the Wisconsin Badgers the NCAA team title. And I was an All-American, crossing the line in 19th place. We scored 268 points and finished in 11th place, teams in the middle so even that 8th was sixteen points ahead and 13th only five points behind.

Seven of us posed under the NCAA Cross Country Championship banner with arms over each other's shoulders – coach snapping the picture as Anita made the quip.

"Girls, I'm so bloated you could pop me with a pin."

Through the eye piece of the camera coach saw Jennifer on the left side of the picture with an easy smile, her meet uniform zipped up and neat; an intermittent bit of sunlight highlighting Anita's auburn hair, a big smile outlined with red lipstick; me leaning into her with my jacket unzipped, a grin stretching from ear to ear; Becky's 36th place finish making her bedroom eyes glow; 5'9" Joanne towering over her teammates with a soft grin; Alena's straight blond bob blowing over one eye as she grinned; Jackie's one-eyed squint making for a crooked smile.

I was in heaven.

Chapter 12

November 24, 1984

The Saturday after Thanksgiving mom took Annette and me to the Brown Bottle in Iowa City, the significance of the get-together not lost on either of us. It was at this restaurant she told us to follow our heart and reach for the moon, turn our dreams into reality. Six years ago, we had to illicitly drink wine from water glasses but as we were twenty-one, we got stemware, our first toast a bittersweet memory.

"To Marie." Mom sighed and turned to us. "And to the dreams of my two precious girls."

Marie's suicide six years ago was still fresh in our minds.

Queried by mom, Annette gave her the latest on their career, pulling a mockup of the album cover out of her shoulder bag, the words inscribed in silver ink. "To the woman who encouraged my dreams. Love, Annette." My best friend leaned over and gave mom a hug, tears rolling down their cheeks.

After the meal we had tiramisu for dessert and drank coffee, mom restating her three tenets as we enjoyed the Italian treat.

"Always remember you can come to me with anything." We both nodded. "Two, you will always seek opportunities beyond your ability." We smiled at the painful memories of mom's seemingly innocuous request. "And three, you will always reach for the moon." She squeezed our hands.

"Okay Annette. Besides alcohol, what drugs are you using?" My mother's boldness always surprised me. I think it's where I got my impulsiveness.

Annette blushed and then smiled, knowing it was impossible to resist mom's interrogation. She talked about marijuana, mentioning she had tried cocaine at post-concert parties, the high from the drug keeping her up all night long. Mom's next question came out of left field.

"How are your grades? Are they over 3.00?"

Annette scrunched her head into her shoulders.

"Okay, the grades are telling. Not what I want to hear." She reached out for Annette's hand. "Always understand that a college degree empowers you. Gives you options a high school graduate doesn't have. So... you're going to do a better job with your classwork...correct." Mom stared until Annette nodded sheepishly. "I'm not as worried about the marijuana...but you understand there is a reason they call it dope."

A burst of laughter erupted from us, Annette and I covering our mouths.

"As to the cocaine." Mom rubbed her forehead. "It doesn't make me happy, but I'm not going to berate you for your choices. You have a good head on your shoulders." Mom took a deep breath. "But promise to tell me if it becomes a problem...please." Annette nodded contritely.

"Sarah." Mom's eyes were smiling. "Did you get as drunk at your post-season party on Tuesday night as you did that summer going into 8th grade?"

My eyes were as big as frisbees, thinking of the incident buried in my past.

"I'm not as clueless as you think." Mom grinned.

"I...I...I." I didn't think she was aware of that dreaded experience. "The girls and guys team...we had a party...but..." I was so embarrassed, my face beet red.

"As long as you weren't swinging your blouse in circles overhead." She put a hand over her mouth to stifle the chuckle, Annette exploding in laughter. "I'm not too worried about you. You don't get out of control like Steve...but just be aware of who you are with. Always have a sober partner."

"Okay, one last toast and it's time to go home." We raised our glasses. "A votre sante."

━━━━━⊷⊶━━━━━

During the two weeks I took off I reflected on the cross country season, acknowledging that if we were going to be at the NCAA Championship in 1985, our three freshmen needed to be faster – because next year Becky, Joanne, and Anita would be gone to graduation. These three teammates were great runners and would be tough to replace. And I would miss them desperately.

The Monday evening after Thanksgiving I met Jackie, Mary, and Amy at our apartment, not stating the reason for our get together. Jennifer sat beside me as I began.

"You are at Northwestern to get your degree. The diploma will open doors you would have never thought available for women." I looked around at the blank faces. The three freshmen had no idea why I called them together. "But you're also here because you are very talented runners." Faint smiles.

"Jackie, you're a two-time Kentucky state champion in cross country, Mary you ran a 5:02 mile and 10:34 two mile double at the Michigan state meet, and Amy, you were a Kinney finalist and Indiana state champion in the mile."

"So, Jackie, tell Mary and Amy what it was like at the NCAA meet."

"It was so cool…I mean, we got to fly. I met Cathy Branta…she was the NCAA champion, and we got shirts that said, *1984 DI Cross Country Championships – Penn State University.*"

"Were you proud to be there?"

"Sure. It made me feel special…like I was an elite runner." She grinned. "Even though I finished 108th." Everyone chuckled. She paused and thought. "But you know what? It also opened my eyes to what I might accomplish, what is possible…so it was a great experience."

"Exactly, and you three will be the ones to help us continue the streak. I remember how challenging it is being a freshman. What with schoolwork and the level of competition…it's tough. That's why I have you here tonight."

We spent the next forty-five minutes going through the expectations and training regimen, about creating a Northwestern legacy, asking each individual to set goals for the indoor season. Our first objective was putting in thirty minutes on the exercise bike beginning Monday at 7am. The girls all nodded.

I ended the meeting quite simply.

145

"Our only goal is to do what is possible every single day. I'll never ask you to do the impossible. Do that and we will be running up in Milwaukee next November."

Finals ended December 21st and I was back in Iowa City. I put my All-American certificate on the bulletin board next to Cindy Bremser's Drake Relays medal, enjoying the fact that all I had to do was relax and run over break. Danny got engaged just after Christmas, Helen, a girl he had dated for three years at Luther College getting a huge diamond. It was hard to picture him getting married. I was thrilled with the news, but his announcement was almost depressing – I didn't even have a boyfriend.

Second quarter classes for 1985 began on January 7th.

Thursday after my 8am Education Psychology class I walked to JK Sweets for coffee, hoping to finish Sandra Cisneros' "The House on Mango Street" before my noon class. I found a table in the back of the cafe, the noise from students up front a little too distracting. The last sip of coffee was cold when I heard the question.

"Aren't you in my Ed Psych class?"

I looked up to see a student with a backpack over his shoulder, steam rising from the mug, his round wire-rimmed glasses, wavy straw-colored hair, and beautiful smile catching my eye. I didn't remember him but...he was cute.

"Maybe?" He could see my confusion.

"Yeah, you sit over on the right side...about two or three rows back. You asked a question today...I can't remember what." He shrugged his shoulders and grinned.

C'mon you idiot. Say something.

"Yeah." I nodded. He just stood there. "Oh. Grab a seat." I gestured. He smiled uncomfortably and sat down, waiting for me to make room for his coffee.

"Sorry, I'm spacing out." I blushed as I moved my mug to the side. "Let's start again. Yes, that was me." He smiled.

"Please have a seat." I flourished my hand with a smile. "Hello. My name is Sarah, what's yours?"

"Justin…Justin Rush." He covered a smile and then took a sip of the coffee. "Man, you're a tough audience."

We talked until I had to leave for class, printing my name and apartment phone number on a piece of scratch paper, praying to God he called me. He did.

In our first meet at Western Michigan the three freshmen joined me on a distance medley and 4 x 800, Coach O'Shea letting me take charge and put together the order. He had planned to sit most of the cross country squad for the first two meets but I had other ideas. He was a bit puzzled when I made the initial request but deferred to my judgement, laughing when he discovered I would be running the four hundred leg on the medley.

I pulled the girls together on the three hour bus ride, the four of us on seats facing into the aisle.

"OK. Jackie, you're going to lead-off the DMR, the 1200 leg." I smiled at her. "I want the first four hundred in seventy-two, and the second one in seventy-five – so you'll be 2:27 with two to go. You're going to hand off the baton to me in first place." I nodded my head and turned to Amy.

"Amy, I'm going to come in fast…so get out quickly." She nodded. "I told coach to get your splits…but I want a sixty-seven first four hundred on your 800. That's thirty-three and then thirty-four." I smiled at her and she smiled back. "Good." I turned to Mary.

"Mary…what state are you from?" She scrunched her nose, certain that I knew the answer. "If I remember correctly, it's Michigan." She nodded, confused at where this was going. "There is no way anyone in this state is going to beat you. You're a two-time state champion!" She smiled. "Amy is going to give you the baton in first place, and I want you to open a gap on the field from the get-go." I smiled. "Make the other girls hurt. So, I want a seventy-two, and then a seventy-five on the second 400…after that just run."

I looked around at every face and then smiled.

147

"And just like that…we're going to win. I guarantee it!"

Fortunately, they followed my plan, and we won by twenty yards, everyone hugging at the finish line, excitement on every face. Three hours later our foursome ran the 4 x 800, Amy anchoring this time but the outcome the same, our 9:15 fourth on the Northwestern list. Their giddy swagger after the race made me happy.

Justin had called after our encounter at the coffee house and set up a date the evening of the WMU meet, my heart beating like the clapper on a classroom bell as we talked, a smile on my face when I hung up the phone. He didn't say what we were going to do but I really didn't care. I had a date!

Jennifer helped me pick out an outfit when we returned from Kalamazoo, eventually settling on my red Fair Isle sweater, the skinny blue jeans, and clogs – my biggest concern was that I wouldn't look cool. I put on mascara and peach eye shadow, wondering if I was wearing too much Opium perfume. Justin picked me up at the apartment, Jennifer sitting on the couch so I could make introductions, throwing on my ski jacket as we walked to his car. I was more nervous now than for my races today.

"There's movie I wanted to see at the Music Box Theatre…'One Flew Over the Cuckoo's Nest'…I hope you like Jack Nicholson." He cringed.

"Oh, I love him." Justin sighed, my enthusiasm just what he wanted to hear. "He was great in 'Easy Rider' and 'Twelve Easy Pieces' was wonderful…so this should be good."

We drove into the city and got off Lake Shore Drive at Irving Park, our conversation about classes and Christmas traditions, Justin laughing when I told him our family always exchanged presents in our pajamas. He parallel parked his old Ford Escort as easily as I maneuvered a lap around the track, my compliment getting one of his beautiful smiles.

I wanted to reach out and hold his hand as we walked up Southport towards the theater, the movie marquee lighting the sidewalk, the smell of popcorn inviting as he held the door for me. *Should I offer to pay for my ticket?*

I was too late, Justin going right to the booth. Instead, I insisted on buying popcorn. We sat on the left side of the massive theater, Justin craning his neck and pointing out twinkling stars on the dark blue ceiling, a red velvet curtain rising as the lights dimmed, conversation fading as the first trailer played.

The best part of the night was when he leaned over in the car to kiss me after I thanked him for the evening, my body tingling as I waved goodbye and walked towards my apartment, the hour well past midnight. I wasn't even tired.

———

The following weekend Coach O'Shea let me train through the Wisconsin meet so I could take charge of the girls. They were running a 3K – but fortunately Wisconsin wasn't running any of their top ten, a call to Cathy Branta confirming the fact.

Just as I did at Western Michigan, I laid out the race plan on the bus, instructing them the pace they were to run, and who was to lead at each point of the race. They finished 2nd, 3rd, and 4th, an anorexic girl from Marquette taking the title over them by a little over twenty seconds. I was thrilled it went so well. The girls were in the palm of my hand.

We cooled down on the snowy streets of Madison, looking for quiet neighborhoods to run in, clear sidewalks a rarity in this college town. I pointed at Chadbourne Avenue and the girls followed.

"First of all…you did a good job today. Your times are equivalent to 10:48-50 for the 3200m, so bravo to you three. I liked how you worked together, not intimidated by a pace that was too quick early on. You three were patient and worked your way up. I'm pleased."

We waited for a stoplight to change and then continued up the street.

"You all saw the winner from Marquette and are probably thinking, thin is good. That she kicked your asses. But that kind of thin is not good." I looked over at the girls, each one listening to my words. "Her 9:39 is an impressive time…but she won't last long." I sighed. "Eventually she'll develop a stress fracture or become anemic, and her meteoric rise will turn into crash and burn. So don't think that's the way to go. You're doing everything right…trust my plan."

On January 26th I ran my first race of the year at the University of Illinois, the ease of my 9:29.2 PR in the 3K shocking. I was only hoping to get under 9:40. No one was with me when I passed the mile at 4:58, Coach O'Shea encouraging me to push the pace even more on the 262-yard track, my last two hundred meters in thirty-three. Alena ran 9:36 and Jennifer 9:38, the Wildcats finishing 1-2-3 on the armory track.

Anita and Becky joined my three *amigas* in the mile, the two seniors first and second, both breaking 4:50, my trio turning in career bests – even though it was on an indoor facility. I was so happy. Things were falling into place. As was my relationship with Justin.

Saturday evening, we stopped at Annette's apartment to pick her up, Aiden planning to meet us at the Fireside Restaurant because he had to deliver an amp to a friend. It was the first time I felt comfortable showing Justin off, a big step in our burgeoning relationship – one that I hoped would continue to blossom. When we arrived, Annette gave him a big hug and then pointed to the couch, asking Justin questions like a newspaper reporter as he sat beside me.

She suddenly jumped up.

"Sarah, I don't like this outfit." *It looked good to me.* "Come in the bedroom and help me pick something out."

Annette peppered me with questions about Justin as she tried on outfits, finally deciding on a cowboy shirt, beaded leather belt, and boots, satisfied that she looked much better. When we returned Justin was sitting at the keyboard in an alcove off the living room wearing headphones, humming to himself as he played, unaware of our presence.

"You didn't tell me Justin could play the piano." Annette looked at me out of one eye.

150

"That's because I didn't know." I tapped Justin on the shoulder and he stopped, embarrassed to be caught unaware. I had no idea he had any musical talent. "I didn't know you can play the piano." He grinned.

"That's cause I'm not particularly good. My mom is a music teacher and made us learn an instrument when we were little. My brother plays the guitar…much better than I do."

"What were you playing?" Annette smiled. "I wanna hear."

He hit a button on the keyboard and played the short introduction, Annette recognizing the tune, a smile filling her face as she joined in to sing the words to Elton John's "Tiny Dancer."

"*Blue jean baby. LA lady. Seamstress for the Band. Pretty eyes…*" I hummed along.

When he played the last notes Justin turned to Annette, a shocked look on his face.

"Oh my God…you are so good." He looked at me and then back to Annette, his eyes as big as frisbees. "Are you a professional?" Annette and I laughed at each other.

"She plays in a band." I grabbed Justin's hand and pulled him up. "I promise to take you some time if we can find tickets." I smiled at Annette. "Let's go, we're gonna be late. I don't want to keep Aiden waiting."

I ran the Bally Invitational at the Rosemont Horizon the week before the Big Ten meet, thrilled to be part of the elite field of runners in the 1500m – Cindy Bremser, Joan Nesbitt, and Sue Addison also competing, all finalists in the 1984 Olympic Trials. I held my own that evening, running a 4:20.6 to get fifth, my heel unusually sore on the cool down after the race.

It didn't seem bad but when I woke up Sunday morning, I could barely make it to the bathroom, the pain intense – as though I was walking on a sharp stone. I called coach, freaking out at the bad timing, worried that maybe I'd broken something. He met me at the Dyche Stadium training room, the head trainer indicating I had plantar fasciitis – an inflammation of the tendon on the bottom of my foot.

"It's not fatal." The trainer looked at me. "But you're going to have to stay off it for three or four days…maybe a week."

It was as though he'd asked me to chop off an arm. The trainer gave me ten minutes of sound treatment and then I shuffled out of the training room with chin on chest.

"Sarah, follow me." Coach O'Shea nodded over his shoulder. "We're going to put you on the exercise bike and do some interval training."

That day and the rest of the week I diligently rode the torture machine for forty-five minutes in the morning and forty-five minutes in the afternoon, my butt bone so sore it hurt to sit on a kitchen chair. But if that's what it took, I was ready to make the sacrifice.

The Big Ten meet had been at Ohio State outdoors and it had been a good meet, so I was pumped to be back, hoping the results this indoor season would be just as good. But I hadn't run a step since the Bally Invitational, the pain there every morning on the way to the bathroom. There was no way I could even run if things didn't change. It was hard to stay positive.

On the bus ride to the conference meet I sat by myself and read, too rattled to relax. It was hard to ignore my worries, the unscheduled break from running an unwelcomed necessity. I needed to be sharp, to get ready with speed work or my Big Ten meet would be a bust. But we couldn't take the chance. The girls tried to engage me in conversation after the lunch break in Fort Wayne, but I pretended to be asleep, not in the mood for trite platitudes.

When we arrived at French Field House on Thursday evening, I was afraid to run, overcome with fear. Worried that if the pain was still there, I would freak out. Coach led me to the training room while everyone else went to the track. I needed to get heat on the bottom of my foot with a hydrocollator, the warmth comforting as I sat on the taping bench, my nerves still frazzled. I put on my shoe and shuffled down the hallway to the field house like a condemned prisoner.

What am I going to do?

It felt okay when I walked, but I jogged the first lap around the track like I was running over broken glass, worried the pain would come back. I couldn't tell if my form was good or bad, far too much thought going into each step. Somehow, I got through eight laps, slowing to a stop beside Coach O'Shea, his words reassuring. But I wasn't as confident. He entered me in the 1500 meters and 3000 meters, aware my strength was much better than it was nine months ago. Now it might be all for naught.

I rested my arch on a bag of ice as we rode to the hotel, unable to say good or bad when I stepped off the bus, my foot so cold I couldn't feel it. Jennifer sat at the desk in our room while I propped pillows against the headboard to read, trying to concentrate on William Kennedy's "Ironwood," the story beautifully written but so depressing I had to put it down.

"I'm going for a walk."

I put on my ski jacket, pulled the stocking hat over my ears, and walked to the far end of the hallway, carefully navigating the steps from the second floor, pushing the side door open and stepping into the cold air. Shivering, I moved forward hesitantly, no destination in mind. It might have been a mistake to put weight on the arch, but I had to burn off my nervous energy or I'd go crazy.

Thirty minutes later I walked through the lobby and up to our floor, pulling the plastic bag out of a random wastebasket and filling it with ice at the machine. I tossed and turned all night, trying to be quiet so I didn't disturb Jennifer, barely sleeping a wink. *Please. Just let me get through this.*

Coach O'Shea motioned to me at breakfast the next morning, glancing at my right foot.

"What do you want to do?" He pursed his lips. "Run or not run?"

"I need to at least try…I got to give it a chance." I started to say more and then stopped.

"Okay then, here's what we're going to do." He washed his hand down his face. "I'm going to wrap your arch…to support the tendon, and then we'll fashion a heel donut that fits in your spikes. Let's warmup on a stationary bike, stretch, and then I'll put the tape on ten minutes before the race."

He paused.

"Then you can lace up your spikes and do some strides. Let me know how it feels." He looked at his plate and then up at me. "Sarah, do what's best for you…not for me…and not for the team. Just for you. I think you can do it but know that I'll support your decision…whether to run or not run."

I sat in a chair on the backstretch of the track, coach wrapping individual strips of athletic tape around my arch, making sure none of them strangled my foot. I looked up as Cathy Branta and Katie Ishmael did a stride-out, the breeze from their speed ruffling my hair. He waited until I laced the second spike and then stood, nodding to him as I forced a smile.

"Good luck Sarah."

I could feel tightness, but the tape really helped, my first stride around the corner smooth. I did a second on the backstretch, adding more speed. It still was good. *This might work.* The first preliminary heat of the 1500 meters was lining up so I walked over to the clerk, and he put me in order, turning to Cathy to wish her good luck, shaking hands with a runner from Iowa – Penny something, to my right.

Sweat was dripping from under my arms, my pulse racing like we had already started, breaths much too quick. *RELAX!* I took a deep breath and let it out slowly, focusing on how it calmed me. *C'mon Sarah. You can do it.* I was ready.

The starter tooted on his whistle.

"Runners set." We all leaned and posed. BOOM!

Cathy Branta jumped to the lead and I followed her blindly, recalling only the top two were automatic qualifiers. We weren't going that fast, but I was relieved it felt comfortable, the rhythm of my foot strikes hypnotic as we circled the track. With three laps to go Cathy picked up the pace and I responded immediately, stationed myself just off her shoulder in second place, running on the white line of lane two.

She sprinted hard when the bell rang but I stayed with her, my bangs blowing back as we raced down the final straight. I instinctively raised my fist and smiled as we crossed the line together, sighing to myself as we slowed. *I did it!*

But when my heel hit the ground, I crumpled to the track like a puppet whose strings had been cut, the sensation in my foot as though I'd stepped on a hot coal. *Oh my God. It hurts so bad.* My eyes were pinched shut as I grabbed my right knee and rocked back and forth on the ground, pain traveling through my heel like a forest fire. *What just happened?*

Cathy leaned over me, holding my hand, waving a trainer over. Coach O'Shea arrived seconds later, kneeling at my hip, asking if it was my heel. I nodded with eyes squeezed shut, wondering if something was broken. The pain was so intense I couldn't open my eyes, the urge to rock back and forth my only outlet from the agony. A trainer brought a wheelchair and helped get me up and into the seat, rolling me off the track to applause from the crowd. It only made me angry.

They didn't understand. I didn't want their pity applause. That was for losers. There was nothing noble in what they had just seen. I qualified for the final, and yet probably wouldn't go, the injury stealing my opportunity. This was a tragedy that Shakespeare might have written – as though I was haunted by the ghosts of Stacey Hersh and Sue Kennedy, and then slain by the Macbeths. I cried in the wheelchair until there were no more tears, coach accompanying me to the hospital for X-rays after the meet.

Two hours later I was back in my hotel room, the doctor seeing no break on the film, only a slight rupture of the plantar fascia, expecting me to recover with two to three weeks of rest. My Big Ten meet was over. For the second night in a row, I slept poorly.

The next morning the entire team was in the breakfast lounge as I trailed Jennifer on crutches, everyone applauding as I entered the room. I hung my head. I no more deserved this than I did the pity applause yesterday – but somehow it felt better today. Anita quieted everyone and then spoke.

"Sarah, whether you know it or not, you have been an inspiration to all of us. Always had our backs, giving encouragement when we're down, praising us when we succeed…your contribution to the team is immeasurable." She wiped tears from her eyes. "Yesterday I made the final in the 1500 because of you. The last straight I could feel your presence. You gave me the courage to push even harder…and it worked." Anita was smiling through tears reaching out to hug me. "Although you'll need to kick me in the ass even harder today." We both laughed.

Then Amy stepped forward.

"And Sarah. You didn't see us run but Mary, Jackie, and I broke ten minutes in the 3K…our first time. Career bests. You were the reason. We were *so* happy after the race, finally feeling like we contributed to the team. It's all thanks to you."

I smiled for the first time in twelve hours.

———◦———

Riding a stationary bike for four weeks was one of the most torturous things I'd ever done, the twice daily efforts testing my resolve each session. Occasionally the temperatures were nice enough that I could ride outside, but for the most part the work was completed alone in the weight room, head bent forward staring at the sweat dripping off my chin onto a towel resting on the handlebars, the wet oval growing larger with each passing minute. *I must be nuts.*

If you had asked me whether I would rather go in for my annual checkup or ride the bike…it would have been a toss-up. The only reason I put up with it is that Northwestern was hosting the 1985 Big Ten meet in May and I had plans for something special.

The one good thing to come out of injury was that Justin and I had more time to spend together, my weekends filled with a myriad of exciting activities, the thrill of having a boyfriend erasing the setback in my running career. His presence made the unwanted hiatus tolerable...but barely.

Over spring break Justin took me for an evening at the 'Hideout,' Annette and Aiden playing a two hour set at the stage she sang on just four years ago. Hard to fathom how fast time had passed. Last month she was on MTV with Aiden and their band, the new album with I.R.S. expected to be released sometime this spring. Annette would be a recording artist at twenty-one.

We had a wonderful time but stayed out much too late talking with Annette and Aiden after the performance, Justin convincing them at 1am that he had to take me home.

The next morning, I woke up feeling lost, still in my jeans and blouse from last night, Justin across the room at the kitchen table eating cereal in his bathrobe, my last memory the smell of Herbal Essence shampoo in his hair and a kiss on the forehead.

I sat up, feeling my head to see if I had bed-hair.

"Oh my God…did I fall asleep on you?" I blushed, Justin smiling as he turned towards me.

"Good morning sunshine. You are such a lightweight!" He covered a smile. "Two glasses of wine and you're a goner. When we got home I had to go, so I headed to the bathroom and then brushed my teeth." He shook his head side to side, a sly grin on his face. "I couldn't have been gone two minutes and you were already out cold. So, I covered you with the bedspread…but your snores kept waking me up."

I was aghast, too ashamed to look him in the eyes. He started laughing.

"I'm kidding…just kidding." If looks could kill Justin would be dead. He was suddenly contrite. "If you want to take a shower there's a clean towel under the sink…and I got you your very own toothbrush – the purple one." He gave me his best smile. "When you're done, I'll make you some breakfast – my famous French toast with bananas and strawberries on top…and of course some freshly brewed coffee."

On March 29th the doctor said I could resume running. In my mind that meant I would be at 100% and ready to go March 30th. It couldn't have been further from the truth. The first week I ran ten minutes on the grass and felt like I was going to die, my breathing far too heavy after such a meager effort, the lack of significant work forcing me to bike for an hour immediately after. *I hate biking!*

I passed the initial week with flying colors and was allowed to run twenty minutes on week two, each day my foot's response to the training good. I was religious about treatment – icing in the morning and afternoon following workouts, performing the stretches and band work trainers set up, doing all of those little things I hoped would add up. Anything to get back training.

It had been challenging when the girls were in Arizona while I was suffering through the Midwest weather, and especially tough sitting out the first April meet when my teammates were racing, but standing on the sidelines for the April 13th Northwestern Relays was a bitter pill to swallow. Yet, those were the cards I was dealt. It was like watching someone enjoying an ice cream cone while I stood outside the front window of Dairy Queen.

On Tuesday, April 16th coach put me on the Dyche Stadium track and I got through my first interval session in racing flats without a hitch. My fears vanished. Mostly. Still, it gave me hope that everything was going to work. But repetition training and racing are two different beasts. One gives you a break and the other presents relentless demands.

That initial day I did 8 x 200 at a 1500m race tempo with a 200m jog between, the opportunity to open my stride a wonderful feeling. It was like a phantom limb had been restored. I was tempted to do more, but he insisted I stop after eight, instructing me to call the next morning for an update. My arch was good the next morning – but all I could think about was I still couldn't race.

Three days later I did 5 x 300m at the same tempo, my jog between still 200m, the effort tougher but doable. The following Tuesday it was 4 x 400m, Coach O'Shea sticking with the 200m jog between each repetition. While I was doing the Friday workout of 3 x 600m, the rest of the team was at Drake Relays, only the football team's field goal kicker watching me perform the session. It was the first time I'd missed competing in the Relays since my sophomore year of high school – five years ago. *Sigh.*

On Thursday morning of the third week coach added a pair of 10-minute steady state runs at the track so he could assess my aerobic fitness. I ran both of them at a 5:30 pace, the efforts challenging but doable. He must have been happy because all he did was smile after the session.

The following Tuesday my intervals were 3 x 800, on Friday 2 x 1000 – at the end of these workouts 4 x 200m at 32-33 seconds to assess my finishing speed. That weekend, the first Saturday in May, all the other distance runners raced at a small meet at North Central. I just did another interval workout, my impatience tested yet again. I was tired of the training. I wanted to race.

On Monday Coach O'Shea caught me before practice.

"Sarah, I'm going to have you race this weekend." He could see the look of uncertainty on my face. "But not at Stanford." He gave me a fake smile. "Instead, Coach Dahlquist will take you with the sprinters to IUPUI for a smaller meet…one with easier competition. I want to see how you look before I throw you to the lions." There was a huge smile on my face.

"To be honest…I much more comfortable with this." I nodded. "To jump right into a big race might be too much. Possibly a…" I didn't say the next word. "So, I like your plan."

"Good. And I want you to race in your training flats." He paused. "Just like you've done each day in practice. That way I'll know if the trainers are good for competition. The spikes make me a little nervous."

On May 10th I was standing at the 1500m waterfall line on the IUPUI track, so nervous I wanted to pee again – even though I just had, instead bending over to re-check the laces I had checked one minute ago. The massive lights created an eerie glow over Carroll Stadium, shadows dancing in two directions as I did a last stride on the backstretch.

None of the girls in my first heat had that look, at least the ones I'd seen so far, but I had been fooled many times over the years with the assumption that I could tell with a glance. I checked my laces one last time and then the clerk placed me in position two, as I waited, adjusting my necklace so that the clasp was in back.

The clerk turned to the starter clad in a red blazer and nodded, the official raising his pistol overhead.

"Runners set." He paused. BOOM!

I was too nervous to lead so I ran off the shoulder of the girl from Wabash College who shot to the front, staring at the Indianapolis skyline as we entered the homestretch a first time, from twenty meters away glancing at the finish line clock "55...56...57." As we rounded the corner, I could feel someone immediately behind, her shoes nicking my heels three or four times. *Back off!* I could hear the clerk shouting as we neared the 1500 meter starting line.

"73...74...75."

A girl in a white Nike uniform zoomed by me, blond hair bobbing up and down as she increased speed, my eyes locked on the tag sticking out of her jersey as I took off in pursuit. *Go get her.* I finally closed the gap to three feet by the steeplechase pit on the south corner of the track, deciding it was smarter to sit on her heels right now. *See how she likes it.* Down the homestretch there was no question we were running faster – but I didn't have a clue how much faster, anxious to hear the next split so I could make up my mind.

At the discus cage the clerk shouted.

"2:25...2:26." *Damn, that was a seventy-one!*

I was beginning to get tired, my breathing no longer relaxed. *C'mon Sarah. Stay on her.* Around the corner we entered the penultimate straight with five hundred meters to go, the girl in white pushing the pace again as the bell rang for the last lap. The thought of another four hundred sounded impossible. *C'mon Sarah. Just a little longer.*

I was breathing too heavily to hear the 1200m split, pain crushing me as we raced down the backstretch in tandem, somehow finding myself halfway into the last corner, the announcer calling out names. *This is it.* I didn't know if I could find the willpower.

"Come on darling...you can do it."

160

I slid out to lane two and pumped my arms hard, running side by side with the girl in white, barely able to see the finish line through the slits of my eyes. She began to struggle, and I pulled by her with fifty meters remaining, a fisted hand above my shoulder as I crossed the white stripe.

Chapter 13
May 18, 1985

The Big Ten meet was at Northwestern.

On Saturday afternoon I stood at the waterfall line on the backstretch, staring down the long straight towards McGaw Hall at the open end of the stadium. Justin was in the stands with mom and Annette, my girlfriend shouting at the top of her lungs from a spot near the finish line, holding a big sign that said, "Go Sarah Go." I laughed to myself; aware she was the only spectator in the crowd holding up a poster – just like she had when I was in junior high. Annette always kept it light-hearted.

I qualified for the final with yesterday's effort in the 1500m, my finishing kick amazingly strong despite the meager training, capturing one of the two automatic spots for today's race. It was hard to fathom I'd only raced once since the Big Ten *Indoor* Championships in Ohio, the February date feeling like a million years ago.

The last two weeks Coach O'Shea worked on my finishing kick, insisting I could be in the top three or four – maybe higher if my turnover was good. Since February 15th there hadn't been a seven day tally that exceeded twenty-five miles, all my focus on footspeed and not endurance. He claimed my races would be "sit and kick," my aerobic fitness from all the biking more than enough to get me through the prelim and final. I worried nonetheless.

At my recent track workouts we'd included sets of 800's with the first lap at seventy-two and the second at sixty-five, along with repetitions of 150m at ninety percent – even some flying 50's with all-out efforts. I'd never put so much into this type of training, but it gave me the needed confidence.

The starter waited until the announcer finished with introductions, tooting on the whistle as we toed the line, my eyes locked on the white Nike Waffle Trainers on my feet as he said "Set."

BOOM!

It was just as we expected, the early pace at a turtle's tempo, fourteen girls within five yards of each other on the first eight hundred meters. *Perfect. Who's it going to be?*

It was Michigan's Cathy Schmidt. She took off with six hundred meters remaining, five runners chasing after her like she was a purse-snatcher at the train station. I was in position as the caboose of the breakaway group, the speed work I'd done making this effort seem easy.

The announcer called out names as we entered the penultimate homestretch.

"That's Schmidt of Michigan, then Wisconsin's Branta…and the Gopher's Eder, freshman Penny O'Brien of Iowa, McNee of Illinois, and Northwestern's Tucker."

We raced down the homestretch in single file, the bell clanging as we leaned into the penultimate corner, three-hundred-fifty meters of real estate before us when we crossed the 1500 start line. Halfway down the backstretch I gunned it and slid by McNee, my sights immediately set on the Hawkeye's O'Brien, passing her in the middle of the last turn, one-hundred-fifty meters remaining. *C'mon Sarah. Dig-dig-dig.*

Schmidt and Branta were in lanes one and two, only steps in front of me, from the infield Coach O'Shea windmilling his arm like Pete Townsend on the guitar, my breaths so loud his shouts went unheard. I swung out to lane three to get around Eder, the Gopher so close I could have tapped her on the shoulder. *C'mon. Get her.*

Three of us gave it all we had but Branta just wouldn't quit, the four of us crossing the line separated by less than ten feet, so close together we would have fit in an elevator. I was completely spent, hands resting on knees and staring at the beige track, recognizing Cathy Branta's voice as she patted me on the back. "Good job Sarah." I stood tall and smiled, reaching out to shake hands with the two other girls, all of us waiting for the other runners to finish.

Coach Dahlquist rushed over, a big smile filling his face.

"Great job Sarah! Awesome. You got third."

"Did you get my time?"

"It's not official but I had 4:17 flat." I sighed contentedly. He shook my hand as Coach O'Shea rushed up, from the stands Annette's unmistakable voice filling the air.

"You're awesome Sarah. Way to go. Yahoo!"

I turned to my three fans and smiled, Annette waving arms overhead like she was trying to scare away a bear. I waved back, Annette's efforts even more vigorous. Coach O'Shea patted me on the back.

"Amazing. Simply amazing." Coach raised both fists and shook them in the air. "When you came off the corner I knew it was going to be close." He smiled. "Great performance, one I'll never forget."

Coach Dahlquist pointed at the scoreboard over my shoulder and I turned.

1.	Branta	Wisc	4:16.47
2.	Schmidt	Mich	4:16.60
3.	Tucker	NU	4:17.02
4.	Eder	Minn	4:17.11

That night the four of us celebrated at Giordano's in Evanston, mom relaying dad's congratulation on my new PR, the Little Hawk boys winning their conference meet by eight points at Kingston Stadium in Cedar Rapids – the site of my earliest running memories. Fortunately, mom didn't tell Justin too many embarrassing stories while we waited for the food, and she only asked him a few personal questions, pleased when she discovered he wanted to teach high school math and physics.

We finished the pizza and the night was winding down.

"I had no idea…" Justin was at a loss for words. "I mean, you are *so* good. Cathy Branta was the national champion in cross country…and she's won like, a zillion Big Ten titles." He stretched his arms wide. "And you were only this far behind her."

"And you thought *I* was good…Sarah is even better." Annette held my hand and smiled. "Look what two girls from Iowa City have accomplished. And it's all because of her mother." Mom smiled.

"On that note let's raise a glass to my girls…and to a boy who gets my Good Housekeeping Seal of Approval." They all laughed but I blushed, mom covering her smile with a hand as we raised glasses.

"A votre sante."

We hugged outside the pizzeria door, mom driving Annette back to her apartment in Lincoln Park, the hotel my mother was staying at only four blocks away from there. I leaned into Justin with an arm around his waist, reaching to hold his hand as we ambled the four blocks to his apartment, wondering if he felt what I felt. I hadn't been this contented in a long time. I had a boyfriend who I really cared for and wouldn't have been any happier if I'd won today's race. Well, maybe…but life was good.

While we waited at a corner for a car to go through the intersection, Justin bent down and looked into my eyes, holding the kiss until I thought I would melt. I hated couples who showed public displays of affection but at this moment I could have cared less – even if my brothers were watching. The pace picked up as we neared his studio apartment, our thoughts in sync.

I'd made up my mind after today's race. This was the night.

I woke with Justin's arm over my waist, sunlight finding another shortcoming of his dusty curtains, the room so peaceful in the soft light that I was reluctant to get out of bed. But I had to pee. I tiptoed to the bathroom, returning to sit on the edge of the bed wearing only his bathrobe, leaning over to kiss him on the cheek.

"Good morning sleepyhead."

It was hot in Austin. Eighty-five degrees when we landed.

Even though this was the Thursday evening session of the NCAA 1500m preliminaries it felt more like mid-day temperatures, heat still radiating off the track at 8pm. The thermometer said it was eighty-three degrees while we waited in the clerking tent, everyone sipping water, a few with ice bags on the back of necks.

My prelim turned out to be a replay of the Big Ten 1500m, the early tempo at a snail's pace, the last half of the competition like the track was on fire. I finished in seventh with a 4:19.63 – a good time but a little worrisome. After we caught our breath everyone waited in the shade of the scoreboard, sipping on cups of water, anxious to see results from the second section. Seventh place wasn't what I had in mind.

Jacobs, Warren, and Krebs were the automatic qualifiers in our prelim but the rest of us would just have to sit on pins and needles until they posted times from section two. Officials tried to coax us from our position, but no one would move from the shade, the non-auto people holding ground, hoping the next section would go out slower than ours.

From where I stood after the gun fired their pace looked about the same as ours.

When they put the final qualifiers on the scoreboard I stared at my name, afraid that if I took eyes off it officials would discover a mix-up, and Tucker would be removed. Eventually the reality soaked in. I qualified! With Cathy Branta's third place in the second heat she got an automatic spot; Jody Eder and I the final Big Ten runners to make the Saturday final. Michigan's Cathy Schmidt was on the wrong side of the line. I knew how it felt.

That evening coach and I ate supper at Terry Black's BBQ, walking along the river afterward as the sun dipped into the horizon, waiting for the big event. Despite Coach O'Shea's claim, I was uncertain if watching the ascent of Mexican bats from the Congress Bridge was going to be as exciting as he thought. If you asked me, it sounded pretty creepy.

On Saturday I ran in circles around the empty throwing expanse just outside the stadium, the only area that was covered completely in shadow at 6pm. I was soaked in sweat after seven or eight minutes of jogging, coach handing me water and putting an icebag on my neck as I stretched.

"I want you near the back after the gun…maybe nineth or tenth. Typically, they get out too fast and a bunch suffer because of the heat. Don't freak out if you hear seventy."

Jody Eder went by and I shouted, "Good luck" and coach resumed.

"After the first lap…on the backstretch, I want you in eighth place and then settle in." He looked at me. "Don't let anyone pass you." I cut in.

"I want to keep my eyes on Jody. She's always a good gauge." He nodded.

"Your kick is good so just hang on when you hear the bell…don't go too early. With one hundred fifty meters left give it everything you got. No sooner."

I was in last place when Regina Jacobs heard her first split for the 1500m from the announcer, "66.3 for the Stanford Cardinal" the field strung out in a long line, proof the pace was fast. Even though coach told me to move up on the backstretch the tempo was too quick to make a stab at moving up, my certainty that I would pay a steep price for such an effort holding me back.

Regina Jacobs continued to push the tempo, but Cathy Branta doggedly hung on, my 2:18.8 at the eight hundred still in last place, nervousness starting to prey on my mind. *C'mon Sarah. Just hang on. Don't let them get away.*

Down the shaded backstretch and around the corner no one was giving in an inch to my entreaties, twelve runners flying down the penultimate straightaway like a taut shoestring, Branta grabbing the lead as the bell rung. Regina Jacobs was struggling.

Coach O'Shea shouted from the shade on the turn.

"Eyes up…get the Wildcats." I presumed he meant Kansas State.

As we came out of the corner at the 1500m starting line I slid by the Wildcat into eleventh place, Jody Eder only five yards in front, running side by side with the Villanova runner in white, the pair coming back to me as I charged across the backstretch. *Should I go or should I wait?* If I waited, I would have to pass them on the turn. It was much earlier than coach instructed me, or even what I wanted, but the momentum was on my side, and I had to move.

Go-Go-Go!

I took off like a bat out of hell, sneaking by the two just before I entered the final corner, the chance to navigate the turn from the rail an advantage I would need if I were to catch more. *C'mon Sarah. You can do it.*

Six meters ahead of me a Texas Longhorn battled the LSU runner down the final homestretch, the home crowd cheering the girl from the Lone Star State, the three of us only eighty meters from the line. *Which was should I go? Inside or outside? Stay on the rail.*

Sixty meters remained and I was three meters behind, inch by inch the Longhorn sliding from the curb in a desperate attempt to hold off the LSU runner. It was exactly what I needed. *C'mon Sarah. Everything you got!* With ten meters left I squirted through the gap between the rail and the runner in burnt orange like a watermelon seed between thumb and index finger, dipping my chest as I crossed the white line.

I sat in the stands on the shady side of the stadium, enjoying the sensation of being barefoot and drinking iced water, so exhausted it was tiring to sit upright.

"You know what coach." I laughed. "I didn't do a single thing you told me to do. You said move up to ninth and I stayed in twelfth. You said to wait on the kick until one-hundred-fifty meters...I went with two-hundred-sixty."

"And I glad you didn't." He smiled. "It's easy to make plans, but in the heat of the moment you did the right things." Coach smiled again. "Your instincts were impeccable. You're an All-American Sarah. Congratulations." He chuckled to himself as I reached out to slap his open hand.

"Oh, and by the way. Villanova's mascot is also the Wildcats…so you were the top kittycat in the race." He started laughing and pointed. "Now go get cooled down."

I had two English papers due before finals, one that I finished in Austin on Jennifer's portable typewriter, only two tests remaining the week after the NCAA meet. Then I would be in Iowa City for a week, unable to be away from Justin any longer than that. Since the Big Ten meet, it seemed we were attached at the hip, all my free time spent with him. Even though we hadn't said the words yet, I was in love with him.

The bike ride to St. Joseph's Cemetery in Iowa City was awkward, the tinfoil over the four roses not enough to keep the thorns from poking my hand. I coasted towards her plot, laying the bike in the grass, crossing my feet, and sitting down akimbo, leaning forward to put the flowers on her grave.

"Guess what Marie?" I smiled at her headstone. "I'm in love." I giggled. "I met a boy at a coffee house in Evanston…his name's Justin. And he has the cutest smile…oh gosh, I spend all my time with him." I looked over both shoulders to make sure no one was around and whispered. "I slept with him." I sighed, recalling one of our conversations so many years ago, laughing at the memory.

"Remember when we thought it was so gross…well, let me tell you…it wasn't." I laughed loudly with a hand over my mouth. "It was wonderful." I giggled. "In fact, it gets better each time." I took a deep breath.

"Annette is doing so well…she's a rock star. Literally. I mean she's been on MTV and even has a record. Right now she's on tour with R.E.M…they have something like twenty concerts around the US." I suddenly teared up at the thought. "It's too bad you aren't there singing with her…we both miss you my darling."

I was quiet, saddened by my thoughts, staring at the roses until I finally sighed.

"Well…dad said he'd be grilling brats at twelve, so I better be heading home." I paused. "I miss you so much. And thanks for all you do for me. Bye."

My summer fell into a routine, during the weekdays practice with the girls at 7:30am, continuing my position as counselor for the Northwestern sports camp from 10am – 3pm, on Wednesdays volunteering at the Evanston food pantry. Although I had lots of time with Justin, I missed Annette, her friendship keeping me grounded, our relationship like the old Girl Scout song.

Make new friends but keep the old.
One is silver and the other gold.
A circle is round, it has no end.
That's how long I will be your friend.

Annette was my gold. The most precious of all. She called one night after a concert somewhere in New York, the red numerals on my alarm clock showing 1:34am as I rushed into the kitchen to pick up the phone. This better not be some teenager playing phone pranks or I was going to curse them out. Suddenly I worried it might be bad news.

The background noise around her was so loud it was difficult to understand what she was saying.

"Sarah. We rocked tonight…it was *so*…awesome. You should have heard us." I could tell she was drunk, words slurred but the euphoria was real. "They loved me." Someone was shouting in the background. "We played three encores. Sarah, I'm so drunk. The crowd here was like nothing I ever experienced." She paused, distracted by something in her room.

"Tell your mom I love her…I couldn't have done this without her." Someone was talking to Annette. "Okay…okay. I gotta go, but I wanted to tell you I love you. I miss you so much. Come see me in Indy. I need you."

"I'll try. Let me…" I started to say more but she cut me off.

"Okay, love you." And then she hung up.

Jackie, Amy, and Mary met at our apartment on a cloudy June morning, memories of Anita making me sigh as we greeted the girls. I missed her so much. Today a 4-mile run was scheduled on the lakefront at a 6:15 pace, skies threatening rain as we jogged down Sheridan Road towards Boulevard Park to stretch.

"My parents took me to see 'Cats' last night." Amy was so excited to see her mom and dad. "It was awesome."

"Where was it at?" A flash of lightning broke over the lake, every head turning simultaneously.

"At the Shubert Theatre." The sound of thunder rolled across the water. I turned to the girls.

"We better get going."

Everyone stood, following Jennifer and me towards the mile marker, starting my Timex wristwatch as we got underway. The first mile was comfortable, my muscles finally feeling loose, the dark clouds hanging low over the lake moving towards us as we ran down the sidewalk along the giant limestone boulders on Sheridan Road. Around the bend at the cemetery and then past Biddy Mulligan's tavern, we maintained the 6:10 pace to the Loyola campus where we would turn around.

The Rambler's campus was quiet as we approached the northern edge, going past the tall dormitory, and over to their horseshoe track, using its curve to redirect us north. As we returned to the sidewalk on Sheridan Road, we could hear the southbound L up above nearing the Loyola stop, a blast of cold air hitting us as we raced through the stoplight at Pratt Ave. *Oh shit. Here it comes.*

Ten seconds later a torrential downpour erupted, rain coming down so hard it bounced off the sidewalks, everyone soaked to the skin before we had gone two blocks. Bangs were plastered to my forehead, rainwater dripping off my nose, the tank top clinging to my body like a white swimsuit. Instinctively we picked up the pace, heads lowered as we continued back towards campus, the exposed area by the cemetery forcing us to turn trunks towards the west as we continued the tempo.

Back at our starting point I slowed to a stop, laughing at the girls when I saw their pathetic state, everyone with a miserable look on their face. The rain was finally spent, the dark clouds continuing westward.

"Well, that sucked." I shuffled towards my teammates and held out an open palm to slap. "But guess what? We ran those last two miles in 11:22…not bad for a bunch of drowned rats." Everyone smiled.

———————

From the middle of June to the ides of July, life was quiet and peaceful, the routine of running, sports camp, and Justin falling into a nice rhythm. Annette called me when she could, often at strange times – sometimes while I was eating breakfast and she was ending her evening, other times after the concert when she was still excited from the high of singing in front of her fans. Every call ended with an "I love you" and my concern that her life seemed too crazy to maintain.

I had a key to Annette's apartment so the five of us slept there Saturday night before the race. That way we didn't have to get up early, the Run for the Zoo 5K/10K beginning at the Grant Statue in Lincoln Park. Sunday morning, we jogged over from her apartment, three of us wearing Kinney XC tank tops from years past, our running shorts a variety of colors, everyone anxious to ascertain our fitness. It was going to be hot one, the sun already uncomfortable at 6:30am.

Five minutes before the start I led the girls through the crowd to get into a good position, weaving around bodies like a snake in the grass, eventually stopping behind the front row of guys. A few glanced back but there was one blond, dressed like he was modeling the latest running outfit, who wrinkled his nose at us, obviously wondering what we were doing so close to him.

When he faced the starter I motioned to the girls – pointing at him with an index finger, mouthing the words that this was the one. Last night I told them to expect one guy to give us that look, and that he was our target. I laughed to myself and then smiled at the girls, rubbing my hands together in glee.

Runners filled Cannon Drive with a lot of male BO, the back of the pack stretching south of the footbridge over Lake Shore Drive. When the airhorn went off we chased after the lead vehicle with a burst of speed, the field finally spreading out as we crossed Fullerton, blue wooden sawhorses protecting the intersection as we continued northward behind a police car. I looked around to make sure the girls were close, pointing at the blond asshole on the other side of the street, a grin filling my face as I nodded.

It was hard to tell who was running the 5K and who was running the 10K, the split at the tennis courts deciding the fact. I prayed to God the blond was running the shorter race. There were maybe fifteen male runners just in front of us as we left Cannon Drive and joined the asphalt path under Lake Shore Drive, the initial mile near the totem pole at Addison.

I watched numbers change on the clock.

"5:30…5:31…5:32." *Perfect.*

Our moment of truth was at hand as we approached the split just past the Waveland tennis courts, a woman with a large cardboard arrow motioning the 5K runners east towards the lake. From ten yards away I watched as the blond guy made the lean for the 5K course. *Yes!*

I checked behind as I made the corner, Jennifer, Amy, Mary, and Jackie right on my tail, only three males in front of us as we took another right turn onto the gravel path along Lake Michigan, the look on blondie's face when he saw us priceless.

I motioned to the girls and we closed the gap, running right in his wake where he could hear but not see us. This was going to be *so* much fun. Around a grove of trees and back towards the totem pole the blond asshole refused to acknowledge us. So we just traded smiles with each other, biding our time. The two mile was just ahead.

"11:03…11:04…11:05."

Racing down the gravel path on the east side of Lake Shore Drive the blond guy made a surge, all of us covering the move, resuming a spot behind his shadow in a matter of seconds. I turned to my teammates and spoke loud enough so he could hear. "Stay together girls." I wanted to make sure he knew the surge didn't work.

At the Belmont Harbor boathouse he tried it again but was no more successful than the first time, the smile on my face the only thing he saw from the quick glance over a shoulder. I hadn't had this much fun at a race in a long time.

Back under Lake Shore Drive we flew down the gravel path past the driving range, my eyes watching the blonde's technique for flaws. I checked the girls again, blank stares on every face, lines beginning to crease the edges of eyes. Past the horse trough, the males in first and second were one now hundred yards ahead, our blond prey in third unable to escape us. As we neared the Fullerton underpass he turned his head slightly, the sign I was waiting for. He was tired.

I raised my fist as we climbed the slope on the far side of Fullerton, five of us charging en masse past the blond, his feeble resistance far too meager to provide a challenge. At the boat house we broke clear of him, the Run for the Zoo finish line banner blowing in the gentle breeze two hundred yards ahead. I waved the girls together and we crossed the line five abreast, 17:04 showing on the overhead clock, the announcer a little shocked to see us finish so high.

"Let's give 'em a big hand. Wow. These ladies are the real thing…third place overall. Amazing."

The official photographer shot pictures of us at the back of the chutes as the blond walked by with his eyes cast down, my smile so big it hurt.

On the third Saturday in July mom called me at 7:30 in the morning.

"I knew you would be awake." She paused. "I got a call this morning from the IU Hospital in Indianapolis saying Annette is suffering from exhaustion…she's doing fine but they are giving her IV's and letting her rest." I collapsed on the kitchen chair, recalling a phone call about Marie years ago.

"I know this brings back bad memories, but Annette is fine." Mom's voice was firm. "She'll be up and at 'em in no time. But she needs rest. Her parents are in Europe so I'm going to drive to Indy as soon as we get off the phone."

"I'll meet you there." I spoke immediately. "I know Amtrak has a route through Indy…Amy takes it all the time."

"Thanks honey. But you don't have…"

"No…I'm going." I was resolute. "I'll call Amy, but I seem to remember her on a train around noon. Give me the hospital number and I'll try to leave a message with Annette. But regardless, I'll let dad know what time the train arrives in Indy…so just call him when you get there."

I wished there were a way we could be in constant contact with each other.

Eight hours later I asked for directions from the Indianapolis ticket agent and walked to IU Hospital from Union Station with only a backpack, rushing to greet mom with a hug in the third floor lounge.

"Oh honey, I was so anxious to hold you." She kissed me on the forehead. "Aiden was here but he just went back to the hotel to shower and change. I checked on Annette ten minutes ago and she's still asleep. The nurse said she'll be awake around suppertime…so let's get something to eat." Mom smiled. "I'm going nutso just sitting around."

At St. Elmo's restaurant mom told me what had happened.

"Apparently Annette collapsed at the end of her set at The Vogue. They rushed her to the hospital in an ambulance, uncertain what happened. Aiden called me because her parents are in Paris and he didn't know who else to call." Mom sighed. "He said she hasn't been sleeping well…taking quaaludes to get rest, and then using amphetamines to get her up for the performances. A bad combination." She stared at her glass of wine and shook her head.

"You know. It's sad." She sighed. "But it just occurred to me that the pursuit of success can have such negative

175

consequences…even if the intention is good. For you, the devil is anorexia. For Annette, it's drugs."

Thirty-six hours later they released Annette and we drove back to Chicago to drop me off, mom taking my best friend on to Iowa City. It was hard to say goodbye, an irrational nervousness spinning around my brain, tears falling steadily as I gave her a last hug, waving to the car as they drove away.

The rest of the summer our training was consistent, repetition ingraining the work ethic and toughness we would need down the road. Cross country camp started on August 25th – Carol Bjornson and Darleen Rutkowski our new teammates. I was both nervous and excited for the coming season, my last chance to achieve goals I'd dreamt about for so long. I sighed.

Where had the time gone?

Annette missed the last two weeks of the summer tour with R.E.M. while recovering in Iowa City, her weekly updates on the daily walks with mom always informative. She bragged about weeding our vegetable garden and mowing the lawn, coming up with a couple of ideas for songs in her free time.

When Aiden finished the tour and was back in Chicago, Annette joined us in the Windy City, everyone concerned about leaving her alone. I was glad to have her so close. After Marie's death I was never the same. She was the yin to my yang and I couldn't live without her.

Chapter 14
August 22, 1985

"I'm so excited about this." Annette clapped hands in front of her face. "I called Earl's of Old Town, and they said I could play Friday night at 8pm, so I want your kitty-kats to come down." I laughed at her reference to my teammates. She put her hands in prayer. "I need your support. Please, please, please."

"Of course." I smiled. "I presume I get a ten percent cut."

"Yeah…of nothing!" Annette hugged me.

I borrowed Justin's car and drove the girls to Old Town, the Escort just big enough to hold the four of us who were twenty-one. All the way from campus I worried about parallel parking but somehow found an easy spot space on Clark Street, everyone jumping out of the car, excited about a night on the town.

The lights in Earl's finally went down, the spotlight encircling Annette like a halo as she stood in front of the microphone. The sight of her made me so happy. A glance around the room showed the place was packed, tables crowded around the small stage, fans leaning against walls eager to hear her sing.

"I want to thank Earl Pionke for letting me play tonight. It means the world to me." She pointed at the back of the room and smiled. "I'm going to play a lot of songs that you've heard before, but I want to introduce a couple for the first time."

She opened with "Angel of Montgomery" as a tribute to John Prine, the same song she had opened with four years ago as a seventeen year old. A lot has occurred since then. Annette was wearing blue jeans and a white Ernie Banks baseball jersey, her hair pulled back in a ponytail, eschewing her traditional look. But she still looked as pretty as ever.

Mom had never mentioned what Annette disclosed while she recuperated in Iowa City, but I knew it had something to do with a guy from the I.R.S. label. I wanted to know…but I didn't. I was certain the story would be tawdry.

It was fun to watch the reaction on the faces of teammates, especially the ones who had never heard Annette in-person, all of them shocked with how good she was. The trio played for forty-five minutes, the heartfelt response of the crowd a soothing balm for my friend. They took a break.

"I'll tell you…Chicago fans are the best. I love you." The room filled with applause; hoots and hollers from all over the room. She waited until it quieted. "This next one is called 'What it All Comes Down To'…a song that hasn't been released yet. I think you're going to like it."

Todd started on the three-piece drum set, Aiden joining in with his six-string guitar as Annette swayed back and forth to the upbeat rhythm.

"I'm tired but ecstatic, I'm happy but sad, adrift but I'm grounded…darling.

I'm drunk but I'm gettin' high, sleepy but wide awake, I'm bored with my life…baby.

But everything is good right here…cause it's gonna change, change, change.

Cause I got one hand on my guitar…the other hand waving good-bye.

"I'm bored but I'm overworked, clueless but wise, sick of the BS…darling.

I hate all the groping, I'm pissed at the veiled threats, holding on a thin thread…baby.

But everything is good right here…cause it's gonna change, change, change.

Cause I got one hand on my guitar, the other hand waving good-bye.

So what it all comes down to…is…he can stick it where the sun don't shine. Yeah.

Cause I got one hand on my guitar, the other one waving bye-bye.

The audience roared after the first chorus, my teammates jumping to their feet, singing the second and third chorus with Annette, "he can stick it where the sun don't shine" everyone waving bye-bye, the applause deafening when she finished.

————•————

Our first meet was at UW-Parkside on September 7th. A course that I considered my second home. A close friend. It had always been good for me, the place where I qualified for the Kinney XC Championship in high school, the same venue I discovered I could compete with the best collegiate runners in the nation.

Coach O'Shea wanted to keep everyone together today, to cross the line in a pack of seven, so I led the team through a 5:31 first mile and a 11:04 two mile, only three opponents in front as we crossed the line, the clock showing 17:22. As I walked through the chute I computed our score, the 30 points earning our third trophy in three tries.

Ten days later we were on a plane to San Francisco, Stanford hosting the third 'Meeting of the Minds' in Palo Alto. Regina Jacobs and Alison Wiley were back, as was Jenny Stricker of Harvard, but this was a year we could win it all – the other teams lacking the depth we possessed. I had a good feeling about Saturday's race, excited to get it underway. There was something special about stepping off a plane in California – I'd always had good luck.

On Friday we warmed up on the Stanford Golf Course in NU t-shirts and shorts, the blue skies and ocean breezes our last chance to hang onto summer. The venue was beautiful, small rises on the golf course puckered like gentle folds on a curtain. It was as pristine as a surgical room. After the warmup, we stretched while Coach O'Shea talked about race strategy, instructing Alena and I to go out with the lead pack, asking Jennifer to work with the rest of the team the first two miles.

Saturday morning, I shook hands with Regina Jacobs, the fifth place finisher at last fall's NCAA meet, the Stanford senior looking as thin as I'd ever seen her. After three years of finishing in the top ten it was hard to think that in her last season she wasn't pulling out all the stops to grab the national title in '85. Regina certainly had what it took.

BOOM!

Though the tempo was quick as we approached the first mile, I was surprised to find only six in the lead pack, Harvard's Stricker running to the side of the Cardinals, Klassen of Rice riding in their wake along with Alena and me. The rumors of Stanford injuries must have been true, neither Ceci Hopp nor Christine Curtin running today, their absence remaining unexplained. *Wow.* There was a new undercurrent on the Stanford team, and it left me feeling uneasy, something weird about the squad hovering in the background.

Alena had been in Atlanta all summer, so I was uncertain of her top-end fitness, but she had a toughness that always impressed me, so I expected a good race. In the early workouts she stayed alongside but I could sense she was working a bit harder, breathing a little heavier. Today would be a true test of her fitness.

We floated through two miles in 10:11, none of the four faces belying signs of fatigue as we curled around a tee box near the start and headed out on the final loop. A quick glance over my shoulder showed Jennifer about one hundred yards back leading the trio of Amy, Jackie, and Mary, the runner from Rice, and a pair from Stanford in the cardinal red strung out behind. *We can win this.*

The course made a turn to the left and Regina made her move with about eight hundred meters remaining, my response instantaneous. Alena was the only one to join me as we looped around the 16th green, a five yard gap between us and Regina up front. Past the 17th tee and a sign which said "363 yards, par 4" she surged again, pushing me to my limit.

At this point in the race, it was every woman for themselves, all focus on doing whatever it took to get to the finish line first – even though I was way past dead. But my desire to win made the issue moot. I would do, as in Annette's song, "anything" to make the race exciting. Alena was falling behind as I gave it my all, Jacobs continuing to pull away despite my best efforts, the 17th green just a few yards away. *C'mon Sarah. Keep her close. One more fairway.*

I was completely spent when I crossed the finish line, Regina beating me by forty yards, standing at the back of the chute with the cute pixie haircut, looking fresh as a daisy, her big smile and a cup of water greeting me as I exited the red and white pennants.

"Good job Sarah. You ran a great race."

"Thanks." Alena joined us, slapping my extended hand. I turned to the winner.

"Good luck down the road." Regina smiled as she greeted her teammates.

It was clear we won as the purple shuffled through chutes, our number six in the top twelve. Everyone was giddy as we huddled by the water table sipping on cups of Gatorade, a huge smile on Coach O'Shea's face as he neared. *This is so cool.* I smiled at the girls.

"Ladies, we're rock stars." I ruffled Amy's hair with my hand, looking around to make sure no one else heard. "You're a bunch of bad asses!" I laughed like a lunatic at the smile on every face. *We just fuckin' won! We beat the Stanford Cardinals!*

It was the most enjoyable cool down of my life.

On September 28th we won the Chicagoland Championships hosted by the University of Chicago on the lakefront course, sweeping the top five spots, the 8th place NCAA ranking filling heads with hubris. But I should have remembered the Greek tale of Icarus – the son who ignored words from his father about flying too close to the sun.

A week later at the Minnesota meet I had the most miserable cool down of my life.

We expected Wisconsin to win the meet in Minneapolis – although hoping we might put a scare in them. Instead, the Badgers, along with Big Ten rivals Indiana, Indiana and Michigan squashed us like a bug, the embarrassment of the thrashing akin to childhood spanking. It rained Friday night before the meet and I slipped at the start Saturday morning, landing face-first on the grass, my rivals disappearing into the crowd of runners, the rear ends of athletes I typically never saw filling my vision.

I would like to say I ran smart and bided my time, but I ran like a rookie, frantically trying to close the gap in the first mile. The hill at the two mile ended up burying me like an arrogant gunslinger in Tombstone Arizona, my wooden marker at the top of the climb engraved with the words, "Here Lies Sarah Tucker – October 5, 1985." Dad's adage echoed in my head.

"They don't give out awards for potential – only results."

I trudged through the chutes with runners who didn't break twenty minutes, berating myself for the stupidity, aware my big dream had gone up in smoke. That I could be in the top five today. Now I worried that my senior year would end like a wet firecracker, the soft 'poof' so lame.

Instead of turning towards the team gear I slipped out of the chutes and ran down the grass pathway on Larpenteur Avenue, ignoring the stoplight at Cleveland, slowing to a stop by a small strip mall, leaning against the wall of a bar that hadn't yet opened. I was still wearing my spikes. Tears rolled down my cheeks in a steady stream.

What in the hell just happened?

Finishing second at Stanford was so cool, but this meet was a much bigger stage, fourteen of the top twenty-five teams in the nation here today. It was a chance to display my talent, to prove to the others I had the right stuff…but I blew it. I was crushed.

A white van pulled into the parking lot, stopping twenty yards away, Coach O'Shea jumping out and shuffling over to me, sliding down the wall to sit alongside. He was quiet at first. Finally he spoke.

"Sarah, I know it sucked. That you had a terrible race. I'm sorry." He sighed and looked at me. "But you have to remember you're a captain. That the girls depend on you. To walk away when they need you…" He shook his head, his lips pursed.

I was suddenly embarrassed, the truth of his words striking me like a slap.

"I'm sorry coach...I...I. You are one hundred percent right."
The tears resumed. "I...I...I wanna go back. Let's go back."

He stood and helped me to my feet, both of us walking
silently to the van, only the clickity-clack of my spikes on the
asphalt making a sound. When the girls returned from their
cool down, my hope was that they'd think my red eyes were
from the race. The fake smile didn't fool them, but they
followed me anyway, everyone settling into the grass under a
maple tree.

"First of all, I want to apologize for my race today." Some
of the girls shook their heads. "I let you down...and I'm sorry."
Jennifer cut in.

"Sarah, no one is mad at you...just sad that you had such a
shitty day."

"Coach told me we got 5th...that everyone ran tired." I
smiled through teary eyes. "I'm still so proud of you." I
nodded. "You all work so hard...are so dedicated to the
program. I want you to know that I feel lucky to have you as
teammates. I've never had a group that invested so much." I
took a deep breath.

"But we need to learn from this. That we're all human. That
maybe we can't give one hundred percent every day." I sighed
again, the words sounding right, but having no impression on
me.

"Some days ninety percent is the smart thing to do." I
smiled, aware that I was really talking to myself. "There isn't
one of you whose judgement I don't trust. If you need a day off
always...always let me know. I believe you. I trust you." I
nodded.

A gaggle of geese flew overhead, everyone's eyes following
the honking.

"So...let's take tomorrow off and restart on Monday...and
I'll bet we kick ass at the Big Ten meet. Okay, circle up for a
team cheer."

I called Justin from the Minneapolis airport before we left,
telling him I needed to see him tonight, that I had an issue to

unload. He was concerned but I said we would talk later. I needed time to battle my own demons alone.

It was wonderful to wake up Sunday morning with Justin's arms around me, my troubles disappearing after lots of talking, fudge ripple ice cream, and a good night's rest. He made me his famous French toast for breakfast, and we planned an afternoon with Annette and Aiden, finally able to joke with them about my performance before we parted that evening.

Justin was my rock over the next two weeks, the salve for an injured ego full of past misgivings and future doubts. He was such a practical person, laying out the irrefutable facts so I could see that these marks led to this conclusion. It all sounded so clear. Before we separated each day he made me repeat the words to him before I got a kiss.

"I am a good runner and will overcome every obstacle placed in front of me."

It sounded hokey but it's amazing what the self-affirmation did for my ego, the words getting easier each repetition.

Like I hoped, we kicked ass at the Illini Meet in Champaign, easily defeating a team that had crushed us in Minnesota. Our good karma was back on track, the move from 8th to 13th in national ranking only making us hungrier. We continued to run Mt. Trashmore each week in preparation for the hilly Michigan course, the strength work what I considered to be the deal breaker between first place and fifth in Ann Arbor.

The 1985 Big Ten meet.

It was cool to read my name in the Big Ten program as an athlete who had a shot at the individual title tomorrow, Cathy Branta always a sure winner whenever she was racing – but thank God she graduated. I'd waited three years for this chance, every year feeling like the bridesmaid and not the bride. Now, I wanted to be the one in the white dress. But I was certain Jody Eder, Katie Ishmael, and Sue Schroeder were just as anxious and certainly good enough to take the title. And there was always that unknown.

Saturday morning, I stood motionless in our starting box, the weight of the final Big Ten cross country meet sitting heavily on my shoulders. I wasn't nervous about racing, more a feeling of dread for what the outcome would be, as though I was walking along a narrow ledge, hoping to get to safety. *Let's get it done – everything you got.*

After the gun I remembered little of the early portions of the race, my blank stare and the sounds of runners breathing the only thing registering in my brain. But I knew these were the leaders.

"At-a-way Sarah." It was Coach O'Shea. "Looking good...keep it going up the hills."

I glanced to the side for the first time, Wisconsin's Ishmael, Wolters, and Herbst, flanked by the Gopher's Jody Eder in our lead pack, four other runners, including Michigan's Sue Schroeder to the side. We circled behind the finish chute and went back out on the last loop, all of us dreading the hill one more time.

Kate Bush's song ran through my head as I stared up the incline.

"I'd be runnin' up that road, be runnin' up that hill...with no problems..."

I charged up the long hill, everyone's breathing much deeper, arms swinging in bigger arcs, the pain of the effort making me wonder how much longer I could hang on. The hill leveled out slightly and then climbed again, halfway up some of the group dropping away like a fallen skier on the slopes. First Christensen and Herring of Wisconsin, then Goudreau of Indiana, the lead pack thinning until there were five.

The Badger's Herbst took a clear lead off the top of the hill, none of us able to respond to her herculean effort. She wasn't the one I expected the push to come from, but she was the one who demonstrated the courage. Ishmael and Wolter had finished 1-2 at the Minnesota Invitational four weeks ago – spots I'd aspired to that day. They were the ones I expected to make the move.

I was exhausted and didn't know how much longer I could last, teetering on the edge of a precipice, uncertain whether I was able, or willing, to go into the dark place to get what I desperately wanted.

"C'mon darling, you can do it."

I don't know Marie…it hurts so bad.

"Don't give in."

Somehow, I closed the gap on Herbst, suffering through the crushing pain as we looped around a green, heading back towards the finish banner. *It hurts so bad.* On the long downhill my legs were battered by each foot strike, as though my thighs were passing through a gauntlet of blows by unseen pillows. Yet I endured, continuing to stay on Stephanie's hip, my relief from the last steps off the hill a misguided notion.

Unfortunately, gravity was no longer helping. And with three hundred yards remaining I had almost nothing in the gas tank. There was no hill to push me and I couldn't coast any longer. My engine sputtered with two hundred yards of real estate ahead, Herbst pulling away despite my attempt to hold on. I began weaving side to side, spots dancing in front of my eyes as rhythm slowed, the banner just ahead seemingly out of reach.

Get to the line Sarah. Get to the line.

I closed my eyes and punched my arms forward, using what little reserve I had in my upper body, the effort producing pathetic results. Then I collapsed, my last memory of a thud and a chalked white line under my chest. After that there was nothing.

A face I didn't recognize was leaning over me, the head of a stethoscope resting on my chest, a smile filling the bearded face. I was laying on a cot in a white tent, just next to me a Michigan trainer wiping blood from the spike wound on a Purdue runner's calf. *Where am I?* The medic understood the look.

"You fainted…but you'll be fine." He grinned. "That was quite a dramatic finish. You went down like a ton of bricks."

"What place did I get?" It was the first thing that popped into my head.

"I think second…but let's sit up and see how you feel."

We turned as Coach O'Shea stuck his head through the tent flaps.

"Oh my God Sarah. I'm so glad to see you're fine." He squatted down next to me. "I don't know how you made it the last straight. I mean…you had nothing left, but somehow you hung on. The courage it took." He grimaced. "Well…I'll let you rest and then I'll tell the girls you're okay.

The award ceremony was special, loud applause from everyone in the crowd as I walked up on the riser to get the second place award, each of the All-conference girls hugged me as I walked to my spot with a medal around my neck. I imagined the ovation was what Annette experienced at concerts.

Jennifer and I held the second place plaque as the team posed for pictures, arms around each other's waist, smiles plastered on every face. It would have been nice to beat the #1 ranked team in the nation, but even Jeff Spicoli didn't smoke enough dope to think it would happen this year.

It was a joyous ride to Evanston, the boys' team finishing 3rd – their highest finish in Wildcat history. We turned up the radio in our van and sang to Madonna, Pat Benatar, and the Eurythmics – Coach O'Shea so ecstatic he put up with our craziness.

"Would I lie to you? Would I lie to you honey…"

Things quieted down after our rest stop at Kalamazoo, heads leaning against windows or staring at the ceiling with eyes closed, from my seat behind coach I glanced at empty pastures as we flew westward on I-94. My dream of winning a Big Ten title was gone but I was happy with the effort today, the runner-up spot a fact I could live with. I had worked my ass off this summer – giving one hundred percent on the Mt. Trashmore hill, diligent about weightlifting and speed work, my training consistent. *But something is still missing.*

There was one thought I couldn't banish from my mind.

Chapter 15
November 20, 1985

We got through the Region IV Meet in Bloomington Indiana with flying colors and qualified for the NCAA Championship in Milwaukee on Monday, November 25th. It was a long season and I was tired, but workouts were much shorter, and Coach O'Shea let us run on our own on recovery days, his main focus that we be rested and ready to race.

I did the easy run before classes on Wednesday, throwing on gloves and a headband to cover my ears before I stepped outdoors into the cold, running up Ridge Road and towards the Baha'i Temple, the intricate design on the dome and pillars always capturing my attention. The leaves were mostly gone from trees, winter temperatures just around the corner.

Continuing northward I stared at the sidewalk, in the dim light looking out for cracks in the cement, thoughts drawn to the Wisconsin squad. They were invincible at the Big Ten meet, scoring a Big Ten record of twenty-two points, almost repeating the same score at the Region 4 meet. This may have been their best team ever – even without Cathy Branta. But there was a different vibe with this group. One that left me with a feeling of disquiet.

When Cathy Branta captained the team, they all seemed so light-hearted, her leadership creating a positive environment, one that valued fun and enjoyment. She always gave hugs like you were her best friend and not a distant aunt, handing out compliments like candy. Even though the squad might have been better this year, it seemed like the Badgers had no rudder, no one steering them in the right direction.

I could see the "thinner is good attitude" had spread over the Badger squad, just as it had on many other national caliber teams, far too many taking the motto to unhealthy extremes. The skeletal hugs at the Big Ten award ceremony creeped me out that day, reminding me of Stacey Hersh and her high school anorexia, the unfortunate downfall despite her good intentions, a tragic story.

Yet four of the Badgers kicked my ass in Bloomington. So maybe there *was* something to the idea. That losing a few pounds might work for me. Get me the elusive title I so desperately craved. The incompatible facts drove me crazy. Was there some alternative world where it would all make sense? A galaxy where I could still succeed – without having to resort to such drastic measures? I was lost.

I phoned mom.

"Honey, I've been reading up on weight loss in young women so you can take this to the bank." She paused, recalling the exact words." Active girls between the ages of 18-22 should be eating *at least.*" I could hear the emphasis in her voice. "Twenty-five hundred calories/day. This is not a suggestion…it's a necessity."

"But it's the skinny ones who are beating me." I was exasperated despite her attempt to help.

"Yeah, and it the anorexic ones who develop anemia, lose bone density, have a higher incidence of injury…and suffer from depression. Do *any* of those sound good to you?" I sighed while she continued. "I've said it before, and I'll say it again. Dad and I won't love you any more if you are good runner or a bad one." I could hear her chuckle. "And I'll bet a dime to a dollar Justin feels the same way. So, trust old mom on this one and you'll get through this fine."

"Okay, I love you. Thanks."

On the Sunday morning before Thanksgiving, we did a run-through on the keyhole loop of the rolling Dretzka Park course in Milwaukee, forecasts predicting 1"- 4" of snow in the early morning hours, the ground expected to be covered in white on Monday. It was wonderful to be such a short distance from campus, only ninety miles away – almost like it was a home competition. Another long flight was not something I looked forward to.

Race morning, we woke to two inches of wet snow covering the grass, at breakfast everyone discussing the miserable conditions, laughing when Coach O'Shea mentioned NCAA rules required that any tights had to be worn under our bun-huggers. I'd like to confront the person that came up with such a stupid rule. It made us look like dorks.

My feet were frozen before we finished the Monday morning warm-up, a vague patch of green grass finally visible from athletes running the course – although there were still lots of slick spots. Our team had a mishmash of stocking hats and mittens on heads and feet – like we'd rummaged through a grade school lost and found box for clothing. I laughed at the picture in my head.

The race time temperature was 33 degrees, northwest winds making me shiver when I stripped off sweats, everyone piling them behind our starting box by the trash bag. I'd never raced in snow before. I wasn't looking forward to the cold.

We leaned forward on the whistle and posed, a gust of wind knocking one of my hip numbers off before I'd taken a step, the blast of a pistol sending one-hundred thirty-four runners on their way. *I hope these one inch spikes work.* The red and white uniforms of Wisconsin and North Carolina State shot to the front, the rest of the field racing down the first fairway in a palette of colors, someone just in front wearing the distinctive scent of Jovan Musk.

As we neared the culvert over the creek Coach O'Shea shouted, "top twenty-five," my quick glances around the pack identifying Jacobs and Wiley from Stanford – Suzie Tuffey, Janet Smith, and Kathy Ormsby of NC State with a slight lead on the large field of runners. Wisconsin's top four were to my left – a UCLA runner in an all-white uniform racing without tights or long-sleeved undershirt. *She's a nut.*

The pace was quick, so I was contented to hold position, my heart suddenly racing as I slipped on the turn near the mile mark. *Be careful Sarah. Stay on your toes.* There was no question we were running a 5:15 pace, an Iowa State runner wearing socks pulled her over forearms sliding up as we approached the initial split.

The timer had to shout to be heard over the wind.

"5:14…5:15…5:16…5:17…"

Although the rest of my body was fine, my feet were rapidly losing heat, the combination of melting snow and wet socks making it feel like I was running on two blocks of ice. Jody Eder of Minnesota was suddenly at my side, a familiar face comforting me in these icy conditions. She slipped as we made a U-turn behind the starting line and I instinctively reached out to grab her elbow, shouts from fans unrecognizable as we passed the halfway point.

Across a creek, spectators lined the pathway as runners scattered left and right on the uphill, searching for sections of the grass where the footing was good, everyone praying they didn't fall. We crested the slope, turned to the right, and headed back down, a runner in the burnt orange of Texas slipping to a knee on the icy downhill, somehow maintaining her balance.

Up ahead I spotted Lori Wolter, the Badger only twenty yards in front. She beat me at the regional meet. *C'mon Sarah. I'll be damned if she beats me again.* My feet were getting so cold it was hard to ignore the throbbing, every footstep torture, only my determination driving me to push through the pain. By the two mile I pulled just behind Wolter, the effort nearly killing me. *I'm dead.* My breathing was rough and ragged, doubts creeping into my mind as we passed two miles.

C'mon Sarah, remember your mantra – I will overcome every obstacle placed in front of me.

I took a deep breath and charged, counting out twenty steps on my right foot. *1…2…3.* She didn't even fight me as I went by her. *8…9…10.* Coach O'Shea was suddenly at my side, pointing with his right hand, with the other cupping the side of his mouth as I continued to count in my head. *16…17…18.*

"Sarah…it's Ishmael…c'mon, it's Katie Ishmael. Go after her." He slid alongside as I ran, the shouting more emphatic as he slid from my peripheral vision, his encouragement now at my back. "Katie's thirty yards ahead. C'mon, you can do it."

Coach knew the words to motivate me. If he had said Tove Lutdal or Carole Roybal, neither of whom I had ever met, I would have been content to stay where I was until a final kick.

But Katie Ishmael…I *had* to get her. The thought of it riled me. To let a rival, a Big Ten runner I bested at the conference meet beat me today was…well it just wasn't going to happen.

I will overcome every obstacle placed in front of me.

I stared at her brunette pixie cut, the headband covering her ears making hair flop up and down with each stride. We made a U-turn near the creek with just over a half mile remaining, Coach O'Shea rushing over to encourage me.

"That-a-way Sarah. Ten yards…you can do it." He clapped his hands together. "C'mon, you can do it."

When we made the final U-turn the northwest winds hit us dead in the face, Katie's tiny frame struggling in the gusts of wind. I was closing the gap, my hill work on Mt. Trashmore paying off. Running into the wind took leg strength, and I definitely had it. Fifteen feet…then eight feet…and finally I was half a step behind her.

Make it big.

We crossed over the culvert and I was free of my rival, five-hundred yards of frozen grass all that remained in the 5K, eyes traveling to the finish banner billowing in the wind. I was so exhausted I didn't know if I would get there, the pain and fatigue gnawing at my courage. *I'm so dead.*

Marie's image appeared before me like a desert mirage, memories of our time together filling my thoughts. A big smile was on her face as she danced like a hillbilly around her bedroom playing 'Clementine' on her ukelele, Annette and I sitting on her bed laughing our asses off. I sighed.

"Oh my darlin'…Oh my darlin'…Oh my darlin' Clementine…"

And then I was under the banner and shuffling through the chute, the blue and gold Marquette pennants fluttering as I took a deep breath and sighed. An official handed me a notecard with "13" and I smiled. Four years ago, I finished 17th at the Big Ten meet. Now I was 13th at the NCAA meet. Thirteen was my new lucky number!

Mom phoned Tuesday morning before we left for classes. We had gotten home late Monday night and I was too tired to call. Dad was on the upstairs line. I could hear him clearing his throat in the background. Something about this was kind of weird. They should be at school.

"How you feeling today?"

"Happy but sore." Jennifer was eating cereal beside me, studying a textbook at the kitchen table. "I'm just glad to be warm. I was freezing my butt off at the meet. I've never run in such miserable conditions."

"Congratulations are in order." It was dad. "You must have run a heck of a race. I'm proud of you." He paused, waiting for mom to speak.

"Honey, I can tell you haven't heard the news." *Oh shit. Oh shit. It must be something bad.* "After the NCAA meet one of the Iowa State planes crashed when they landed at the Des Moines airport." I gasped, Jennifer's eyes suddenly on me. "They were in a seven-passenger plane…and everyone died."

"Oh my God…oh my God." I closed my eyes, memories of Marie's death haunting me. "Who…who…"

"Both coaches, three of the girls on the team, and a trainer." She paused. "It's so tragic…" I cut in.

"But I was just with them…they were at the award presentation. The girls were so happy." Tears rolled down my cheeks. "And now…"

We talked for ten minutes, and then I hung up, giving Jennifer the sad news, both of us heartbroken as we shuffled to classes. I couldn't imagine what their parents were going through. Even though the season was over, Coach O'Shea got us together that afternoon, all of us signing a card for the Iowa State team. It gave me a new perspective on life.

The Saturday after Thanksgiving mom and I drove to Ames for the memorial service at Hilton Coliseum, the second place trophy sitting beside the lectern on the basketball court, both of us amazed to see a thousand people in the stands. Bill Bergan, the Iowa State men's coach spoke first and gave tribute to coaches Ron Renko and Pat Moynihan, teammates sharing stories of Sheryl Maahs, Julie Rose, and Sue Baxter. They all mentioned the rustic cross country camp in the northern Minnesota woods – Julie's toughness and tell-it-like-it-is attitude, Sue's sweetness and her surprising humor, the grit and determination of Sheryl, her signature treat a Tootsie Pop. It was heartbreaking to listen to the tributes.

After the service we walked down to the basketball court looking for Dawn Lentsch, a member of the cross country team who was injured, and one who I'd competed against in high school and college. She rushed up and gave me a hug, reaching for mom after I made an introduction.

"Thanks for coming." She wiped tears from her eyes. "We got the card from your team. It was so nice of you to think about us."

"I didn't really know any of them..." I sighed at the awkward reference. "But we were together at the award ceremony, and they were so happy..." I didn't know what to say. One of the ISU runners approached from the side.

"Sarah, I'm not sure if you know me...I'm Bonnie Sons." I smiled. "I ran beside you for some of the race...around the halfway point."

I reached out and gave her a big hug, introducing mom. She hugged Bonnie.

"Sure, I do. You had socks on your hands." She smiled and nodded.

"Thanks for coming. It means so much."

"Well, we just wanted to offer our condolences."

We walked back to the car with heads down and arms around each other's waist, the bitter northwest winds chilling us to the bone.

———— ◦◦ ————

I finished my last final on the 19th of December, looking up high school teammates in Iowa City when I returned to town, meeting them in the Wheel Room at the Iowa Memorial Union for some quiet conversation. Even though we were good friends, I hadn't really talked with Mary Kate since we graduated, her running career continuing at Grinnell College, our the brief interactions at the Drake Relays too short. Rachel and Emily were Tri-Delts at Iowa, well versed in the social life of sororities and the bar scene in Iowa City, their lifestyle nothing like mine. It was hard to remember when I'd seen them last.

Mary Kate and I met outside the IMU on the sidewalk and hugged, finding a table by the windows facing the river, finals completed and the campus dead. I asked about MK's older sister, surprised to hear Eileen was a nurse in Chicago. We began talking about running and then I spotted Emily and Rachel by the doorway, waving them over, both squealing as they rushed to our table with arms extended for a hug.

"Oh my God, it's so good to see you two." Emily smiled as she draped her ski jacket over the chair. "How long has it been?"

"Too long. I don't get into Iowa City as much…too busy running." I gave them an apologetic shrug.

"I am so over finals…" Rachel sighed. "I had four in three days…it sucked. But there was a party at my boyfriend's frat, so I let loose." She rolled her eyes and smiled. "I don't know how I survived."

"Have either of you bumped into anyone on the team." Mary Kate leaned into the table. "I saw Coach Raffensperger at the mall…he was buying beer at Osco's." She chuckled. "So, I just turned around and left. It was too weird." We all laughed.

"Hey. Is it true Annette is a rock star?" I nodded and smiled at Emily, taking a sip of water. "I heard she had a breakdown or some drug overdose." I scrunched my nose, anger erupting in my brain.

"No, no, no. You heard it all wrong." I hated to hear this BS, girls always wanting to cut down a female who achieved success. "She had been sleeping poorly and took medication that made her faint." I could tell Emily and Rachel didn't believe me.

"I was at the hospital in Indy." I was exasperated with them, trying to control my voice. "The doctor just had her there for

195

observation. She skipped the last two weeks of the tour with R.E.M., but she was back at DePaul in the fall."

I changed the subject, sad to think that my former teammates could be so petty. They probably presented me as a loser after my pathetic indoor season as a freshman.

"So, Mary Kate, how's your love life?" I grinned, knowing she would blush.

We talked for two hours before parting, replaying our track experiences four years ago, each story better in the retelling. After we parted I was aware of two things. That Mary Kate would always be somewhere in my life. And that my friendship with Emily and Rachel was a thing of the past. Their lives were boyfriends and booze. Parties and puking. Both of them were pursuing a MRS degree – neither with any intention of using any of their studies in Marketing or Communication. Only a husband.

The fact was sad to acknowledge.

<hr />

Justin and I celebrated the New Year quietly, all my time spent with him until classes resumed on the sixth.

On Monday Barbara Sandy left a note on the new Radio Shack answering machine I got for Christmas, asking if I could stop by, leaving no mention of what she wanted to talk about. I fretted about the meeting for two days, wondering if I'd done something wrong, dragging my feet when I entered her office before practice. She motioned to the chairs in front of her desk and sat down opposite.

"Sarah, I was so impressed with your performance at the NCAA meet this fall and have been looking for a way to reward you for the result." I took a deep breath and finally relaxed.

"I spoke with a woman I know at the TAC offices in Indy, and she mentioned the trials for the World Cross Country Championships are in Waco, Texas on February 16th." Barbara smiled. "So, we are going to send you down there. How's that sound." My eyebrows went up.

196

"Oh my gosh...yes." This was hard to believe. "That would be so cool." *Oh my God!*

"I already talked with Mike, and he gave you the okay...but you'll probably miss a meet or two."

"That's no problem. To run against the best in the nation...is so cool." I was already dreaming about the race.

Despite the snow lining the outside lanes of the track I attacked the workout that afternoon with a renewed vigor, my thoughts drifting into the clouds, a dream that I might make the US team leaving a smile on my face. *Yeah. Right. And pigs might fly. And it's still twenty-four degrees outside.*

The workout was up and down the ladder: 400m-800m-1200m-1600m-1200m-800m-400m, a ninety second jog between each interval, the goal to run the last half of the workout at a faster tempo than the first. I led the girls through a sixty-six on the initial four hundred meters, and a 2:18 on the two-lapper, Alena still on my tail, tired but good when I finished the 1200m at 3:38.

Now it was the 1600m – four laps. *Hoo boy. This ain't going to be fun.*

I would have sworn that only forty-five or fifty seconds had expired on the stopwatch when coach shouted, "You're up" eight of us jogging towards the line, taking a deep breath before we took off. Around the corner and down the back stretch I had time to ponder what I might do. *Could I break 5:00?*

All I heard was Coach O'Shea shouting "2:28" as I flew by after the second lap, my only focus on the effort it would take to break five minutes. *C'mon Sarah. You can do it.* I circled the track a third time, the arcs of my arms more vigorous, coach holding the stopwatch in front of his face as he shouted.

"3:46...3:47..." *Damnit!*

At that moment I had to make a choice. Go for it or don't. Calculate the effort necessary, the gas still in my tank, and the price such a bold move would drain my battery for the subsequent intervals – a formula with far too many variables. In that split second, in the blink of an eye, there was only one answer.

Spinal Tap!

Although the knob on my speed only went to ten, I invented an eleven, hoping my body would give me the extra response I needed on this important lap. Around the corner and down the backstretch I kept repeating to myself. *You can do it Sarah. Stay relaxed. Make it look easy. You can do it.*

I stared down the long homestretch at Coach O'Shea, reeling him in like a big fish on the line, praying the first word out of his mouth started with a four. His head went from me to the watch and then back to me, from ten yards away a loud shout.

"Four-fifty-eight..." *Yes!*

The thrill of a sub-5 faded quickly, a big gorilla riding on my back. Now I was faced with a challenging 1200m interval, the reality hitting me twenty seconds after the 1600m was completed. *How am I ever going to manage the next three intervals?* Dad had a saying for this.

"You read an eight hundred page novel one page at a time."

I got through the 1200m, 800m, and 400m by taking it one lap at a time, each of the three finishing splits faster than the initial marks I'd established. After the final four hundred I slowed to a stop and stared at the track with hands on knees, my body tingling in response to what I had just accomplished. It was the best workout of my life – indicating I might break sixteen minutes for a 5K...and hopefully soon.

Coach O'Shea smiled at me and nodded. I knew exactly what he was thinking.

Two weeks later I ran a mile in the Shell at Wisconsin, Coach O'Shea suggesting I run 2:24 the first half of the race and then finish out with a 2:16. I liked the challenge so much I did him one better, closing in 2:15, my 4:39.16 a new meet record. I felt immortal but reminded myself – so did Icarus.

That evening I celebrated with Justin, sharing a pizza at his apartment, falling asleep halfway through 'Ghostbusters' on his VCR. I remembered my embarrassment on one of our earliest dates, his appreciation for the demands I put on my body making me love him even more.

Many guys would have been dismissive, ditching me like an empty beer can because I was never around, but his support was unwavering despite my crazy lifestyle. Just like Aiden did for Annette. Or girlfriends did for guys on the men's track team. I wasn't a women's libber, only asking to be treated as an equal, provided the same consideration. That's what Justin did.

There was nothing better than waking up in his arms the next morning, sharing breakfast, meeting him at the library after my morning run. Life was good.

———————

All I knew about the 5K in Waco, Texas was that the Cottonwood Creek Golf Course was flat and fast, average daytime temperatures were in the sixties, and that Lynn Jennings would be there. *Oh my God.* She won the TAC XC championships last November 30th at Meredith College, bested Lisa and Leslie Welsh, Nan Doak, *and* Cathy Branta by more than thirty seconds! There was even a Sports Illustrated article on her in the latest issue because she was so good.

Friday afternoon I took the shuttle bus out to Cottonwood Creek, talking briefly with Nan Doak and Cathy Branta before they headed back, Cathy asking for my room number so we could eat dinner together. I was so relieved, worried I would have to eat alone. I picked up my race number at the clubhouse, two girls along the wall bent over, looking at the course map, both obviously clueless.

The one in a Virginia sweatshirt looked up and smiled, waving me over.

"Sarah. Can you help us?"

"Sure." I hoped all the hiking our family did would help me figure this out. "Let's go outside to get oriented." *How does she know me?*

"I'm Patty, Patty Matava…and this is Ellen Reynolds." Now I was the clueless one, Patty acting like I should know her. "I was in the same pack with you at Nationals…with Jody Eder and Karen Dunn." Oh, now I remember.

"Oh yeah…you run for Virginia!" I immediately blushed; the word clearly emblazoned on her sweatshirt. We all burst into laughter. Ellen looked at both of us and smirked.

"This course run-through is going to be like the blind leading the blind." We laughed again.

Saturday morning, I rode the shuttle bus out to the course, sitting in a seat alone, reminding myself six would qualify for the World Championships. *As if I had a shot.*

"Is it okay if I sit with you?" I looked up, Lynn Jennings pointing at the seat next to me.

"Sure…yeah." *Oh my God. Oh my God.*

"I'm Lynn Jennings." She paused, waiting for me to say my name.

"Oh, Sarah Tucker." Lynn reached out to shake my hand.

" Nice to meet you Sarah. Where you from?"

"Chicago…well, Iowa City. I guess Chicago."

"Wow, two cities. You must be a jetsetter?" She laughed with a hand over her mouth.

"I go to school at Northwestern…but I'm from Iowa City."

"Wasn't John Irving in the Writer's Workshop in Iowa City?"

"Yeah." I nodded. "He wrote 'Setting Free the Bears' and 'Water-Method Man' there." Lynn smiled, letting me continue. "But I like the 'World According to Garp' the best." I paused and added. "I went to his reading in Iowa City…it was cool. He was so funny."

"I really liked 'The Hotel New Hampshire'…something about the story resonated with me."

We talked about John Irving the whole way to the course, Lynn wishing me good luck before we separated. The girls on the team wouldn't believe this encounter.

I was content to warm up alone, the good vibes I got from talking with Lynn keeping me relaxed. When I showed up at the starting line there were only about twenty-five or thirty runners – a little surprising. I expected at least fifty, maybe even a hundred. Wow. I mean, the six qualifiers would get to represent the US in Switzerland. If that wasn't a reason to show up, I didn't know what was.

The gun went off and I charged down the fairway past the large pond, the entire field running together like a swarm of bees, weaving around the course as though this was a training run and we were teammates. I didn't bother to listen to splits – times were irrelevant – only places counting today.

Although Doak, Dornhoffer, Webb, and Branta were running at Lynn's side at the 2K, all of them were responding to her efforts rather than dictating them. She was definitely the alpha wolf in this pack. I was fifteen meters back as we passed the starting line, the second big U-turn just ahead. Something told me Lynn was going to take off there. *Be ready.*

I was right. There wasn't a quick surge – only a steady increase in tempo, my only concern that she would never back off the gas pedal – that each kilometer would be five seconds faster than the last. The first two kilometers had been at 3:15, but on this one Lynn upped it to a 3:10 pace, the field splitting into two pieces like a taffy pull, ten runners hanging on to her punishing tempo, the rest falling behind.

Somehow, I was near the front pack, holding on by fingertips.

Another U-turn and she pushed again, five going with her. This time I couldn't respond, the leaders easing away despite my best efforts, their lead on me thirty meters as we passed the fourth kilometer. A brunette from St. Olaf College was halfway between me and the lead pack, Patty Matava, and a runner in the red and white Athletics West uniform at my side. *C'mon Sarah.* A little over two minutes and I would be done. *Stay tough. You can get in the top ten.*

Even though the finish line was only one hundred-fifty yards away as the crow flies, we still had four hundred meters – a last sweeping U-turn before we crossed under the banner. The St. Olaf runner was only twenty meters ahead. *C'mon Sarah. Go get her.*

I pumped my arms and charged after the girl in black and gold, my efforts to overtake her agonizingly slow, only two hundred meters of green grass before we were in the chutes. I gave it my all but came up short, crossing the chalked line two steps behind, shuffling down the flagging with fingers interlocked above my head, proud of what I accomplished. Eighth place.

I didn't make the US team…but a girl can always dream…can't she?

Chapter 16
February 19, 1986

I picked up the letter and read it again, still not believing the words, certain it was a hoax. The truth of my new status seemed as accidental as a car crash.

Sarah Tucker,

Congratulations! You have been selected to represent the United States at the 1986 World Cross Country Championships in Neuchatel, Switzerland on March 23, 1986. Two of the runners ahead of you elected not to participate, so on the receipt of your phone call, you will join the Women's 5K team and be competing for the USA.

You will need to provide your passport number when you call and then flights will be arranged to get you to Switzerland on March 18th. Please fill out the National Team Information Form and the Uniform Requisition Form and return them as soon as possible. You should have the clothing before February 27th if you decide to join the team.

We hope that you enjoy this truly unique experience as a member of the US National Team!
Jimmy Carnes
President TAC

One week later I got the USA team gear – the same outfit the American squad wore at the 1984 Olympics. I busted open the box and stood in front of our bedroom mirror wearing the clothing, smiling like a kid in a candy store, posing in the red Kappa singlet and bun-huggers. After I got a good eyeful, I put on the USA competition sweats, layering the rain jacket and pants on top, turning this way and that to see how I looked. Awesome!

Then I tried on the USA t-shirt, boy shorts, and socks, putting on the white Medal Presentation outfit over them, holding the red travel bag embossed with the USA logo, trying various poses, pretending I was modeling for a poster. *This is so cool!* It was difficult to sleep that night.

———◦———

It was strange to see Christine McMicken at dinner the first night in Neuchatel. I felt like I was hallucinating. Moreso, because I had jetlag after a long day. She finished ten spots ahead of me at the NCAA meet last fall, now wearing the all-black of New Zealand instead of the orange and black of Oklahoma State. She waved and smiled, mentioning she wanted to trade t-shirts after the meet, wishing me good luck before she rejoined teammates.

After dinner we had a team meeting, our coach distributing information on the week ahead – when to eat, where we would practice, and the functions the team was expected to attend. There were all kinds of extra activities available if we chose – the Olympic Museum in Lausanne, a sightseeing cruise on Lake Neuchatel, a bus ride to Kilchberg for a tour at Lindt Chocolates – the factory promising free samples.

Wow. This was like my experience at the Kinney Cross Country Championships.

For some reason Lynn Jennings took me under her wing that week – even though we had little in common. She was three years older and from New Jersey, well-versed in New York City street smarts, while I was a naïve girl from Iowa. But we bonded on the shuttle bus in Waco discussing John Irving and it continued here in Switzerland. She pulled me aside after the team session.

"Sarah, it's important you stay focused on the meet. I know how easy it is to get caught up in sightseeing and the plentiful food...but remember, you're here to run, and run fast."

I nodded, listening intently.

"Pick one activity, and only one. You can't do them all. I saw you brought your books, so I would encourage you to set aside two to three hours every day to use them. Maintain a routine. Keep your lifestyle just like it is at Northwestern – eating, sleeping, and running.

She paused.

"And one last thing. I realize this is the World Championships, and you may feel a little overwhelmed, so come to me if you have issues with anything. I'll help. But don't be intimidated by the setting. You'll be surprised how well you do. Expect to be in the top fifty." Lynn smiled and nodded.

Finals week at Northwestern coincided with the week in Switzerland so I had to take two finals before I left, both English professors allowing me to submit papers when I got back to campus. The only issue was that I would have to find a place to type them.

On Thursday, I went to the Lindt chocolate factory with Leslie Seymour and Betty Springs, the chance to sample the finest chocolates in the world an irresistible choice. But it was only because I finished typing the two papers, certain the professors would give me A's. I also made sure to send postcards to my parents and Coach O'Shea, Justin getting a scenic card each day, his included with a heart by my name.

The day before the meet I saw Zola Budd running barefoot on the sloppy course despite the cold, mud, and water, the South African now representing England, apparently immune to the wretched conditions. None of the other girls took notice but I was awestruck, trying to reconcile that this was the runner who accidentally tripped Mary Decker in Los Angeles. I mean – she was an Olympian at eighteen!

The course was a hilly 4.65 kilometers – two snake-like circuits nestled in foothills of the Swiss Alps, the orange fencing lining the loops with signs of sponsors – Mita copiers, Adidas, Rivella, SBS Bank, and Longines. It was such a unique event – nothing like I'd seen anywhere in America, the crowds twice the size of the NCAA meet. And it was *so* weird to see clusters of girls wearing the national uniforms of countries like West Germany, Australia, and Brazil – just a few of the thirty-six nations represented at this international meet.

Race day each country positioned runners in a double line at the starting box, teams assigned to long narrow chutes, corralled in between red and white surveyors' tape like cattle waiting to get branded. I was one of the cabooses on our 6-member US team, shivering as we waited for the start, rubbing upper arms with gloved hands, the brisk winds rapidly stealing heat from my body. I would have worn an undershirt but none of my teammates did, so I imitated them, afraid to stand out.

I looked down at my red USA competition uniform and smiled, the same singlet and bun-huggers Mary Decker wore at the 1984 Olympics in Los Angeles. *This is so cool.* I was proud to be on the team – even if it was because they passed up two qualifiers. Half of me was nervous, the other half calm, the reminder of Justin's last words before I left O'Hare making me smile.

"Why should you be nervous – no one expects *you* to win." He laughed.

The starter was to the side on a platform, shouting "Runners set" in English before he fired the pistol.

We took off like a pair of six-legged centipedes, everyone agreeing to Lynn Jennings' suggestion that we put the right foot forward, so we didn't step on a teammate's foot. Although I tried not to think this was the *World* Championships, in many ways it was much like the NCAA meet last fall, the quality about the same. All I had to worry about was getting in good position after the gun – because if I did, as Lynn said, things would fall into place.

One thousand meters into the race there couldn't have been more than forty or fifty runners in our swarm up front, meaning over two-hundred fifty runners were trailing behind, the simple fact enough to keep me calm. On turns I could see Lynn's red uniform about forty meters in front, running with the leaders from France and Portugal, Nan Doak just off her shoulder, Zola Budd already leading by fifty meters.

I ran alongside Sabrina Dornhoffer and Betty Springs, grateful to have someone to hang with, my eyes traveling up and down to stay aware of the footing and the direction of the next turn. We wove around the course, splashing through puddles that were ankle deep in some spots, the grass so saturated it felt like we were running on a wet wrestling mat.

As we approached the halfway point near the starting line the Alps were visible through a break in the clouds, the jagged peaks covered with snow. It was so beautiful. I glanced down and took a deep breath, legs and race number speckled with mud, my white spikes the color of the Lake Michigan water after big waves.

Even though I'd expected an early pace that was fast, in these conditions running a 3:15 kilometer was tougher than a sub-three on the track. Way tougher. But I promised myself that Lynn's faith in me would not be a wasted effort.

There was nothing about this race which was easy. Lots of turns, short-steep hills, the turf saturated with water – everything frustrating my efforts to close the ten meter gap on Sabrina and Betty. I searched for good footing in an effort to catch them, but it was all for naught, the strong wind on the final straight stealing my speed, crossing the finish line ten spots behind the pair.

I finished in 49th place. Lynn Jennings finished 2nd.

The trip to Chicago wasn't anywhere as exciting as the one to Switzerland. We left Neuchatel at 9am, the train ride to Geneva taking ninety minutes, many of us buying an Engadiner Nuss torte at the airport and some strong Swiss coffee, the delicious shortcrust pastry filled with caramelized sugar, heavy whipped cream, and chopped walnuts heavenly. *Yummy.*

Lynn and Betty flew to New York; Sabrina, Nan, and Leslie, joining me on the plane to Chicago – all of them with a layover or a two hour drive before getting home. I was the lucky one. Our flight landed at 6pm, the eleven hour trip reminding me of camping on a rainy day – much too confined. I felt like a zombie as I walked through the terminal, stopping to pee and brush my teeth before I headed to get my bags.

Before I left for Switzerland Justin had promised to pick me up at the airport, so I was thrilled to see him sitting on the rim of the baggage carousel reading a book, looking up and smiling as I rushed over for a kiss and a hug. At least my breath was fresh – because I knew my pits were another story. We talked for five minutes, but then I was exhausted, so tired I could have fallen asleep in his arms.

I took a shower at Justin's and was in his bed at 8:15pm, waking up Tuesday morning well after the sun had come up. There was coffee on the table, and he began putting together his French toast, listening to my stories as he whisked the eggs, cream, and cinnamon in a cake pan, describing the race conditions in Neuchatel as he carefully dipped slices in the mixture, and transferred them into the frypan.

After finishing the French toast, we sat at the table and talked about what we were going to do this week, savoring our second cup of coffee.

"You have to be bummed that the Northwestern team is in Tucson and you're in Evanston." He looked over at me and pursed his lips.

"Not in a million years. I'd much rather be with you over spring break." I smiled. "Plus, you'd have to put a gun to my head to get me on another plane." We laughed.

On Wednesday we rode the L into the city, walking up the stairs at the Jackson stop and towards the Art Institute on Michigan Avenue, amazed to discover Grant Wood 's 'American Gothic' was much smaller than I thought, and that Seurat's 'A Sunday Afternoon on the Island of LaGrande Jatte' was *way* bigger. But we liked Hopper's 'Nighthawks' the best, promising ourselves to get a poster as we walked up Michigan Avenue afterward, stopping on the bridge over the Chicago River to enjoy the view, the scent of Garrett's Popcorn drawing us towards the Magnificent Mile.

The rest of the week I stayed at Justin's, doing my workout first thing in the morning, the afternoons filled with 'Desperately Seeking Susan' at the Century Theatre on Clark Street, a trek to the Lincoln Park Zoo and Botanical Garden, and Friday evening with Annette and Aiden.

My first outdoor meet was the Chicagoland Championships at the University of Chicago – an open 3K on the Hyde Park track – the same track that Jessie Owens had run on fifty years ago. The last time I'd run this distance was at the Big Ten Indoor meet March 1st, finishing second to Stephanie Herbst, my 9:09.01 one step short of a victory. Today I took it easy, pulling Amy and Jackie to sub 9:45 times, my 9:29.92 enough for the win. Their performances were the most satisfying thing for me today. These girls were part of a legacy I hoped to leave behind.

More and more, I caught myself reliving my moments at Northwestern – the first meeting with the team, my 5th place Big Ten finish in cross country junior year, being selected for the US team, all of them turning points in my life. The friends I had gained, the pride I developed, the importance of speaking up for principles, and appreciating that the more I gave, the more I got.

It was hard to comprehend this was my last quarter of classes at Northwestern, that next fall I would be student teaching at Evanston HS and finishing my degree in Education. Weird. I looked forward to teaching English in high school, contemplating life as a coach, sad to lose one aspect of my life I'd invested so much into.

The next weekend Annette and Justin cheered me on from the stands at the Northwestern Relays, watching me anchor the 4 x 800 and distance medley relays to victories, my final races on the oval in Dyche Stadium ones I would cherish. That evening we joined Aiden and Annette for some Ranalli's pizza, walking over to their place after for a game of Monopoly, savoring the quiet evening.

Sunday, I studied in Justin's apartment while he watched the Bull's playoff game on TV, my boyfriend closely following Michael Jordan after he returned from the broken foot last fall, the former Tar Heel capturing national attention for our Chicago team. Justin turned off the television after the game was over and sat with me at the kitchen table.

"I swear, Jordan is the best." I glanced up from my book. "How many did he score?"

"Forty-nine." My eyes got big. Justin shook his head and smiled. "He's like all-World. Unstoppable."

"Did the Bulls win?" Justin grimaced.

"Nope. The Celtics have too much." He sighed. "But just wait and see. The Bulls are going to be the best in the NBA…and soon."

Drake announcer Jim Duncan called out the big names in the 5000 meters.

"In position four in the purple and white, she was a seven-time state champion for East High, just a month ago she represented the US at the World Cross Country Championships in Switzerland – it's Northwestern's Sarah Tucker."

Wisconsin's Stephanie Herbst took the lead from the gun, despite the eighty-four degree temperature she ran seventy-fives with the steady rhythm of a metronome, nineteen athletes following behind like ducklings trailing their mother. By the fifth lap the field separated into two groups, the heat, and her tempo too much for most in the 5K field. Somehow, I hung on.

"Folks, that's Herbst leading the pack through a 5:01 first mile." Duncan paused as he went through the field. "Then it's Betty Springs of Athletics West, Seymour, Knisley, K-State's Struckhoff, Neubauer of Club Sota, Tucker of Northwestern, and Becky Kirsininkas, the former Purdue runner now competing for Reebok.

By the halfway point I knew I couldn't hold the torrid pace much longer, passing the eight-lap mark at 10:13 in fifth place. Sweat was dripping off my brows in a steady stream, my face and chest as red as a beet, the track surface so hot it felt like I was running barefooted across an asphalt parking lot. *Why in the heck did I ever decide to run the 5K?*

With three and a half laps remaining Herbst was a hundred meters in front of the field, Struckhoff and Knisley just in front of me, with Springs at my side, the others another one hundred meters behind. The heat was brutal. Struckhoff and Knisley pushed with two laps remaining, but I had no response, Betty Springs, my teammate on the US squad, was still at my side. Discomfort hit me from every direction – from the blazing sun, a throat screaming for cool water, skin desperate for faster evaporation, feet tortured by the heat radiating off track surface, and lungs screaming for relief from the effort.

I have no idea how I got to the line, somehow sneaking by Springs on the last straight, crossing the line two steps in front of her, sweat falling steadily at my feet. It felt like I was standing in front of an open oven door.

Everyone hustled down into the infield grass, and pulled off spikes, pouring cups of water on bare feet, the sensation the most wonderful thing in the world. *Sarah, you must be some kind of stupid to have run this race.* We looked up at the scoreboard, a 16:07.22 behind my name – a career best.

I congratulated Stephanie Herbst on her victory, the 15:34.84 tough to fathom. A year ago, I could beat her but now…well, today she beat me by thirty-three seconds. *Would I ever beat her again*? I cooled down with Leslie Seymour and Tori Neubauer on tree-lined University Avenue, the shade from giant oaks and cottonwoods keeping us out of the sun.

"That was the most miserable race I've ever run." I looked over at them. "I debated whether to run the 1500 or 5K…it was stupidest decision of my life. I must be an idiot."

"17:51…I can't believe it. You know…if I was a racehorse." Tori sighed. "The owner would have shot me." She smiled and shook her head. "At least Leslie had the good sense to drop out." We all laughed.

"Girls, let's put this one behind us and focus on the future…and hopefully it involves some ice cream!"

This outdoor season was a time of lasts – my last Northwestern Relays, last Drake Relays, last Big Ten meet. The initial years at Northwestern I lamented the slow-pace of my life as a runner, impatient with the never-ending intervals between opportunities – though now my only thoughts were to slow things down. To avoid the rush. Savor all the moments. *Sigh.*

The 1986 Big Ten meet was at the University of Wisconsin on May 23-24.

I got two 2nd places – Indiana's Parrott outkicking me in the mile, and the Badger's Stephanie Herbst repeating the indignity in the 3K – quite a shock after she set the Big Ten record in the twenty-five lap 10K the night before in an astounding 32:54.37. If my math was correct, that was a sub-5:20 pace. *Wow.*

Saturday after the 3K I cooled down with Minnesota's Jody Eder on Saturday afternoon, our Big Ten careers having traveled on parallel paths, commiserating with her as we ran around the Madison campus – our last conference championship. I was still frustrated.

"You know what...just once...just once I'd like to win it all." I was so exasperated.

"Sarah, you know what really sucks?" Jody smirked as we ran along the path on Lake Mendota. "I'm a five time All-American, ran at the '84 Olympic Trials...and yet I've never won a Big Ten title. Believe me. I know how it feels."

She looked at me as we waited for a light to change on Walnut St.

"Sarah, there isn't one Big Ten runner who doesn't respect you. Not Tina Parrett, or Stephanie Herbst. Or even me." She smiled. "Yes, it stinks, but those are the cards we've been dealt."

I smiled at Jody as we approached the gate to the track.

"Damnit. As always, you are right." I reached out and gave her a hug. "You know what my dad would say?" She shook her head. "Suck it up buttercup."

Jody burst out laughing and my bitterness was gone. The truth hurt but she was right. After all, I was a three-time All-American and got to represent the US in Switzerland. And got an athletic scholarship to boot. How many girls would kill to say those words?

I was on the track that I would forever look back on fondly – the IUPUI stadium in Indianapolis. The one where I regained my mojo after the plantar fasciitis injury at the Big Ten indoor meet. We arrived on Tuesday evening, leaving Evanston after the day's classes were finished, Alena and me bringing along books so we could study for finals next week.

We stayed at the same hotel mom and I did when Annette was in the hospital for exhaustion, the memory of that time bittersweet. That first evening, I ran along the White River by myself, confident we had made the right choice. Coach O'Shea and I talked about doing a 1500/3000 double, but I told him I would rather be master of one than so-so in two, the debate only on which one was the best option. Ultimately, I chose the 3K, reasoning I could handle any type of race strategy at this distance. My endurance was good and I had a kick.

Wednesday morning, I did a fifteen minute shake-out with Alena, running down New York Ave. past the Carroll track facility, listening to the announcer introducing women competing in the heptathlon for their two-day competition. When we got to the bridge, I pointed down the embankment to the White River path, talking about the Chernobyl accident in Russia as we continued towards the Hoosier Dome, and then back to the hotel.

The rest of the day was studies and then to the track at 6:30 for my 3K prelim at 8pm, followed by Alena's 10K final at 9:40pm. Even though it wasn't fast, the 9:24.49 in the second heat got me into Friday evening race. The first heat went out slow and finished fast, only four from the other section getting into the twelve-runner final.

Though the sun still had a presence at 9pm, the stadium lights were beginning to supplant the setting sun as we waited for Alena's race, the scene redolent of nighttime baseball games we used to attend when I was little. Spectators were leaving seats as Coach O'Shea and I sat down on the backstretch, everyone who remained true fans of distance running, excited to watch the final event of the evening.

I looked at the stadium video screen as the camera panned the field three minutes before the race, recognizing many of the athletes – although there were a few I didn't know. In position one was Kathy Ormsby of NC State, next to her Wisconsin's Holly Herring, Ellen Reynolds of Duke, Connie Robinson next to my teammate, Patty Matava of Virginia, Christine McMicken – who ran at the World XC meet in March, my Big Ten nemesis Stephanie Herbst, and the Hawkeye's Jenny Spangler, back for her final outdoor season.

The sight of so many rail-thin bodies on the big screen was unnerving.

Coach O'Shea said the big battle would be between Ormsby, Herbst, McMicken, and Reynolds – the only four he believed could break 33:00 tonight. The foursome hammered the pace from the gun, running seventy-nines like a stopwatch was implanted next to each heart, the field separating as they passed 3200 meters at 10:36. *Oh my God!*

At the halfway point Alena was already struggling, the fast pace too much for her today. Up front, there were only seven, the announcer identifying the lead pack as they came down the homestretch with twelve laps remaining.

"It's the Badger's Herbst, Reynolds of Duke, McMicken of Oklahoma State, Ormsby of NC State, Jamrozy of Clemson, Welsh of Boston College…"

I shouted encouragement at Alena, but it was clear my effort was a lost cause. It was as if she was sitting in a sailboat on a windless night, the tilt of her head, and empty look in her eyes telling the sad story. My focus went back to the leaders – Herbst pushing the tempo as Reynolds and McMicken struggled to hold on with only six laps remaining.

"Coach, what happened to Ormsby?" He hunched his shoulders.

"She must have dropped out."

With four laps to go Herbst pushed again, steadily pulling away from Reynolds and McMicken, five minutes later crossing the finish line with a new NCAA record of 32:32.75. *Whoa.* It was hard to fathom. Back-to-back 5K's of 16:16, my PR of 16:08 indicating I could have only run with her for thirteen or fourteen laps. *Wow.*

It was impossible to rid my mind of Kathy Ormsby as I warmed up for the 3K final on Friday evening, yesterday morning's news in the *Indianapolis Star* hard to fathom. The

214

reason I didn't see her finish was that she had left the race after four miles, exiting the stadium, running down New York Avenue, and jumping off the bridge over the White River – all while the 10K was still in progress.

Coach heard through the grapevine that she was paralyzed from the waist down, somehow surviving the forty foot drop to the riverbank. It was the same spot Alena and I had run on Wednesday morning. The thought freaked me out.

Why did she do it?

The smell of hotdogs drifted from the concession stand on the backstretch, twelve of us shuffling back and forth as we waited for the 3K to start, waiting impatiently for things to get going. My last collegiate race. I thought of all the trite clichés I'd heard over the years – "Make it a good race" or "Give it one hundred percent" - all so stupid. So trite.

I always gave one hundred percent. Always wanted a good outcome. The trouble was that you never knew if one hundred percent would be enough. Whether I had the right stuff at the right moment. The truth of the matter was that the dice had already been rolled. I could only give what I had today.

I gazed across the field of runners, aware of certain realities – half of the athletes were dealing with some issue before the race even began. More than likely three of the twelve were running with an injury – maybe a stress fracture, severe case of plantar fasciitis, or a slight hamstring pull. Two may have experienced a recent emotional difficulty – a breakup with a boyfriend, loss of someone close or mental fatigue from overwhelming expectations. Even a last workout that gutted their confidence.

And then there were the complications during the race – probably eight runners who could handle laps of 72, but only two who could withstand splits of 71, the outcome for these eight dependent upon a leader who didn't push the pace from the gun. Alena's first mile in the 10K Wednesday night had settled her fate, the 5:36 fourteen seconds faster than coach wanted her to run – though she was in last place at the time.

From the stands the race always looks so coordinated, as though choreographed by Alpha Beat Jam – yet it couldn't be further from the truth. There were millions of race scenarios. I could be tripped by some klutzy runner, sprain an ankle stepping on the curb, get my shoe removed by some asshole just behind – all of which I'd experienced at some point in the past ten years. It wasn't worth worrying about.

Thursday morning when I went over the 3K prelim results, noticing so many unfamiliar names – and that there were four freshmen, two sophomores, and five juniors. Half the field were novices. I was the only senior. *Wow.*

Yet, I shouldn't have been surprised. My only Drake Relays win was as a sophomore in high school, at the time when I was too naïve to appreciate that I had no business finishing at the front. In reality, the only thing I controlled at each race was staying in good position throughout, keeping my wits about me – playing the cards I was dealt.

C'mon Sarah. Make it happen.

The starter tooted his whistle, saying "Runners set" watching as everyone inched a foot towards the white line, his assistant scanning toes.

BOOM!

I was tempted to take the lead but knew the leader never won – unless of course, they were Stephanie Herbst. So instead, I followed Polly Plummer and Liz Natale around the steeplechase corner from the outside waterfall, running out wide on the lane two line as we passed the finish line for the first time. Seven laps to go.

Down the backstretch the announcer called out the runners.

"That's Plummer from UCLA, Natale in the burnt orange of Texas, Breiding from Kentucky…Ohio State's Monard, Olafsdottir of Alabama, Tucker from Northwestern, Ljungberg of UTEP…"

Coach O'Shea shouted from alongside the steeple pit.

"Seventy point seven. Great Sarah. Perfect."

I was transfixed by the ponytail on the blond Alabama runner as it swished side to side, the hypnotic effect keeping me focused as we circled the track. I zoned out. The pace was quick enough that everyone was content to maintain their position, coach's encouragement on the second lap omitting my split.

"Good Sarah, keep it up." Then there was a gap I remembered nothing.

Five laps completed and a thousand meters remained, cracks in running technique beginning to show as I slipped by Plummer and into fifth place when we entered the long homestretch. Coach O'Shea shouted "seventy-two point one" at the steeple pit. It left me wondering. *Were the other splits seventy-ones?* By the depth of my breathing, it sure felt like it.

From above the announcer called out the field.

"The lead pack is now six…it's Natale of Texas, Breiding of Kentucky, Olafsdottir of Alabama, Monard of Ohio State, Tucker of Northwestern, and Ljungberg of UTEP."

Past the finish line with two laps remaining, we circled the corner in single file, from front to back less than ten meters of separation. *C'mon Sarah. Eyes on Monard.* I squinted in reaction to the pain, my breaths coming in rapid fire, driving arms rapidly as we crossed the waterfall line with 600m remaining. *Stay relaxed.*

"At-a-way Sarah. You're good." I heard coach's words as if they were from a dream.

Up above the announcer's voice went up a notch but had no idea what he was saying as we raced down the penultimate homestretch, the bell ringing in my ear as I leaned into the corner, another lap seeming to be an impossibility. *I don't know if I can do it.* Into the backstretch I moved off the rail, pulling up on Monard's shoulder, the effort nearly killing me.

"*C'mon darling. You're doing great.*"

I was by and back on the railing just before the final corner, Coach O'Shea windmilling his arm as I passed the steeple pit in fourth place. *I'm trying Marie. I'm trying.*

"*Keep going darling.*"

Olafsdottir and Natale were side by side just three meters in front of me, both chasing after Breiding as I entered the final homestretch. *Could I catch all of them? One at a time.* Driving my arms as hard as I could, I swung out to lane three, eyes locked on the blond in the burnt orange uniform, praying I could get past her.

"You're doing great darling. Keep going."

Fifty meters to the line and Natale and Olafsdottir were only one step ahead, Breiding still ten meters in ahead as we sprinted at the finish line, the runner in Kentucky blue and white unbeatable today, her arms wide as she crossed the white stripe in first place.

I leaned and looked to my left as we flew past the finish line, Natale's head two feet in front of mine, Olafsdottir falling to the ground in an attempt to hold us off. Slowing to a stop, I rested hands on knees, from my peripheral vision aware the Alabama runner was still prone on the track, officials hustling over to get her off the ground. I turned to Natale.

"Good race Liz." She gave me a quick hug. "I can't believe a freshman beat us." She shook her head and smiled.

I patted her on the back and then we separated to congratulate the other runners.

Chapter 17

June 17, 1986

"Well Marie. I did pretty good in Indianapolis." I sighed as I stared at her headstone, a cardinal chortling in the background. "I got third. For a second, I thought I might win but…" Another thought hit me.

"Guess what? Justin and I moved in together." I giggled. "We got a one-bedroom apartment four blocks from campus. He graduated last weekend and is looking for a teaching job in the north suburbs…at least someplace close so he can commute from Evanston. I'm so excited." My face lit up.

"And I'm going to student teach next fall…so I will get my degree in December." I smiled. "Can you imagine me as a teacher?" I chuckled. "Will I be a dork like Mr. Englert? Or cool like Ms. Liebowitz?" I grinned. "I know…you probably think I'll be a dork." I chuckled.

"I'm still trying to decide whether to continue running." I sighed. "What do you think? There's something about it that I'm not ready to give up." I paused in thought. "But I won't decide until after I get my degree."

"Well…it's great to see you." I took a deep breath. "I'll stop by later this summer. See ya."

I glanced back at Marie's gravesite before I hopped on the bike, a stream of memories flooding my mind as I coasted down the long hill on Dodge Street – the summer before 7th grade competing in the 100m, 200m, and long jump at the Iowa AAU Championships in Cedar Rapids; laughing at Marie and Annette wearing their one-piece gym suits backwards in Mrs. Pundt's PE class; the chance meeting with Thorsten at the coffee shop my sophomore year, and our first date at an Ingmar Bergman movie.

Those experiences seemed a lifetime ago.

As I rode past Nagel's lumber yard I stared at the roadway over the front tire, the whine of a circular saw in the background blocking out other sounds as I pondered the past ten years.

Joining the girls cross country team as a seventh grader was the most profound decision I'd made. Was the basis for the direction my life traveled. It's hard to imagine what I would have been like without running. How I would have turned out.

My friendship with Annette and Marie in junior high was serendipitous, their precocious maturity the roadmap for me to pursue running with the same drive and dedication – each of us going above and beyond, happily accepting the demands of a path few chose.

Running was the activity which helped me avoid the pitfalls of teenage years, those who were consumed by drinking, drugs, and a social life that revolved around how you dressed and who you knew. Without running I probably would have been just like my high school teammates Rachel and Emily – sorority girls focused on getting drunk and finding a husband, rather than utilizing their degree to pursue a dream.

Yet running also took me to many of the lowest points in my life – the painful loss in cross country my junior year of high school, the frustration of failing to qualify for the Olympic Trials, my exasperation at being the bridesmaid and not the bride throughout my Big Ten career. But these were the things which taught me how to handle life when I wasn't given a bowl of cherries - when all I got was the pits. It taught me resilience, a belief in my personal value, and the understanding you wouldn't achieve success at the highest level until you failed – and many times.

In fact, these experiences may have been the most important lessons in my life – that learning to get up every time you get knocked down is the greatest gift. Creates a toughness that victories don't. Winning always seems nice, and getting better without stumbling sounds good, but the truth of the matter is that everyone fails – even Mia Hamm, Sue Bird, Serena Williams, and Simone Biles.

Dad always said, "Failure is like a callous – it's not much fun to develop, but there will be hell to pay if you don't have one. It's necessary for success."

I had many to thank over the past years. All the coaches – Coach Raffensperger and Coach Forwald at East High, both of them welcoming me with open arms and treating me with the same respect they gave the boys, encouraging me to pursue goals too many might have thought foolish, providing the constant support needed in a sports world where females were treated as second-class citizens.

And at Northwestern there was Coach O'Shea who gave me direction, encouraged my big dreams, was there for me whether it was his Sunday morning day off, or for a solo practice when I couldn't train with the other girls. He was a constant – the one won whom I could always rely.

Barbara Sandy, the Associate AD at Northwestern, took our concerns seriously, making sure things were equal, the playing field level. She was a woman who didn't treat her position as though she was a figurehead – instead standing up and fighting for us at every opportunity – always in our corner.

And to my parents. A father who accepted nothing less than my best whether in academics or athletics – reminding me that excuses were for losers, and that I would get nowhere in life without his favorite adage – "Suck it up, buttercup."

He gave me love but never coddled me – laughing at every trivial complaint, with a glitter in his eyes, always ready to explain lessons in the School of Hard Knocks. He expected hard work and dedication from *all* the Tuckers but always listened to my issues. His tough love is what made me such a tough runner. Helped me succeed when others didn't have the courage to continue.

And to my mother who was there for support when I needed it the most, encouraging me to continually challenge myself no matter how painful it might be, expecting me to "reach for the moon" and follow my dreams despite any discouragement. She got me through the lowest times in my life – was always there to lean on when I was down.

It takes a village to raise a child.

———————

The 1972 Title IX legislation was a game changer – opened doors which were closed for females, forced equal funding for women's sports, demanded facilities which were equivalent to the males, guaranteed equal athletic scholarships at each institution, and mandated that high school and NCAA sports be similar to the boys – one of the reasons events like the steeplechase and pole vault are now a part of women's track and field.

Today females take all this for granted, as well they should, but need to be aware of the struggles, all the lost opportunities, all the indignities faced in the 60's and 70's, when girls and women faced so many obstacles to follow their dreams. Katy Schilly was a real person, and her fight to participate in cross country actually happened – her membership on the boy's team in New York a true story.

Other than Sarah Tucker and her teammates, all these women in these stories were runners in the early 80's – competed at the highest levels across the US, producing phenomenal results, and turning in performances which would rival the efforts of collegiate athletes in this new millennium. In many ways, these women and girls were part of the Golden Era – the apogee of women's running.

But the fight is not over.

Epilogue

Over one hundred years ago, in 1911, Northwestern offered men's track and field for the first time, in 1976 the university initiating a women's program as mandated by the 1972 Title IX legislation. Twelve years later, in 1988, NU's 14th President Arnie Weber cut men's and women's XC/TF – all in the name of additional funding for men's football and men's basketball. To this day Northwestern is the *only* Big Ten school which does not have women's track and field, nor men's cross country or track and field. Shameful.

In 1988, after a ten year hiatus, women's cross country was reinstated – though the NU president wouldn't include the addition of women's track & field in the equation. There were consequences as a result of the decision – opportunities for women denied. Northwestern was (and is) a member of the Big Ten, yet league officials refused to allow these athletes to compete in distance events at the track and field conference championship meet, claiming NU doesn't have a *track and field* team.

Imagine how you would feel if your own conference refused entry into this annual competition – simply because Northwestern couldn't find the wherewithal to argue inclusion *for their own athletes*. This travesty has not been addressed by the current president and is a blemish on the school – a Title IX requirement unmet. For an institution which prides itself on Ivy League ideals, Northwestern does not care to meet that standard. Disgraceful.

As of this date, Northwestern has plans to renovate Dyche Stadium (sans a track oval) to the tune of $800 million, nowhere in this venture are funds earmarked to make up for the 39 athletic scholarships the women have been shortchanged since 1988, or the unequal stadium facilities between baseball and softball (guess which gender got swindled), or even the inequities in men's and women's budgets within individual sports – i.e. especially basketball.

The requirements of Title IX law mandate that universities provide equal opportunities, proportional scholarships, and equal treatment – regardless of a team's success or revenue. Data from Northwestern for 2021-22 shows that $12.4 million of the athletic budget goes to male athletes, while women receive only $10.1 million – *a violation of federal law*. That $2.3 million is certainly enough to fund a women's track and field program. Unconscionable.

The real story of Northwestern, not the one in this book, is that in 1983 and 1984 the Wildcat women finished fifth at the Big Ten Cross Country Championships, taking 2nd in the 1985 *and* 1986 conference championships – proof that Northwestern *can* successfully compete in the Big Ten if given the chance. In fact, at the 1985 NCAA Championships the women finished 13th in the nation.

Every few years there is talk, but that's as far as it ever goes, the powers that be unwilling to follow the 1972 law which was established to provide equality for women. I coached at Northwestern from 1984-1986, the final track meet held at Dyche Stadium, the 1986 Central Collegiate Championships on May 30-31. A sad ending to a storied program.

When will things change?